REVENGE OF THE
FALLEN SONS

PRAISE FOR DAWN OF THE TRADE (DOORMEN 1)

"*Dawn of the Trade* grabs you from the first page. A compelling story you shouldn't miss."
    —Brian Drake, author of the Sam Raven series'

"An exhilarating, high-stakes crime story with twists and turns from start to finish."
    —January Bain, author of City of Lies series

"Jarrett Mazza writes in a distinctive style that hits like a punch in the gut and yanks the reader into a vividly realized blend of thrills, excitement, and compelling characters. DAWN OF THE TRADE is a great debut novel, and I look forward to seeing what the author comes up with next!"
    —Best-selling author, James Reasoner

"Following in the footsteps of *Roadhouse*, Mazza's *Dawn of the Trade* is all action. It tells the story of a man with a code who makes himself at home with a community of like-minded warriors: the Doormen. The night club setting—NYC's the Conquistador—is so atmospheric that it's a major character all on its own!"
    —John Corr, author of *Eight Times Up*

"Jarrett Mazza has written one hell of a good book with *Dawn of the Trade*. His protagonist, Jon Haze, a tough-as-nails former marine, is the kind of guy you'd want next to you when your back's against the wall. This one has it all: excellent writing, fabulous action scenes, intriguing plotting, and best of all, it's the first in a new series. Do yourself a favor and pick up this first Doorman novel. You won't regret it."

–Michael A. Black, author of the *Trackdown* series

REVENGE OF THE FALLEN SONS

DOORMEN
BOOK 2

JARRETT MAZZA

ROUGH
EDGES
PRESS

Revenge of the Fallen Sons
Paperback Edition
Copyright © 2024 Jarrett Mazza

Rough Edges Press
An Imprint of Wolfpack Publishing
1707 E. Diana Street
Tampa, FL 33610

roughedgespress.com

Paperback ISBN 978-1-68549-732-3
eBook ISBN 978-1-68549-730-9
LCCN 2024940505

For Mom.
Always there, always prepared.

REVENGE OF THE FALLEN SONS

PROLOGUE

HE WANTED TO BURN THE EMBLEM IN FRONT OF their eyes, see the smoke rise, and let the putrid smell of flesh waft through the air. He had his words, and they were clear.

"You are no more."

Four men kneeled before the man in the suit while Larry Thomas, the owner of the legendary nightclub known as The Conquistador, gawked at these men.

"You betrayed me. You betrayed this place. You disobeyed our code, and you refused to play by our rules."

The men, all bowed in shame, were completely silent...for now.

"You have lost yourselves and so you will all now lose your privileges, your ability to *access*."

Next to Larry Thomas was Addison Krowe, who stood just as stoic as his lord.

"You are all gone. You are all *fallen*, do you understand? No more bouncing, no more guarding..." Larry stepped in between the men, all of whom refused to

look their employer in the eye. Now punished, the cere-
mony of these fools' excommunication was something
long foretold, and there was little they could do to
prepare. "No more *club*."

Larry clapped as he approached his former
employees.

While he was the one who had the ability to strip
them of their rights, these men were losing more than
just their jobs. They were losing their titles in the most
elite security unit in the entire nightclub business.
They were losing their right to access and enjoy all the
privileges that came with working at such a respected
location. They were relinquished and shamed. They
would no longer be known as the Doormen.

Now, they were fallen. *The Fallen Sons.*

"Do you have anything else to say to us?"

Not one had the guts to speak up or defend
themselves.

Once a decision is made at The Conquistador, a
decision is made. It's final.

Addison Krowe remained by his father-in-law and
didn't say a word.

"Yeah." Among the four men, only one decided to
speak.

It was a man with a dragon tattoo, dark eyes, and
sharp teeth. Of all those kneeling and about to be
outcast, he was the only one dressed in a muscle shirt
rather than wearing one with sleeves.

"You can take our crest," this man said, "but you
can't take our creed or our oath. One day, this game
you're protecting...it's all going to change. I'll see you
when it does."

"Strong words," said Larry Thomas. He held the

lighter and the crest. He dipped his head and nodded at Addison, who stepped forward. "Strong words, Rex. Very strong words. Now burn these motherfuckers," Larry ordered, "and make sure they never step foot in my club again."

With that, Addison raised his hand and fired up the torch. A blue flame hissed from its mouth, and the burning of The Conquistador crests commenced. The one called Rex glowered.

"Someday," the head of the Fallen stated, "we will return, and we will finish what you started."

"Whatever you say," Addison replied with ice-cold intent. "Whatever you say."

CHAPTER 1

THE OLD WAR

No matter where Jon was in The Conquistador, he could see everything.

After many months spent working in the same location, Jon's memory was now sharp as a razor. And, as he stood near the railing that overlooked the dance floor, Jon flinched when he heard a peculiar sound. He was not alone. Standing with Jon was Addison Krowe, the club's cooler and Jon's boss and friend.

"See anything yet?!" Addison shouted.

Jon surveyed the space below. Gazing through the flashing lights, Jon did his best to hear over the blaring music.

"Southside!" Jon said to Addison. "Two knuckleheads!"

"Got 'em!" added Addison.

Normally, Addison wasn't on the floor. Normally, he was up in his office getting frequent updates from the rest of the Doormen and watching the cameras. Addison was always the Doormens' eyes in the sky, and the bouncers were the club's hands and feet.

They walked, talked, and fought.

Right now, Jon was eyeing a gang of boys huddled in the center of the dance floor. It started off as something casual, with four guys and four girls swinging back and forth and having a good time. Yet, it changed course when one of the girls pushed one of the guys into the crowd. This caused an uproar. And a noticeable altercation began boiling in plain sight.

Jon was the first to spot it.

Tonight, he was assigned to the second level. When the altercation was noticed, Jon was by the railing, where he heard a girl yelling and a guy yelling back. When viewing this back and forth, Jon made his assessment. Facial expressions appeared hostile. Tones were emphatic and loud. This didn't mean a fight was certain, but it didn't mean one wasn't either.

"You can move in any time you want to." Addison gave Jon permission to step in. Although Jon didn't require Addison's approval or his permission, it was still a nice thing to have. In fact, when Jon or any of the other Doormen received such from Addison, it made them all feel good.

It let them know their judgment was suitable and their actions justified.

Jon nodded.

He stepped to the right and then to the left. He hustled up the stairs and reviewed the space around him. Soon, Jon spotted Danix and Li and even saw Kya too. Now at the bar, she was serving drinks to the many patrons who waved their hands and demanded her attention.

Kya, who always delivered, handed over whatever beverage was requested. Much had changed these last six months. Originally, Kya and Jon were only just friends. They were coworkers. Now, however, something new had hatched between them. Jon didn't want to push things too far too fast, so he decided to keep things simple.

He asked her out to dinner, and thankfully, Kya said yes.

Their first date was great, at least Jon thought it was. They discussed everything from work to school, from life to future goals and plans. The second time was just as fulfilling as the first. As things were going well, Jon decided to take things further. He wanted to know as much as he could about Kya. He even asked her about her last name.

Kya told Jon it was Garner. She said it was Kya T. Garner, and Jon made no other queries about it after.

Now coming closer, when Jon passed the bar, he waved at Kya.

Sometimes she noticed and sometimes she didn't. Tonight, she did.

Kya didn't just wave back at Jon, she smiled too.

She didn't know what Jon was up to, but here, he was always up to something.

Jon stood at the top of the three steps that led to the dance floor and observed the escalating altercation happening between a group of six people. Often, Jon was a shadow. Now, he was a weapon. Danix and Li were working their own spaces while Addison stayed where Jon had been. So far, this was nothing Jon couldn't handle. He motioned between three guests dancing near the stairs. Jon's expression was vacant. He might as well have been a robot going about its business. In fact, at this exact moment, Jon found himself feeling and acting like Arnold in *The Terminator*.

When Jon drew nearer to the fight, he stopped to examine the setting.

He had his plan. Based on what Jon could see, it was the ideal situation. He was going to politely ask the people to make their way away from the dance floor. He was going to escort them elsewhere and make sure the girls stayed out of the commotion. Basically, Jon was going to lean into being more of a teacher than a bouncer. Often this was the route he and the other Doormen would take.

Strategy first, words second, and fists are always last.

Jon also learned a lot since his previous encounter with a difficult patron.

Even now, Jon Haze could still picture Frankie Castellani and his plot to corrupt his club. Jon thought about Frankie and then he thought about Sam too. Jon reflected on his betrayal and how he wanted to destroy The Conquistador and create a new future.

It was a future that, even today, remained a mystery.

This was the thought that plagued Jon most of all. He'd lay awake at night thinking about it.

The Conquistador was many things. It was the best nightclub in New York, for one. Everyone knew this. It was also the place that employed the best bouncers—the best security in the world of clubbing and everyone was aware of this as well.

What they didn't know was the same question that Jon had yet to answer.

How did The Conquistador become the best club in the city?

How did its past shape it into what it is today?

Again, Jon was forced to review all these questions on his own time. He recalled what Sam had said. He also recalled what Frankie said too, on the day of his arrest. An argument had occurred between Sam and Addison. It was Sam and Frankie Castellani, a son of the notorious New York gangster, who both made remarks about *making changes*. They spoke about this and about a so-called *truth*. They wanted a revolution within the club industry, and they were prepared to do whatever it took to get it done.

At the time, Jon was focused on protecting the club because that was his job. He wasn't there to solve mysteries or do anything other than his duty as a Doorman. And yet, he still had questions. Today, those questions remain unanswered.

Jon cut through the crowd of dancers. He was gentle as he nudged them all aside. As he eyed the arguing pair, the girl with the red hair pushed the guy in the turquoise shirt. She yelled while he shook his head to show his displeasure.

Then, bingo. Arms shooting out, she shoved, and Jon grinned.

Once contact is made, it provokes immediate intervention and grounds to do something before it gets any worse. Verbal exchanges are one thing, but physical contact is something else.

Now that contact was made, Jon's pace quickened.

He proceeded toward a man in the crowd, but it was the female who struck first. Therefore, she was the one who required the most attention. Should the man strike back, then Jon and the other bouncers would have a much bigger problem on their hands.

However, at this moment, the man had yet to retaliate. He just glowered while biting his lips. Jon shuffled. Now inches from the man and the woman, by the time she raised her hand to hit him again, Jon was on the scene.

"Stop!" Jon's shouts penetrated the rowdy group. He decided to start with the woman. "Is there a problem here?"

The music was loud but Jon could hear through louder.

"No, just some personal shit we're workin' through!" The woman screamed at Jon while the man stayed where he was.

"Yeah, just some personal stuff!" screamed the man.

"Well, let's take it off the floor then, yeah?" asked Jon. "Resolve your issues away from the other guests." It was a solid suggestion. Always, the goal was to take an argument to where there were fewer people. This was Jon's only intention now.

"Come on!" shouted Jon. "I'll walk with you!"

Jon eased closer to the girl. Opening his stance, Jon was carving out a path for this woman to follow. This female glanced Jon up and down and then sighed. Her jaw slacked and she looked at Jon as if he wasn't even security.

She continued to show her disapproval and Jon found this reaction to be strange.

He was, after all, here to help.

But the girl didn't move. She stayed exactly where she was and gawked at the guy who was standing right in front of her. She nodded, and suddenly, all the animosity and aggression that once filled her face was gone.

Now, this girl was smiling.

Jon squinted. He was confused but also irked by the sudden change. He was also uncertain what to make of it, and most of that uncertainty translated into fear.

Jon was afraid.

"Like a mouse," said this unknown man. "Like a fucking mouse."

The statement was a clear insult directed at Jon himself. More than this, it was a threat. Still reeling, Jon peered over his shoulder. The three girls stepped back and merged with the crowd. They vanished the same as their once angry faces. The man who called Jon a mouse began to breathe down the Marine's neck. In the presence of seeing this frightening act, Jon abruptly turned and looked at the man.

"I think it's time for you to leave."

"Leave?" barked the man. He grinned at Jon while two more knuckleheads stepped forward. "Hell no, this is exactly as I planned. This is exactly the trap I set. Fucking bouncers. They read every situation except the ones that are the most obvious."

"What?" Before Jon could get an answer from this menacing man, he was smacked with a hard kick to the chin.

"Ah!" Jon had taken a solid hit before, but this one was goddamn impressive.

After knocking Jon's chin, his vision became hazy. He shuffled back and adopted a basic, solid fighting stance. Jon was to never start anything inside unless it was necessary. It couldn't be more necessary as of now.

Jon raised his hands to block. Shoulders solid and

feet spread, Jon hoped some of the other Doormen saw what was happening. Jon wanted Danix and Li on the floor now too. He wanted them here as soon as possible. Yet, none of them had come...yet.

However, this left Jon alone to handle the conflict. He glared at the man who hit his face. Now making his intentions clear, his opponent—whoever he was—stood by and smirked.

"Don't do this, boy. You're so out of your element you don't even know it."

After hearing this, Jon grinned. "We'll see about that."

The people on the floor began to back away. They made space for the bouncer and this now rebellious customer. If it was going to happen, then it was going to happen now.

Jon glared.

He didn't care if more Doormen arrived or if he was expected to do this all by himself. It was three against one. Nevertheless, Jon had training. He also had more experience than when he first began working.

Therefore, Jon was ready. He was goddamn fueled.

The first attacker snapped three succinct punches directly into Jon's midsection. Evading the next strike, Jon avoided the other two. However, as he made his move, the man kicked again.

"Argh!" Jon snapped as he fell.

The crowd roared to relish in all the violence. They hollered after seeing a bouncer get his ass handed to him. This didn't matter to Jon. Now on his back, Jon gawked at the two men who kicked him. They were big and built wide, like fridges. Their kicks were powerful.

Whoever they were, there was no doubt in Jon's mind that they had training.

They had experience. As one of them came forth, Jon's reaction was immediate and hostile. Sweeping his leg, Jon windmilled himself into a kick. Now with his leg cutting across his torso, Jon popped another attacker in the chest. He rolled onto his feet and kicked the man a second time.

"Ah!" After Jon hit back, this man exclaimed.

Immediately after, the remaining men attacked Jon full force. A cascade of kicks hammered Jon from every direction. The Marine blocked and hit back, and despite these efforts, Jon Haze landed only a few measly strikes.

They did little against his worthy adversaries. When Jon ducked again, the first man who started everything sauntered over to where the bouncer was kneeling. With a smug grin, the man relished. "Where's Krowe?"

The question was appropriate.

In fact, it was the same question Jon had too. He wanted to know where Addison was as well as the rest of the bouncing legion.

"Wherever he is," uttered the man, "I hope he's watching. I want him to know that reckoning is coming to The Conquistador. A new age is dawning..." The man pulled Jon's hair. Jon gasped. "The past has come back to fucking haunt him."

"What?" Jon was confused again. These men were spewing words and phrases that shook him to his core. He didn't know what to make of any of them.

Right now, he didn't want to make sense of it.

At this moment, all Jon desired was to get back into

the fight, although the outcome was clear. His loss was inevitable. Nevertheless, Jon would rather lose a fight than run away from one. A decision like that didn't exist here, not in this place.

The lead man cocked his hand back and straightened his fingers. After setting up a critical strike, thankfully, another hand emerged to stop it.

"I don't think so, pal." Abrupt and badass, Danix had arrived just in the nick of time.

Jon was up now. He was doing his best to contain his relief.

Holding the man's hand, Danix didn't hold back. He bent this *leader's* wrist and contorted the arm. Then Danix slid in for a hard and brutal elbow to the asshole's face.

"Ha!" Danix's elbows were like pylons and hurt as if being hit by a mallet.

The three intruders and the three Doormen squared off. With Li on the scene now too, the club's patrons all cheered. Some even removed their phones and recorded what they could. At this point, Jon couldn't care less where this footage went.

These men were deadly. They needed to be handled.

"All the Doormen here at one time!" The leader rejoiced and then shook his head to get his vision back.

Once anyone is hit by Danix, Jon could only imagine the agony their face was experiencing. This leader was beginning to irk Jon. He called out all the Doormen without fear or any show of intimidation or respect.

He was even smiling as Jon, Danix, and Li stood before them.

"Time to take things outside," said Danix. Jon was about to say the same thing.

Still, he was distracted by the man's attitude. He despised his persona.

"Oh, we're not going anywhere," said the man.

"You want us to take you outside, do you?" asked Danix. "Because we can do that."

"We're ready to do that," Li said this next part while poised by Danix, formidable and ready. For Jon, it felt strange to hear Li deliver this warning. Li was a more passive individual. He was the strong and silent type.

"Oh, I know you're ready for another fight," uttered the man in charge. "But are you ready...for this?"

Standing between his two friends, the leader pulled his hand from his pocket. He clutched a sphere the size of a pool ball. Along with his disgustingly confident demeanor, Jon couldn't stand the sight of this man. He questioned what he was seeing. Once, when Jon first started working at The Conquistador, he thought he saw a grenade, but it was just his panic-stricken self experiencing a war flashback. Right now, he wasn't having a flashback as much as he was having déjà vu, and he hated it.

Jon just wanted to know what the hell he had.

"What?" Jon still struggled to catch his breath. Then the man whipped the circular device toward Jon's feet. It clanked against the floor and then broke apart, and the scene felt familiar to Jon. It happened in war, but then this wasn't war.

At least, Jon didn't *think* it was.

He didn't expect to see an actual grenade explode. Whoever this man was, he might be dangerous, but he wasn't stupid. Dropping a grenade in The Conquistador would do nothing except kill everyone on the floor, including themselves.

"Down!" Jon dropped so fast he felt his prosthetic digging into his skin.

Danix and Li did the same. The device didn't create a burst of flame or emit any shrapnel. No, what came after was smoke and only smoke.

But it reeked of something awful.

The smoke cloud was high and fat and concealed this lead man and the two others. The gray spread as Jon gradually began to stand.

"What was that?" asked Li.

Li coughed, but Jon didn't. Jon's lungs quickly adjusted to the chemical compound as he looked at where the attackers used to be.

The spot was empty. They were gone.

"Fucking smoke bomb," said Danix. He took the words right out of Jon's mouth.

"Fucking smoke bomb," confirmed Li. "Shit."

Jon steadied toward the spot where the *bomb* was dropped.

The Conquistador's alarm system was cacophonous. It was so endless and irritating that all the people left the dance floor and made their way to the nearest exit. With more security stampeding the floor, Addison raced from the staircase and approached the Doormen.

"Who brings a smoke bomb?" Li asked.

Jon shook his head. His question was the same.

"Professionals," replied Danix.

"No, not professionals."

Jon's head turned so fast his neck cracked. Addison was on the scene in a typical fashion. He was dressed to impress and calling all the shots. Addison's presence was never determined by size or ability. Addison was not the best fighter or the scariest person around. He was, however, the most knowledgeable and the absolute calmest.

Always, this made Addison more respectable and potent. Jon was happy to see him.

Yet, when Addison said not professionals, Jon didn't know why he said this.

"Rivals," Addison clarified. He marched to where the bomb had detonated and flinched before falling to one knee. The remaining Doormen encircled. Together, they stood with Addison and stared at the same spot while the security escorted guests out of the club.

"Who were they, Addison?" Jon didn't want to ask this question, but he felt he had no choice. After taking the beating he did, he didn't just want answers. He felt as though he deserved them.

"Rex MacIntosh, Brutus Watson, and Cole Hausen."

"You know them?" asked Jon. "Why?"

"Know more than that," said Addison. Still kneeling, he pressed his finger to the floor.

"Who—" Jon was on the verge of asking, but Addison already knew what to say and how to say it.

"*The Fallen Sons*," Addison said.

"The who? The what?" Jon's queries were sharp and relentless.

"Are you sure it was them?" Danix was now standing closer to Addison.

However, Jon stayed on Danix. The topic of conversation was exclusive to them and them alone. Whoever these men were that caused the anguish, Danix was familiar with them too. Jon still had no idea.

"Yes," said Addison. "It absolutely was."

"Son of a bitch," said Danix.

Before Jon could ask more questions, he gobbled back his other questions. Now was not the time to dive into the exact details, but Jon knew exactly how it felt.

What was happening to him and to everyone else felt like war.

The Doormen were at war.

CHAPTER 2
A TALE OF TWO SONS

THE DOORMEN SKULKED ALONG LIKE A BAND OF humiliated teenagers. While it was nearly two, Jon felt like he had only just woken up as he walked up the steps. Next to him was another bouncer. Owen was a new hire. Like Jon was before now, Owen was still learning how The Conquistador functioned as a business and as an entity.

"Hey, man," Owen said to Jon. "Are you okay?"

Jon wanted to shake his head because, at this exact moment, he was pretty fucking far from okay. And yet, Jon nodded anyway. "Yes," he said. "I'm fine."

"Shit," snapped Owen. He and Jon were halfway up the steps now when Owen's tone became louder. "I tried so hard to get down there, but I was dealing with a girl fight near the coat room. I should have been there, though. I'm sorry."

Jon didn't care that Owen wasn't on the floor. Honestly, he was happy about it.

The fewer bouncers in that situation, the better it was for everyone.

"No, it's all right, man. It's fine."

"Fallen Sons," said Owen. He leaned in and whispered this point to Jon. Ahead of him were Danix, Li, and Addison. Everyone was heading up to Addison's office. Jon could still smell the terrible scent of smoke coursing through the club. "Sounds like a biker gang or some shit, right?"

Jon didn't think Owen had more to say, but apparently, he did.

In fact, Jon was learning Owen had a lot of things to say.

He was a talkative guy. He loved his job and was also capable. Owen had a black belt in Shotokan karate and was a very good communicator. Currently, Owen was studying to be a cop but wanted some real world, hands-on experience before getting his badge. Owen was Jon's closest friend at the club now. He was still close with Jamal but had grown closer to Owen. Jon shared his thoughts with Owen about bouncing, security, martial arts, as well as the culture of clubbing.

As it turned out, Owen might have been new, but his knowledge of the industry was sound. It was one of the reasons why Addison hired Owen. He was fully aware of the who's who in the club industry. Owen understood people's interactions and was very good at keeping calm and dealing with customers.

In the end, calmness was the game.

It was and always will be one of the Doormen's primary tools.

For now, Jon had nothing new to say to Owen. However, it wasn't because he didn't want to talk to him. It was only because Jon had one thought on his mind. He was thinking about those men who barged into The Conquistador.

He thought of their names.

The Fallen Sons.

Addison unlocked the door to his office and walked inside. Jon recalled how decorated and unique it was. He recalled the velvet walls, the hot red shades penetrated Jon's gaze and he basked in the savoring scent of cologne that filled the space.

Jon inhaled and goosebumps scattered along his arm. He wasn't nervous, just uncomfortable. What those three men did was not only impressive, it was downright terrifying.

It shook Jon to his core, and his arms began to shiver. All he wanted to do was sit down, so that's what he did.

Jon sat in the first seat he came across. He didn't even bother to see if the others joined him. With all eyes on Addison, he didn't sit in his fancy chair. He opted to go to the back of his desk and pour himself a drink.

"Does anyone want one?"

"On the job?" asked Danix. He sounded surprised.

Addison's rules about drinking on the job were clear. He didn't approve, and he hated catching employees doing it. Should they be caught, then there were to be drastic consequences.

"Not like you to offer," Danix said to Addison.

Jon was quiet, because he agreed.

"Yeah, well," replied Addison. He casually brought the glass to his chin and sipped. He continued to face away from Jon and the other Doormen. "Times call for it."

"Where's Larry?" asked Jon. None of the bouncers answered.

Jon believed it was because maybe the question was not relevant at this time.

"Larry's not here, and he doesn't need to be, not now," said Addison.

"Why not?" asked Danix.

Jon watched Addison continue to face away from his colleagues while drinking more of his Brandy. Jon could wait no longer. He and Owen were sitting next to each other directly in front of Addison's desk. "So, who are they, these the guys that attacked us?" asked Jon. "The ones you call Fallen Sons?"

Addison Krowe didn't answer. He had another drink and his gaze shifted from the glass and then to Jon. "As you know, this club—our club—has a lot of history."

Now Jon was the one who didn't say anything. He knew there were secrets, but so far as the details surrounding the club, he still didn't know all of them. He believed this was another chapter in The Conquistador's complicated past.

"Before you worked here, there were others who did. Before any of you worked here," said Addison, "there were other people who did."

All the Doormen were quiet. Obviously, Jon knew that there were other bouncers before he was hired. He understood this no doubt. He just didn't ever think about them, not until now.

"Other Doormen?"

"*Other* being the operative word," Addison clarified to Jon. "What you saw tonight were *dead* Doormen, in a manner of speaking."

"Former bouncers?" asked Owen. "People who used to work for The Conquistador?"

"Yes," said Addison. He gave Jon a sideways glance. "They did a long time ago, until they were let go."

"Fired?" Owen barked.

Addison didn't answer. Jon watched him the entire time. For some reason, Addison was focusing mostly on Jon. "In a way," said Addison.

Jon continued to inspect his boss. Being fired could happen at The Conquistador, but these men were not disgruntled or upset. They were rebelling. They were vicious. They were concerted in their attack.

"Once someone denies the ways of the club, they betray our principles and our code of ethics, there needs to be consequences. These men faced them."

"Well, what did they do?" asked Owen.

Jon turned so he could see Danix and Li. It was strange that they were so quiet. It seemed to the Marine that they knew the story well.

"They did nothing more than refuse to listen," said Addison. "And for that, they were punished and now they are...*fallen*."

"Fallen?" Jon repeated the word. To him, all of this sounded biblical and strange.

The Doormen were strict and lawful. They were united and they were true. Jon knew they were closer than other bouncing syndicates were, no doubt. Nevertheless, The Conquistador was a family, and every family has rules. And, if certain rules are broken, then consequences follow. And yet, the punishment Addison was describing sounded corporal —*savage*.

The Doormen were not bikers, and they weren't

mobsters. And yet, there were consequences for betraying them, however bad they might be.

"It's what they're called now," said Addison. "It's what they've chosen to call themselves."

"The Fallen Sons," said Jon. He repeated the classification just to be sure it was real.

"Yes."

"And what do they want?" Owen was now a journalist spitting questions left, right, and center.

Jon gawked at Addison, who had turned away from his shelf of alcohol and was now facing his coworkers.

"Vengeance. They want vengeance." Addison had another drink and Jon had another look.

"I don't understand," Jon said. His head was turned and he looked only at the man in charge, and that man was Addison. "Vengeance? *Vengeance for what?*"

"For being exiled," Danix said. "For being dismissed, stripped of their status and their titles.".

Danix spoke with a noticeable degree of regret. His eyes were closed and his head was down. Jon never observed Danix in such a state. This was a man hard as fucking stone. Danix never broke. He rarely frowned or showed any signs of sadness at all. In this case, Jon could see him filled with sorrow. The incident referenced had pained him. Jon was glad it hadn't happened to him.

"They were broken," Danix continued. Jon followed Addison's gaze. It landed on Danix as Addison gave him a forceful look before continuing.

"Yes, and now they've returned."

"And how many of them are there?" asked Jon.

Addison shook his head. "Enough."

"And they know everything we do," said Jon. "They

know how we operate, how we work. They know our rules, and they know how to fight and how to move without any of us noticing."

Neither Addison nor anyone else said a damn thing. Jon was blunt. He was so unapologetic all anyone could do was sit in silence.

"We can't stop them at the door," said Jamal.

Until now, Jon didn't know Jamal was present, but he was. Jon was glad to see him. Jamal was one of Jon's favorite people.

"They'll be able to sneak right in, no problems at all." Jon looked to Addison, who was still drinking.

"They also know all our points of entry, even the ones no one is supposed to know besides us." This comment was made by Danix.

"They know much," said Addison. "Too much."

Jon inhaled and felt cool air cutting his nostrils. "They know everything," said Jon. "And so, we have to stop them."

"Going to be tough," said Li. "They do know a lot."

Jon looked to where Addison was standing and waited for his boss to get the last word in. When Addison chose not to, Jon realized maybe he should.

"Good thing toughness is the name of our game. And it's still ours to play. This is still our home. We're going to do whatever we have to...to defend it."

Being the last words spoken, Jon looked at Addison as he grinned.

"Damn right," Addison said. "Damn *fucking* right."

CHAPTER 3
SUSPICIOUS VISITOR

Since Jon began working at The Conquistador, so much had changed for him.

He was now seeing Kya, and the two were infrequently spending more and more time together. At first, it began with a few casual encounters. They were taking things slow like two teenagers, which they still kinda were in more ways than one. They didn't wish for their relationship to interfere with their jobs and Kya was quite secretive. And, so far as everyone was concerned, the two were just friends.

Although some did have their suspicions.

Addison did, and Danix and Li did too, even Owen often made a few jokes about Jon and Kya, which amused the Marine very much. Nevertheless, what changed the most was Jon's relationship with his mom.

It had improved exponentially since that night he returned after Frankie Castellani.

They had a more open relationship now. Jon shared with her all the time, about everything. He told her information about his life, his job, what he was doing the following week. He would eat with her almost every day. He'd help her with errands too. He'd go to the supermarket and do a few pick-ups. Sometimes, Jon would even cook alongside his mom before his daily nap.

Jon's mom didn't need much help. She just liked having her son there.

Honestly, Jon enjoyed it too.

It was set to be a long night. When Jon woke up, he scurried downstairs so he could join his mom, wherever she was. And yet, as he ventured into the kitchen to find her, he saw she wasn't there. It was weird. Jon's mother was always down there at this time. For some reason, today, she wasn't.

"Mom?" When Jon called to his mom, he waited for her to answer. After he didn't get one, he called to her again. "Mom?"

As a woman who rarely left the house, most definitely, she didn't leave during this time of day. If she wasn't here, then Jon had to ask...where the hell was she?

"Jon, sweetie, I'm in here." Jon was in the kitchen when he heard the sound of his mother's cheery voice. Evidently, she was in the backyard. Why she was there, Jon couldn't say. Again, he was curious but also cautious at the same time.

The tables couldn't be more turned. Jon's place of work was under attack, and now he was the one worrying about his mother. Oddly, the sliding screen door leading into Jon's backyard was opened.

"We're back here," Jon's mom said.

Proceeding to the deck, the wood had wilted and was now chipped. Jon stared into his backyard with the freshly mowed grass. Sure to his relief, his mother was there. She was sitting at the table. On each corner were four chairs and two of them were taken. One was obviously occupied by Jon's mom, while the other was occupied by another man, a *new man*.

"Come on over here, Jon," Jon's mom invited. "We're so glad you're here."

"We?" Jon asked this immediately after he heard his mother use the pronoun. Whenever she did, the *we* usually meant Jon and her.

Now, all of a sudden, the *we* included someone else.

Jon stood before his mom, so joyous and bright. Thus far, Jon couldn't see who this new man was because he insisted on staying seated. Jon wasn't used to his mother bringing people home, especially men. Jon didn't say a damn word.

"There's someone I want you to meet," said Betsy Haze.

Approaching twenty-five years old, Jon was well aware that parents have wants and needs too. They need to express themselves sexually in certain capacities and well, Jon owed it to his mom to be cordial in this regard. He had to be polite despite his preconceived feelings because whoever this man was, he obviously meant a lot to her.

Jon's mom still meant a lot to him.

"Come on over." Jon nodded and did as he was told.

Stepping toward his mother and this other man, Jon shuffled, and the man began to stand. Jon observed a twinkle in his mother's eye—a glint of happiness that he hadn't observed in a very long time. He knew, in that moment, that this was a real thing.

His mother might very well be in love.

And Jon didn't know how to interpret this. He wouldn't know until he shook hands and sat down with this new man. This was precisely why he was here now.

"Jon, this is Michael, Michael Irons."

"Hi," said Jon, sternly. "You met, huh?"

"Yes," said Jon's mom. "See, I was taking a break from work, actually, and decided to take a walk to the market, and well, I met him there. He picked me up in the produce section, actually. Very charming and so, we stayed in touch, and well, we've been seeing each other here and there and well, it's been...really nice so far."

"Right," said Jon. "Nice to meet you."

"Anyway," said his mother, "I wanted the two of you to meet. Come...sit."

Jon stood poised by the table where he eyed this new man the whole time. Gradually turning, this man smirked at Jon before extending his hand.

"Jon, nice to meet you too. I've heard so much about you."

Jon nodded.

While he had yet to offer his hand, he studied this Michael Irons like he was working the door at the club. Jon judged him on very specific details. At first, Jon looked for the small things: jewelry, shoe size, posture. Jon looked at his pupils.

Were they dilated or were they normal?

He also looked for any visible scars, but this man was clean. At least he was on the surface. Beneath? Well, Jon hadn't a clue what was down there and that... that scared him.

This man was also too confident, too slick, and way too handsome to be with Jon's mom.

Still, she said he was charming and so, maybe he was.

"Thanks," said Jon. "It's nice to meet you as well, man."

"Well," said Jon's mother. For a split second, both Jon and this man, Michael Irons, said nothing. It wasn't awkward. It was just quiet.

"Why don't we have a seat, yeah? I have some lemonade."

"Lemonade?" asked Michael Irons. "Perfect. Delicious." He began to sit, and Jon did the same.

"Great," said Jon's mom. "Let me get it. One second."

She roamed back into the house and Jon found this to be quite bold. After all, she was choosing to leave both Jon and Michael to do what, to talk? He supposed he had no choice but to try.

"So," said Michael Irons. He leaned back in his chair. "Your mom told me you're a bouncer."

"Yes," said Jon. "Doorman, technically."

"Cool," said Michael Irons. "I hear it's at The Conquistador."

"It is."

"That's pretty impressive, actually," added Michael. "Place is legendary. I used to frequent the club back in the day, but it's a gold mine for opportunity and access. You're very lucky to be working there."

Jon eyed Michael Irons from across the table. Jon didn't know what to make of him, not just yet. Jon didn't know why he was here or how he met the Marine's mom. For now, Jon believed the best decision was to just keep the conversation going as best he could.

"Yeah," replied Jon. "But I work mostly with Addison Krowe. He's the head of security."

"Right," said Michael. "But Larry Thomas, guy's old school, as I'm sure you know. He's been around since the Stone Age. Actually, surprised to see he's still there, I guess he just can't let anyone take over his baby. Been open for what, almost thirty years?"

Jon didn't say *yes* this time. No, he just glanced at the door to see what was taking his mom so long. He was surprised by Michael's questions.

"It has, yeah. How do you..." Jon wasn't sure how to phrase the next question. At first, he was going to ask this Mr. Irons *how long have you been seeing my mom?*

He wanted to ask this, but declined in favor of asking something more important.

"How do you know so much about The Conquistador?"

Michael Irons's mouth opened as he was about to answer. He didn't when he heard the clinking of glasses. His mother was sauntering out the house. She was literally skipping her way to this new man.

"How do you think?" Jon's mother chimed. "I asked him what he did for a living and he said he was a protection specialist, you know a bodyguard. I told him my son worked a similar job. He was in security too. When he asked where, I told him at the city's most exclusive nightclub."

Jon's mother handed Michael a glass of lemonade and clinked it against her own. "Cheers."

Jon's eyes rolled.

"So you work guard people, huh?" Jon asked.

Michael Irons was lost in Jon's mother's gaze, which was making the Marine immensely uncomfortable. Still, his mother seemed happy enough. She didn't look away at all.

"Where?" asked Jon.

Michael looked away. He took a quick sip of his lemonade before answering. "All around with different people. I run my own agency with my own guys. We do mostly corporate events, but we mostly offer protection to big name celebrities and we sometimes take over for other security teams too, if they need us."

"Whoa," said Jon. "Cool."

"Cool is right," said Jon's mom, sitting at the round patio table while Michael was next to her. "In fact, Michael told me a lot about what he does, how dangerous it is, but he also told me not to worry about you as much as I do. He talked about The Conquistador, how it runs, and how amazing a place it really is. One of a kind, he said, isn't that right?"

"It is," said Irons. "Truly...one of a kind."

Jon scoffed. He'd been telling his mother this since the day he started.

She never listened to him and now suddenly she was listening to what, some new guy?

Why? Jon downed the slick and sour beverage. "Did he now?"

Jon examined Michael Irons like he was a detective. In Jon's mind, he was thinking about the new enemy that surfaced. Former Doormen who were exiled had now come back to the club seeking revenge. And, based on what Jon could recall, they were older, though not quite as old as Mr. Irons.

Still, Jon couldn't rule out any suspicions. All the signs were there.

This Michael Irons knew security. He knew The Conquistador. And now, he knew Jon.

He also had skills and operated his own agency. He worked in the same world as Jon and the Doormen did. He also looked tough and experienced, and he didn't appear to be the same type as those Jon fought in the club. His hair was groomed. There were no tattoos on his neck, and while Jon was never one for making this kind of judgment call, he couldn't resist doing it now.

Most importantly, Irons was here. He was with Jon's mother, and consequently, he was with Jon. He had access to Jon, to everything he knew, and all the special information surrounding The Conquistador. The Fallen Sons planned to hurt The Conquistador, its Doormen, and Jon.

But how could someone hurt someone like Jon Haze?

What was the only way to get to him?

It was here, maybe.

"Yeah," said Michael, "the nightclub world is no doubt a complicated one, but it's all about how you choose to deal with the situation at hand, you know? You use your words. You stay calm. It's actually really good practice for a future in law enforcement. Is that a career path that you think you'd be interested in?"

Michael's question was as direct as it was confrontational.

Jon hated questions like this. He just tolerated them because he had to.

Michael Irons was cool, strong, and very intuitive. Jon was beginning to like him, almost. Not everyone was so friendly and knowledgeable, but Michael was. He was very much. Jon leaned in and grabbed a chilled glass of fresh lemonade.

"Haven't thought about it yet, actually," Jon said to Michael. "Still thinking about a career path."

"Well, it's not a bad idea," said Michael. "I mean, given your situation, it could be quite good."

"Situation?" asked Jon. He didn't know what situation Michael was referring to.

"Oh, I'm sorry," said Michael Irons. "I didn't mean to offend."

Jon's mother was sitting beside Michael. There was no change to her expression at all. It would seem not even she knew what Michael meant. What he was indicating, however, brought brevity to this current situation.

"I just meant with your...with your...uh...*uh*..." Michael raised his hand and pointed at Jon's leg. It was then that the Marine knew precisely what he was talking about.

Jon looked down. He hated when people did this. No doubt, he expected people to notice, sure, but to refer to it as a *situation* was offensive. Jon didn't know Michael Irons well enough for him to bring this up and to do it so casually. Nevertheless, Jon's mother didn't seem to have a problem with it. She said nothing and did nothing.

"Right," said Jon, being as casual as he could be. "I know."

"Oh, please don't put the idea of him being a cop inside his head," said Betsy Haze. "You know how much I don't want him trading one dangerous job for another. I worry about him enough as is."

"I know you do," said Michael. "Believe me, I know." Michael's hand slid down to his mother's thigh and he smiled while Betsy smiled back.

Jon gawked.

He could feel the chemistry brimming between his mom and this other man. It was so palpable it practically had its own smell. And Jon hated it. He hated it so much that he tightened his hand against his glass and hoped it wouldn't shatter, but it did.

CHAPTER 4
WEAPONS AND TACTICS

JON RECEIVED FOUR TEXTS FROM HIS MOM WHILE he was at the gym. He didn't answer a single one. He needed time without any noise and to get out of his own head. Jon arrived at Danix's training center where he stripped down to his gym clothes and began hitting one of the free bags. The entire time, Jon couldn't stop thinking about the meeting he just had with this new man, Michael Irons. Now, his mother was a sweet and kind lady. Jon had been told by his friends that she was also quite attractive for her age, so there was no reason why men wouldn't be interested. She could certainly attract a man who was dynamic and cool.

Michael, however, might be with Jon's mom purely because he wanted to be.

He might also be with her because he wanted to get to Jon, if that was his true intention.

Jon hadn't told anyone yet about the fact that his mother was dating someone he didn't trust. Such admittance was hardly a cause for concern. No kid trusts anyone who is dating their mother or father.

However, Jon didn't dislike Michael Irons. Aside from the comment made about his leg, Michael actually seemed like the kind of person Jon could actually enjoy being around. His personality was affable and he seemed like someone who was in complete control. Jon admired this almost as much as he admired his own qualities.

At the gym, Danix was training some new fighters. Jon felt grateful he was no longer considered new. He had been a member of Danix's MMA gym since he started working the club. Now Jon's floor game was getting better. And, as soon as Danix was done saying goodbye, Jon's eyes popped. He gazed at The Conquistador's biggest bouncer.

"You good?" Danix asked Jon.

"Very," Jon said.

"All right," said Danix. "Let's make it happen."

Danix kneeled and leaned into Jon.

It had been some time since the two sparred. Whenever they did, Danix always pinned Jon quick, fast, and easy. Always, there was little Jon could do to defend himself against such a towering opponent. Then again, this was jiu-jitsu. Even a smaller opponent can face someone twice their size and win. Maybe today, that was Jon.

The sparring began with Danix reaching for Jon's neck. Jon latched Danix's wrists and felt like he was holding onto a sewer pipe. When Jon pulled, Danix leaned back. For now, Jon's goal was to roll. The prosthetic was not ideal for this position. However, Jon couldn't deny that one night, he might be in a similar situation at the club.

So, he needed to be prepared.

On his back, Jon invited Danix to grab hold of him again.

This was an effective strategy in the BJJ game. One fighter stays on their back and continues to roll while the opponent plays by their own rules. The only problem was Danix's strength and power.

Regardless of Danix's positioning, he could generate a monumental force.

Still, Jon stuck with what he knew. He pressed his foot onto Danix's knee and invited him to strike. Danix pushed, grabbed hold of Jon's gi, and held it snug. When Danix pulled, Jon added pressure onto Danix's knee.

Jon's primary strategy was to armbar.

He wanted to fasten Danix's hand, pull him in close, and curl his legs around his arm. While this was only something Jon had hoped for, his chief technique quickly transformed into a reality.

Danix reached, and Jon applied the armbar. Now clutching Danix's hulking wrist, Jon fought hard. Danix flinched and writhed. Despite Jon being on his back, Danix inched closer to Jon. Wearing padded gloves, Danix used his hand to grab Jon's gi. Although Jon fought to keep the armbar tight, Danix had deployed his primary weapon: brute force.

Danix lifted Jon up like a toddler and thrust him down. Jon smacked ferociously into the mats.

"Goddamn it!"

Unleashing a hardened thump, Danix and Jon both made varying sounds. Wind was knocked out of the Marine and Jon coughed violently. The plunge was brutal but not uncalled for. Jon didn't take any of it personally. Danix's mentality always was to treat every fight as if it were the real thing.

Real is pain, and pain is sometimes necessary.

After slamming Jon, Danix lifted the Marine up again. Danix slammed Jon a second time.

"Ah!" Jon shouted. The first time was painful. The second time was brutal.

Jon's eyesight blurred. He continued to cough and continued to fight to catch his breath. Danix huffed and punched. It hurt, no doubt. He could feel the burn and the numbness starting to set in. If not for Danix's gloves, Jon's ribs would have been ruptured if not also broken.

He kept the pain inside and continued to hold on tight to that armbar.

Never had he submitted someone like Danix.

Never did Jon think he could. Danix was his most feared opponent. And what made him even more feared was the fact that Danix was Jon's teacher. Like Addison, he taught him almost everything since he returned home from war.

Still, Jon refused to let go.

After the second slam against the mats, the people training in the gym had all assembled . Now Jon had grown tougher. He was training harder and working longer hours. He was lifting heavier and was striking faster and blocking better. He was rolling and contorting himself to such impressive degrees that Jon was burdened with less pain.

Despite this, Jon's tolerance level was not ruptured, because right now, he was channeling all the frustration and uncertainty that he faced when his mom first introduced Jon to her new friend. He didn't hate this Irons guy, no. What Jon hated was not knowing if he was a friend or foe. Jon was also thinking about the impending conflict. New enemies had risen, and they were the so-called Fallen Sons.

He remembered the fight he had with them, with their illustrious and capable leader.

He was tough but, in the back of Jon's mind, might be almost as tough as Danix. So, his main goal was, if he could pin Danix, then Jon could presumably take on the leader of the Fallen Sons.

If he could submit Danix, then there was no enemy he could not face or encounter.

If he could beat Danix, then all of the other Fallen Sons were fair game too. Jon had it in him to keep fighting. He would not back down, no matter what.

"*Grrr*," Danix grunted, his face red like a raspberry.

Danix was burning. Jon listened to subtle sounds of awe from the crowds watching. He could hear them gasping in shock, knowing the main badass at this MMA gym was about to tap.

Danix never tapped.

But then, Jon understood, there was a first time for everything.

Jon pulled Danix's arm and drove his foot deep into his opponent's side. This was usually when said opponent would surrender. There was a huge window for Danix to do this now. Jon was given the opportunity to finally end this friendly contest, though it was barely friendly.

Jon grunted, and finally, Danix looked at Jon and spoke.

"You're doing good," said Danix. "Real good." He was barely audible, but Jon was also confused. Why was he speaking to him now?

"Thanks," Jon said, a hint of surprise still present in his response.

"But you're leaving yourself open," suggested Danix.

"Oh yeah?" said Jon, still confused. How the hell was he leaving himself open? "How?"

Danix grinned, and then he flipped and contorted Jon's torso. Instead of hitting Jon or lifting him up like before, Danix opted to take Jon's hand. He needed it for leverage. From there, Danix hoisted himself up and off his back. Jon felt the pressure, so he pulled harder. His grip was compromised. He didn't have the same leverage or power as before. The power balance in the fight shifted. Danix clobbered Jon with his elbow and the Marine couldn't hold on for much longer.

He could have, but his letting go was merely an act of giving up.

He couldn't take another hit like the one he just did.

When Danix went to hit Jon again, the Marine let go. He was now in a fighting mood, no doubt. He huffed and puffed and exhaled until his eyes started to burn. He wanted to keep going, but then Danix was not his enemy. In Jon's head, he might have been envisioning a new opponent, but now that opponent was his friend.

And this fight was over.

Breathing longer and harder, Jon sat up and felt his slick shirt clinging to his wet body. He was weak. He was tired but happy.

"Very good," said Danix, taking a few breaths. This was a strange sight for Jon. Danix was never tired, yet he was now. "Really good."

"Thanks," said Jon.

Danix offered his hand, and Jon reached out to take it.

He didn't need to take it. He did because, while technically Jon lost this fight, it was the most learned and important lesson he had participated in so far. He loved every second of it. When he stood, the rest of the fighters clapped to give Jon a bit of praise. Now encouraged, Jon enjoyed the moment. It wasn't until he started motioning across the mat he heard Danix say something else.

"Hope you're not too tired. You know we still got a big night ahead of us."

Until now, Jon had forgotten about this *big night.*

"Right," Jon said, trying to remember. "I almost forgot."

Jon walked with Danix to the locker room. There, he made his way into the stuffy corridor that smelled of socks and Axe body spray. Jon motioned through the space and felt Danix's hand on his shoulder.

"Good," Danix said. "Rest up now. You know you're needed at full strength. Gonna be a *real one.*"

Jon nodded.

This *one* Danix was referring to had almost slipped Jon's mind.

Tonight, The Conquistador was going to be stacked. Tonight, the club was hosting a rap superstar called Restitute. It was to be him and his crew. Restitute was said to be bringing his own security detail with him. Therefore, the Doormen were set to work with a private team. All of this was planned in advance, but Jon considered other possibilities.

He really didn't know anything about the rap star's detail.

They were like strangers to the Doormen. They could be anyone from anywhere.

Regardless, Danix wasn't wrong. It was going to be a big night.

However, Jon's hope was it was big but comprehensible. Then, he was reminded of the Doormen's newest enemies who knew The Conquistador. They knew how the club functioned and operated. And, due to this fact, the Sons might emerge in any capacity at any time.

In Jon's mind, this only confirmed how every night from now on would be a big night.

As Danix said, it was going to be *real*.

CHAPTER 5
THE MANY FACES OF THE PAST

WHAT CONSTITUTED A BIG EVENT?

Obviously, Jon knew most of the details. He comprised all of them the second he stepped through the door.

Rap Star. Entourage. Over three hundred guests. Bottle Service. Live Show.

New Security.

He also included *lots of women* and a *high-risk situation* involving former "Conquistador" employees. Jon knew all of this but had yet to talk about it in detail with anyone.

When Danix was done fighting at the gym, he went home quickly as well. According to Danix, Jon would have a lot of duties tonight so he needed time to plan and think.

Jon didn't ask what these details were.

He'd know once he began his shift.

When Jon entered the club, The Conquistador wasn't open, but it was still packed. There were countless bouncers and employees, some of them Jon knew and others he was just starting to. None of them were members of the tier one unit, which was the Doormen.

Yet, Jon showed them the respect they deserved.

Technicians assembled a new DJ booth on stage. Lots of kitchen staff were hulling in dishes and glasses. The bar was filled with additional bartenders and servers. Addison was there. He was on the floor, looking around to check on everything. He was also on his phone, texting whomever. And, because Addison was preoccupied, almost everyone was too. Owen, Li, and more Doormen were moving, assisting when they could and getting the club ready for the big night.

The time was now approaching seven in the evening.

Jon was fighting a knot in his shoulder as well as in his neck. He rotated his head and stretched as best he could. Having dated Kya more than once, he was now easily on a first-name basis. Therefore, Jon didn't need to be nervous when taking the time to ask serious questions. In essence, Jon had progressed beyond small talk and other menial forms of communication.

Always, Jon felt the unavoidable need to speak with Kya.

He needed to talk to her wherever he was and regardless of whatever he was doing. Tonight, Kya's hair was tied back above her head. The rest of her hair was dangling behind her shoulders. Jon always was infatuated by its black shade. No doubt Kya was on the floor to amaze. All the female bartenders accentuated their appearance. They were more than prepared to sling drinks and count tips. Jon considered the number of men ready to throw themselves at Kya and the other bartenders.

Then again, that was their job. Jon might get a few catcalls himself.

Walking up to Kya, she was loading the glasses with her friend, Marcy.

Like Kya, Marcy too was quite attractive. She was blonde and voluptuous. She had a nice smile, wore bright red lipstick, and her hair was styled similarly to Kya's tonight. When Jon approached the bar, it was still crowded. He didn't really want to talk to Marcy. She was Kya's friend, but he didn't want to be rude, so Jon had to talk to Marcy too.

"Ladies, how's it going?" Jon opened with a casual greeting that wasn't much.

"Hey, Jon!" Marcy was enthusiastic. In Jon's mind, she was maybe too enthusiastic. He waved at Marcy and leaned against the bar.

"Nice to see you, Marcy," Jon said. Playing it cool, Jon looked at Kya.

"Hey," Kya said to Jon. She turned to face him.

"What's going on?" Jon said. "You need help?"

"Help?" asked Marcy.

Jon nodded and pointed at all the boxes scattered about the space. "Yeah, loading."

"Uh, there's a lot, but don't you have to go meet with the other bouncers?" Kya asked.

"Not right now. I can spare a few minutes before the briefing. Here," Jon said, "let me give you a hand."

"Okay."

Before every shift, Kya did a lot of the prep work herself. She was not keen on asking anyone for help. Jon, however, was a firm believer in always being of use when people needed him. Kya, being more prideful than most, didn't ask Jon to lift a finger. Tonight, however, was different. Jon lifted one box, placed it onto the countertop, and joined the girls in unloading.

"Thanks, Jon," said Marcy.

"Don't mention it," Jon said.

"You're such a gentleman," commended Marcy. She was nice to Jon, and he appreciated the compliment. "A sweet gentleman, ain't he?"

Kya was busy adding two more bottles of Jack Daniels to the shelf so she didn't pay much mind to Jon. Still, Jon kept unloading while not caring what Marcy had to say or why.

"Yeah," Kya finally replied, "but then again, I don't know too many gentlemen who have big ass scars on their faces. Still, everyone here does, right?" Kya motioned across the counter and slipped in behind.

Jon didn't think Kya would notice this scar. He checked himself out in the mirror at home. The scar Kya referred to was just past Jon's right eye. It was a fine red line. Actually, it made Jon look like a bounty hunter from a video game. His favorite character was Snake from *Metal Gear Solid*. He was also a huge Snake Plissken fan from John Carpenter's *Escape from New York*. Granted, Jon didn't wear an eye patch like those characters did. Yet, he preferred to imagine that under their eyes was something just as gnarly and just as cool.

And tonight, Jon felt pretty fucking cool. "Shit."

"What?" Kya asked. "Didn't notice?"

Jon's head shook and he replied. "No, I did. I saw it back at home. Forgot about it until now, though."

"Looks pretty new to me," said Kya, eyeing the markings. Jon couldn't see the marks, but he remembered feeling them. Whenever he and Danix were in a friendly match, Jon received some pretty hard licks. Most didn't just leave bruises but a lot more than that.

"It is," expressed Jon.

"From here?" Kya assumed Jon had obtained these marks from when he was in a fight with that rebel a while back. He did receive some marks there too, but this one was not from that altercation.

"No," said Jon. "They're from Danix's gym. Sparring."

"Nice," said Kya. She lifted another bottle and secured it onto the shelf.

"It wasn't at the time," Jon said to Kya, wanting to keep the conversation going. "Danix is a fucking truck."

"Wait," replied Kya. "Danix? Did you say you were fighting Danix?"

Jon nodded. "Yeah, during a friendly contest at his gym, like I said."

"Wow," replied Kya. "That sounds...*rough*."

"Not bad," added Jon. "I mean, I almost got him in an armbar. Pretty close, considering how much better a fighter he is than me."

"Right," said Kya. "Pretty impressive."

"Pretty, sort of," Jon said, and he played casual while Kya kept her distance.

Sure, she and Jon went out to dinner a few times, but this was still work. And, in the club industry, there's a lot of prep and so much time needed before the night begins. It's best if people don't distract one another during said process. Now, Jon did understand this, which is why, when he was done helping Kya and Marcy with the bottles, he stepped away.

"Guess that's it. Look, be careful tonight," Jon said. "You know you're gonna be serving at least sixty people in the first hour, another sixty by the second and third."

"Yeah, I know," Kya replied.

"I'm just saying pace yourself. And keep your eyes open, please. Be careful."

Delivering the stern warning, Jon was advising Kya to be cautious and diligent. While this did seem a little like belittling, Jon was only giving this advice because he was worried. Despite his skill set and despite being part of a brigade of elite bouncers, no one was safe at The Conquistador.

This included everyone who worked there, Kya included.

"I will," said Kya. She licked her lips and delivered to Jon a sultry stare.

Whenever Kya looked at Jon like this, confident and astute, the Marine jittered.

Kya was as caring as she was attractive, and Jon was almost always enamored. He didn't want to leave without saying goodbye, but the setting didn't really make for an affectionate farewell.

Jon kept it simple and subtle. He reached out, placed his hand on Kya's hand, and rested it there for only a second. Doing this let Kya know that Jon and her might be more than just friends. Definitely, they were more than colleagues. And, while Kya was not the kind of girl to commit after a few dates, Jon didn't care.

His feelings for her were real. He needed her to know they were.

"Appreciate it," Jon said. He removed his hand from Kya's and slid back toward the bar. "See you around."

For a second, and Jon still wasn't sure if this was true, Kya's thumb slipped. She changed positions so her thumb connected with Jon's knuckle. It grazed the bone and glided down. Though this happened within a matter of seconds, Jon could swear he felt something.

In fact, he *knew* he did.

By doing this, it was Kya's way of letting Jon know that she enjoyed touching him, even if it was slight and barely noticeable. Maybe Kya didn't care for Jon as much as he cared for her. Still, Jon didn't know her last name or anything about her family, though Kya rarely had much to say in that regard. She would tell Jon, *"I'd rather focus on the now than the then."* Jon didn't argue. He agreed with the philosophy himself. He was all about looking ahead. Yet, Kya was now part of Jon's increasingly complicated life. She appreciated how Jon was looking out for her because few did, none except for Addison and Larry. Kya said she was close to them, though she never specified how close. Yet, now Jon was one of those close people too.

On his way back to the staircase, Jon continued to watch Kya as she worked. Aware she couldn't see him, Jon didn't want Kya to see. All Jon wanted was for her to know he was there.

Were there a lot of men pursuing her? *No question.*

Did she meet other men besides Jon? *Most likely.*

After Jon had engaged in this sweet moment, he pivoted and was about to head up to the conference room. He stopped because behind him was Owen, who almost bumped Jon's shoulder. However, due to Jon's training as well as being slightly on edge today, he spun to avoid any contact.

"Whoa, take it easy there," said Owen. "You good?"

"Yeah, sorry. Fine," said Jon.

"Meeting upstairs. You know, briefing before the doors open."

"I know. Yeah."

"Came to get you," said Owen. "Addison's been asking about you."

"Right," said Jon. "It's still early, though. Have a few minutes, no?"

"Wants to meet with A-Team first," said Owen. "Apparently. You know how it is."

"Okay."

———

Jon followed Owen up the stairs and onto the next floor. Jon walked like he had a purpose. Each step was solid, his pacing was succinct. Jon moved like he had someplace to be, and he did. Soon as he entered the club's main conference room, the entire Doormen regime was present. All of them looked at Jon. Danix and Li were front and center while Jamal stood by the door. When Jon walked past Jamal, he decided to sit in the closest set of chairs he could find. These seats were the two at the back. Jon sat there, and so did Owen.

"All right, we're ready to begin," Addison addressed his employees. "Let's get started."

The conference room design was typical. It included a large table located in the center, with swiveling chairs spaced out all around. Most people wore jackets and collared shirts, and this was Jon's choice of wardrobe for today. Actually, everyone was dressed pristinely. Jon wasn't used to seeing his coworkers without their polo shirts. It was nice, he supposed. Addison Krowe wore a maroon three-piece suit and was showing off his spanking gold watch, maybe a Rolex but Jon couldn't quite tell. The man looked very impressive tonight.

"As you know, our event today is one of the biggest of the year, with Restitute set to come in just under three. Lots of moving pieces and lots to discuss. Let's start at the beginning, yes?"

Jon was now in full focus. With loads of coffee pumping through his system, Jon's senses were sharp as razors. It's one of the many reasons why he and the other bouncers drank coffee so often. It heightened their abilities and gave them an extra shot of energy and power.

"Jamal and Marshall," said Addison. "You're both on the doors. Got the lists?"

"Just picked them up," said Jamal.

Jon peered over his shoulder and saw Jamal holding his iPad. It displayed the lists for tonight. Jamal nodded at Addison.

"Stay tight on this list, will you?" said Addison. "There's going to be a lot of people who want to get on. Going to be intense."

"I got this," said Jamal.

"Excellent."

Addison was carrying an iPad as well. While perusing whatever was on screen, Jon checked his watch. Still wearing his favorite model, which was the Luminox Diver used by Navy SEALs, Jon adored the device. He never went anywhere without it.

"For security, we're going to have most Doormen on the dance floor, more on the second floor, and some others guarding various entry and access points."

Jon nodded. So far, this all sounded like common procedure. He wasn't surprised by anything.

"I posted all your positions. Check to see where you will all be."

Jon hadn't checked his posts. He was going to before Owen whispered into his ear.

"Did you check, bro?" Owen asked Jon.

Jon's head shook. "No," he said. "You?"

"Going to now."

Jon checked his phone using The Conquistador's employment app on Zen Planner. Jon's place was the dance floor. While he waited for Addison to say more, Owen nudged Jon's shoulder.

"Hey," he whispered. "Check this out."

Jon tilted his head and glimpsed at Owen's phone.

The app was now opened. The list of names was visible, as was everyone's positions. Although Jon only glanced at this device, it didn't take too much time to see. Right away, Jon could see his name was not there.

He couldn't see anyone's name, actually.

All the names of the Doormen A-Team were now missing.

There was no Danix, no Li, no Owen, and no Jon. It was strange, though not entirely unexpected. For the level of event, as well as the threat brewing from behind closed doors, the coming of The Fallen Sons was imminent. This changed everything. With all of this adding up fast, Jon couldn't be sure what Addison had planned for his main-level guys. Jon needed to remember he was a main-level guy, top tier essentially. He was ex-military, strong, trained, and extremely capable under pressure. Some of the other guys were strong too, no doubt.

Again, Jon was reminded of the pillars of the bouncing industry.

Calmness, kindness, tone, and focus.

"Our timeline is tight," Addison said. "James and his team will be arriving at eight o'clock, in which case three girls are going to escort him up to the VIP."

"James?" asked Owen.

"Restitute's actual name," said Addison. Jon didn't know Restitute's first name until now, but it struck a chord. James was the name of the Marine Jon lost before coming home. Sometimes, he hated hearing it but other times, he just had to accept it. Working here helped Jon to forget his past because there were battles to fight here too, battles that needed to be won just as much as the ones fought in the desert.

"And his team?" asked Danix. "We know anything about them, do we?"

"Private security firm, bodyguard agency, the usual for someone of his caliber."

"Can't we just use our own guys for this?" asked Danix.

It was an apt question. Jon wanted to know if they could too.

"Not tonight. It's in his contract for public appearances," said Addison. "He works with his own agency, always his own guys first, then the local unit. We have to work around it. We have no choice."

"Right," said Danix.

"And we know who his new team is though, right?" Jon asked.

Finally, Jon became part of the conversation. This part of the exchange was one Jon felt compelled to be part of.

"The security team?" asked Addison.

Jon assumed Addison knew what he meant. Evidently, he did not.

"Yeah," said Jon. "I mean, do we have profiles, background checks, and do we know everything about them?"

Once again, Jon found himself in a deathly silent space. He assumed this was because what he asked was a sound and logical question. Actually, he was surprised he was the one asking. Normally, Jon kept his mouth shut during these meetings.

It was better to listen than to speak, the same as the Marines.

"Well, we're not privy to that information," said Addison. He was speaking matter-of-factly, and Jon couldn't help but wonder why.

He knew they were under attack, didn't he?

He knew that anything could happen at any time?

So far as Jon was concerned, what they needed was as much information as they could get their hands on.

"Why not?" asked Danix.

With the tension rising, Jon wouldn't call it rancor yet, but he would say that the briefing was starting to get "real".

"We should know anyone who's coming through that door tonight, whether they have a reason for being here or not."

"We cannot *legally* ask for background checks, you know that, right?" replied Addison.

"And why not?" asked Jon.

"Well, because we're not police," said Addison. His hands were on his hips and he was now using a no-nonsense voice as he replied.

Jon studied his boss's demeanor.

He looked at Addison's furrowed brows. There was no refuting Addison's statement. No one here was a cop. But the Doormen protected the club and its patrons, yet they did not investigate crimes and they did not conduct their own investigations. They could ask for ID and refuse to distribute alcohol to anyone who had too many and remove those who broke the club's code of conduct and rules and they could guard the doors, but that was it. That was the extent of their jurisdiction. After Addison denied Danix's concerns, the room remained just as silent.

"No, we're not cops, but we do have enemies," said Jon, "and they're coming, whether we choose to believe it or not. We're not police, no doubt, but policing is how we have to start doing our jobs now moving forward. I just want to make sure we're doing all that."

Suddenly Jon felt like he was being tickled.

He never spoke this way. He was being assertive but also articulate and strong. What he was doing was speaking from the heart. Jon respected Addison, always had, and he always would. Jon's intentions, however, were not to challenge or to be disrespectful to his friend and boss. He was just remembering the concerns of himself as well as his coworkers.

After speaking up, Jon looked back at Addison.

He hadn't said anything and his reaction to Jon was minimal.

It wasn't until later that Addison's opinion regarding Jon's comment became clearer.

"Which is why," said Addison and he stared only at Jon. "The other half of our briefing is going to be a little different."

Jon tilted his head as his curiosity piqued. He was looking forward to this next part.

"Consider this next part to be the first phase in our policing protocol. We're not cops," said Addison. "You're right about that. But this conflict we're in...*it's a personal one.*"

Jon gazed at Addison and paused for a beat. Then, he looked around the room.

The enemies mentioned were people who once worked at the club but didn't anymore. They were those with a shared animosity toward The Conquistador and its employees, including and especially the Doormen. They wanted revenge, and their tactics were dependent on sabotage, terrorism, and possibly death.

Jon knew personal battles, and this one couldn't be more personal.

"We're all ears," said Danix,

"Not ears," Addison said to Danix. "*Eyes.*" Addison's position shifted and the images on the screen changed.

Jon and the other bouncers were now staring at photos of three different men.

Jon instantly recognized all of them. They were the same men who ambushed him on the dance floor a few nights ago. They were the Fallen Sons, the great enemies of The Conquistador Doormen. Addison was not pretending anymore. He was here to tell everyone exactly what they were up against.

All of it was beginning now.

"So, you all know some of these men," said Addison. "Some of you more than others."

Addison eyed Jon. Jon *did* know them. He was one of the few who did.

"First name on the list is the bad boy in charge...Mr. Rex MacIntosh. He was known as Rex Mac when he worked here, but he's not that anymore."

Jon gazed at Rex's picture.

He didn't exactly appear as Jon remembered him. His head was shaved now and in this picture, he had hair. It was a shade of dirty blonde while eyes were a shade of deep, eerie brown.

"Rex is smart," said Addison. "Served in the Army Rangers but was discharged and was hired to work here shortly after. Now, he is the main conspirator, no doubt. It was his efforts that got him and others disbanded from the club. And, if we were going to assume anything about this man, it's that he's runnin' the whole revenge show now," said Addison. "He knew every way around this place, which is why we have to be tight and focused. Leave no room for error."

Everyone nodded. Jon thought about what a man like Rex was truly capable of.

Based on what Jon experienced before, with the smoke bomb and other combat skills, Mr. Rex Mac was no joke. Jon assumed the other Sons weren't either.

"Next up...Brutus Watson." The images switched and Jon and the other Doormen were now looking at some Neo-Nazi-looking asshole with a fat fucking neck. Jon remembered this guy too. To Jon, this Brutus was a fucking animal. He was a brute, so the name suited him quite well.

"We can only assume he's the muscle, the right-hand man. He has his hand on the switch and he will do whatever he's asked to do. He's tough as nails this one and can take a shit-ton before he finally goes down.

He was our guy on the door before he was let go, so...he knows how the front works, if you get what I'm saying."

Jon turned to look at Jamal and Marshall, the other dude on the door.

Addison's slick comment was directed at these two men. There was no denying what this Brutus might have in store for them. Knowing this, the two hulking men that were Jamal and Marshall both nodded.

They caught Addison's drift and knew the score. "Aye," said Jamal.

Jon glanced at the front of the conference room, at the screen and at the third photograph.

"Next is Cole Hausen," said Addison, now serious. "This one...this one is a livewire."

Jon never heard Addison use the word *livewire* before. Truthfully, he didn't quite know what the word meant. He had an idea, but that idea was unclear.

"I know this word is thrown around a lot, but psychopath, cold-hearted killer, and murderer, well, let's just say this Cole guy is the real deal. He was fired because he didn't have the temperament and liked to hurt people. He wasn't part of our guild for too long, but he was let go around the same time as the others. So, that means he's roped in with them and is also a hot mess. He's a goddamn joker too, as dangerous as he is unpredictable. He's a chameleon, a solid one. He's there one minute and gone the next. When you see him, do not hesitate to call for backup. Trust me when I say you're going to need it."

The Doormen responded well to backup. The A-Team bouncers rarely called for it. They were on the front lines because their tactics and skills were top-notch. If Addison was advising them to do this, then it was because they needed it.

They had to have it.

"Does everyone understand?"

Jon looked around the room.

There were other Fallen Sons Addison had spoken about but Jon only remembered the first three because, in his opinion, Rex, Cole, and Brutus were the most capable, and so they required the most attention and time. When Addison asked the question, everyone nodded, so everyone was on the same page. Jon no doubt believed he was on the same page too. While it was how he felt, suddenly, Jon felt something in his stomach he did not expect. He didn't want to call it fear, but it was close. He was worried, on edge, and was thinking about several possible outcomes that left him twisted.

These men, these Fallen Sons, were the real deal.

They were deadly.

"All we can do right now," said Addison, "is our jobs. We do our jobs the same as we always have. We keep our eyes open, watch each other's backs, and, most importantly, try to remain calm. If we do that, everything else will fall into place," Addison expressed this next part of his speech with ferocity and passion. He was not talking to his workers but his friends. "We will do it. The Sons versus the Doormen. It's a game of chess, and we all know how to play that, so let's do it, do it again, and do it right."

Jon perused the conference room. Calmness was the Doormen's creed and the very oath of the game they were playing. To keep it now, with this so much at stake, it made Jon all the more fearful. But fear was not always a bad thing. As Jon learned in the military, fear is good. Fear works. Fear is your friend.

CHAPTER 6
THE FIRST MOVE

WHEN THE MEETING ENDED, IT WAS BUSINESS AS usual. The Doormen shook hands and exchanged a few words with one another. There were some queries, but Jon was sure to check in with Danix who couldn't help but comment on the recent fight the two just had.

"Good tap. Solid tap."

Jon appreciated the compliment. He wanted to ask Danix more about the Fallen Sons, the names of the others who may or may not be showing up tonight. The club was cleaned and the drinks were set. The DJ was prepped and ready. Restitute had not yet arrived, but when he did, he'd be entering through the club's *rear* entrance.

This was how VIPs usually entered The Conquistador. It was a single door lined with bright lights.

"You feeling good?" Owen asked Jon. "Feeling up to par, as they say?"

Jon nodded as he scanned the dance floor. "Yeah. You?"

"Yeah," said Owen.

With a deep breath, Jon gazed at his friend. Owen was barely looking at Jon and his right hand twitched into his thigh. Such behavior could only be attributed to fear, and Jon thought his friend Owen might be afraid.

Jon understood this. He was afraid too.

The Conquistador filled in just under an hour. When Jamal lifted the rope, clusters of eager club patrons poured in. All happy, excited, and ready, the bar was stacked. Fat lines of people huddled around and begged for drinks. Kya and the other bartenders sprinted from one to the other, slinging and pouring.

The booths were occupied. The VIP section was loaded. And so far, there was no sign of Restitute or the Fallen Sons anywhere, which was good.

Right now, everything seemed standard and exactly as expected.

Jon thought this would make him more relaxed. Then, he remembered the main thought on every bouncer's mind, here, at The Conquistador. Everyone is just waiting for the first fight to go down.

Everyone is waiting for someone to draw first blood, to throw the first punch so it can end the anticipation and everyone can just be cool for the rest of the evening.

Fights in the club industry are unavoidable.

The more people, the greater the odds of something bad going down. Jon didn't get through an entire shift without some drunk knucklehead getting carried away or some drunk girl getting out of hand with her and her friends.

It was a fast, unpredictable business.

Like a cop, you can't work a single night without some problem arising that requires your swift and immediate attention. Jon knew this all too well. But, here and now, he saw nothing to indicate conflict on the horizon.

He didn't like this feeling. It was too odd, too out of place.

He desired things to be normal, and normal here meant abnormal.

However, nothing seemed to be. Everything was dreadfully normal, and yet, the ominous feeling in Jon's gut returned. It deepened as soon as Jon felt a hand on his shoulder.

He wanted to pivot, grab the hand, and initiate the classic wristlock.

This was always Jon's go-to technique while on the job. Doing this now was reflexive. Yet, Jon didn't actually feel like he was being threatened. Still, he didn't care. As he turned to see who was touching him, someone familiar screamed into his ear.

"He's here!" yelled Owen.

Jon flinched.

"Restitute is here! He's at the doors!"

"Aye," said Jon. He stepped toward the perimeter of the dance floor. Jon was supposed to stay by the back doors while Addison welcomed the main star of the evening. He wanted there to be some Doormen close by, in case they were needed.

The goal was to keep Restitute as far from the people as possible. The rap star said he wanted to avoid the cameras and stay out of sight before the show. Jon remembered Restitute was bringing his own security. Jon's orders were to watch the doors while he and Owen stepped around a crowd of women and men. There were other bouncers close as well. All of them nodded at Jon and Owen as they walked past. They didn't say anything, but the double doors leading to the back were *forbidden*.

Jon remembered this place well.

It was the same section where Frankie Castellani met Sam, who was a former Doormen but was not part of the Fallen Sons. This was odd but then Sam Vaughn was still waiting to stand trial and thus, not free to move around or to come here for that matter. This place contained the so-called *hidden rooms* of the club itself. No one was allowed to go there, none except for Addison and Larry. No one else. When Jon saw it, he was taken back to the day when he had worked to expose Frankie Castellani. Jon remembered how he defeated the notorious son of a notorious mobster. Seeing this door also coerced Jon into remembering The Conquistador's secrets.

There were many. Maybe *too many*.

Once one Escalade pulled up, Jon gazed at the Cadillac's tinted windows to see what he could see.

Jon soon squinted at the shapes of four men. All were wearing suits, which was the standard wardrobe for all private security. Jon gazed and waited with Owen for the doors to open. The crowd so far was contained. No one was getting through. When the car doors opened and Restitute stepped out, he was utterly drenched in bedazzling jewels. He shined as if he himself were a diamond. Restitute's jacket was emblazoned, and his sneakers were blinding white.

After leaving the vehicle, his boys joined him. All of them were dressed the same and each one shook Larry's hand as they proceeded. The owner of the club greeted his guest with humility and grace.

Jon watched Larry bow his head and offer his steady hand.

"Thank you for coming to my club."

Once the initial greetings were completed, Larry and Addison stepped in for a quick photo.

Restitute was surrounded by people and cameras. Now was his moment to reveal himself to the club, but the rap star didn't recoil in the presence of all the flashing lights and screaming fans. He waved, made a peace sign, flipped the bird, and even made a few wise-cracks to some of the giddy girls. Jon was impressed by all the pizzaz, all the confidence. Then again, Restitute was famous, and you don't become famous without being confident.

And this guy had it in kilotons. Restitute had so much of it he practically sparkled. Despite the door being all cleared, the commotion happening inside the club amplified. Jon did his best to stay attentive. He was until another person called out his name.

"Jon?" At first, Jon thought it was Addison, or maybe Owen or Danix. But when he heard the voice again, he knew it wasn't any one of them.

"Is that you? Jon...hello." Facing the one who called him, Jon's shock continued to build. It was someone Jon felt glad to see. He was pleased after encountering a man who was slowly earning the Marine's respect.

"Michael? Michael Irons?" The man who greeted Jon was none other than Mr. Michael Irons himself. He was in fact the same man who Jon met yesterday at his very own house. He was the man who was dating his mom and he was also the same man who owned his own security company.

It was for this reason he was here now.

"Hey!" Michael's voice was high. He seemed genuinely excited to see Jon now. "Nice to see you! I knew I'd be running into you," Michael said. "Kinda glad I did."

"Right." Puzzled by Michael's enthusiasm, Jon eyed his mom's friend.

Usually, security are stoic while on duty. Michael was standing close to Restitute and was paid to guard him, no doubt. However, his eyes weren't on his man, they were on Jon and only on Jon.

"So, you're the security he hired?"

"Aye," said Michael. "Our reputation precedes us, so we're guarding this superstar while he works."

"I can see that," said Jon.

There were five bodyguards, all of whom were Michael's employees. Both Jon's job and Michael's were tight. Focus was to be expected. Always, it was this way, no matter who was in attendance.

"Look, I know we're both busy," said Michael, "but I just wanted to say that I'm happy to see you. When things slow, if they do slow, I'll stop by, say hi."

"Right," said Jon. "Sure."

Jon didn't expect Michael to have much time.

Guarding was a constant endeavor. There were few breaks, and tonight, given the sheer scale of this event, Michael wouldn't have time to take a piss, let alone stop and say hello to Jon. Still, Jon appreciated Michael's sentiment.

He was being nice and Jon appreciated the niceness.

Given how Michael was with Jon's mom, if he was willing to be nice to her son, then he was likely being incredibly nice to her. This sat well with the Marine.

"Anyway," said Irons, and he moved toward the door. "We're moving in now. Catch you on the flip side, eh?"

Michael offered Jon his fist for a pound. Jon popped Michael Irons's knuckles, stepped back, and let Restitute go on. Everyone followed, and Addison gave Jon a touch on the shoulder. Whether it was to acknowledge he was doing a good job or if he was just happy to see him, Jon wasn't sure.

Maybe it was both.

"Okay, we're making our way upstairs now," Addison said.

Jon could hear his boss through his walkie. Jon could hear Addison as well as some static too. Jon eyed the moving security team. He could see Restitute stepping up the stairs and proceeding to his suite.

Jon and Owen continued to guard the doors. Not saying much, Jon heard Owen whisper.

"Time to move back, yeah? Wanna go?" The question wasn't rhetorical, but Jon treated it like it was. He wasn't ignoring Owen. He was just focusing on something else because something strange caught Jon's attention.

"What's the matter?" Owen noticed Jon's alertness. There was an alteration happening within The Conquistador.

Primarily, this setting was comprised of dumpsters, other doors, recycling bins, and a rear parking lot when the front one was occupied. It was not filthy by any means. It was just quiet and sealed off. Sometimes, employees would use it for smoke breaks and occasional conversation. It required a key for reaccess, though and was only accessible to a slight few.

It was not used often nor by many.

Jon crept with his nostrils flared. He found himself feeling drawn to this one difference that, to the naked eye, wouldn't mean much. Yet Jon was now an experienced bouncer. He was using his skills of deduction to sniff out anything he deemed suspicious. This was Addison's recommendation. It was advice Jon would follow until the very end.

"Jon?" Owen called his friend again. However, Jon continued to ignore Owen. "You can't be leaving the floor, man. We need you. We need you to..."

Jon proceeded like Owen wasn't even there. He wasn't doing this to be disrespectful or rude, it's just what Jon saw he couldn't ignore. It was a critical clue that, to any bouncer, would have been overlooked.

But not Jon.

"What is it?" Owen hurried to catch up to his friend. "What do you see, man?"

By now, Jon was completely outside The Conquistador. He passed through its back doors, but *one* in particular had caught his attention. This door stood apart from all the others. It had no handle and no color. It was bordered with thin lights, and the only way this door could open was from the inside. So, it was connected to The Conquistador's notable *forbidden section*.

In fact, it was directly linked to *this* place.

And, right now, it was opened. *The door was opened!*

"What do you see?" Owen asked again. He caught up to Jon, somehow.

It was only after hearing this question that Jon finally snapped back and realized there was another

Doorman standing next to him. Jon could only hope Owen noticed what Jon did. Now kneeling, Jon pressed his elbows against his thighs and gawked.

"Door," said Jon. He was so matter of fact he didn't know how Owen would react.

"Door?" asked Owen, confused.

"It's opened. See?" Jon pointed at the opened door.

"Shit," said Owen. "How? How the hell did that happen?"

Hearing this, Jon could only shrug.

"Don't know," said Jon. "Can't open from out here, only from inside."

"So, someone walked through it," stated Owen. To him, the result seemed obvious.

Then again, he was new to The Conquistador. Owen didn't know about the zoning or the sections. Jon only came across this hidden wing because of his run-in with Frankie Castellani.

"Someone must've walked through it though, right?" Owen asked.

"No," Jon quickly dismissed. "No, this door leads to a very specific part of the club, a part only few know about."

"Specific?" said Owen. "How specific?"

Jon didn't have time to explain to Owen exactly what he was referring to. Now was not the time whereby Jon elaborated on things like the forbidden wing, the club secrets, or how The Conquistador was a layered entity.

All Jon knew for sure was this door had been opened from the *outside*.

And, if it was opened from the *outside*, then someone on the *inside* knew about it. They knew where it would lead and they knew how to access it. Such information was only shared among the most experienced Doormen. Although Jon was one of these people now, he knew those who weren't. He knew the best Doormen and those who might have been responsible for accessing said door. They weren't friends. No, they were enemies. They weren't current members. They were those exiled and outcast. They were the ones *fallen*—The Fallen Sons.

"They're here," said Jon.

"Who? What?" snapped Owen, a hint of fear clinging to his voice. "Who's here?"

The admittance of the Sons was only just a hunch. Jon didn't know for sure if they had arrived, then again, instincts are key.

And, if the signs are there, you stay calm before you react.

You take action. You fight.

CHAPTER 7
SICK BEATS

When Jon discovered the opened door, the first decision he made was to radio the rest of the team. Jon wanted Danix and Li, but not Addison. The cooler was too busy accommodating Restitute at this time. He was working with club promoters and PR people to ensure the main event was moving fluently and effectively. Jon knew he could hear him through the mic, but so far as expecting him to get involved, it was unlikely.

He called out to Danix, who answered shortly after.

"I hear you. What's the issue?"

The issue at hand, Jon didn't know quite how to describe. Then, he channeled his inner Marine and pulled out an old word from his vocabulary.

"Breach."

"What?" The voice belonged to Li.

"We've been breached!" Jon felt silly saying this out loud. Still, it was the truth. The club was accessed by enemy forces.

"Someone opened the black door to the west wing. They knew where it was and how to open it."

"*You sure someone opened it from the inside?*" asked Li.

"Did any of you?" Jon snapped back. If it wasn't any of them, it had to be someone else.

Jon believed the connection was obvious.

"Had to be someone who knew about it and the only people who could know are the Fallen. They have to be."

"*Right,*" Danix spoke through his radio.

"Do you see anything on your end?" asked Jon.

"No," said Danix. He was on the floor, scoping the setting and looking for anything suspicious. "Nothing. Shit. They knew right where to hit us too. They knew we'd be preoccupied. Goddamn it. They also knew the only way in was through that door, the one no one uses."

"Yeah, but it was locked," snapped Li. "There was no way to open it."

"Unless they knew," said Jon. "They knew *how* to open it, and clearly, they did."

The comms suddenly fell silent. Every bouncer was performing their own tasks and duties.

Right now, Jon wasn't a bouncer as much as he was a secret service agent. An incursion had occurred. A threat was made against the president's life, so to speak, and it was up to Jon and the other Doormen to prevent this attack. While there was no telling where this new enemy had come from. On the floor, Jon could see Danix, Li, and Owen. They were posted out at certain locations. However, The Conquistador did consist of multiple levels, some seen and some unseen.

Jon needed to open a line of communication with the other bouncers.

As of now, Jon was by the dance floor. And, standing at the bottom level, he checked everyone's hands and cross-referenced the photos of the Sons. Jon studied the faces. Given the blinking lights and the incoherence that came with the radically changing shades, Jon couldn't quite make out the appearance of anyone.

He could move in closer, no doubt, but Jon opted for another option.

"We need our *Shades*. You have them?"

"*Yes.*"

"*Yes.*"

More Doormen joined in on the comms. Jon plunged his hand into his pocket. He pulled a pair of sleek, fat sunglasses. Jon slipped the lenses on his face. They were what the Doormen referred to as *Shades*. They were another tool gifted to all the bouncers working at The Conquistador. After Jon placed these *Shades* over his eyes, everything he saw instantly brightened. Now, it wasn't quite night vision. It did alter color coordination and added additional light onto all the seen faces.

From farther away, it was more difficult.

Jon stepped closer. He was now able to make out more faces and determine the identity of more guests. And, with Danix, Li, and Owen wearing the exact same devices, Jon raised his hand and made a rotating motion.

This was the signal to move in.

The rest of the Doormen were positioned at the four corners. Jon wanted to ensure they moved in at the same time. He wanted them to start from the outside and gradually narrow their search. Jon glanced at as many faces as he could but had yet to see any that fit the descriptions of Rex MacIntosh, Brutus Watson, and Cole Hausen. Jon saw nothing he recognized and certainly nothing he could use to assist him.

"Anything?" Jon asked.

"*Negative*," said Danix. He was closing in too.

Actually, he and Li weren't far apart, but the dance floor was exploding. Now among a perpetual swarm of bodies, all bouncing and swaying, it gave Jon little room to move or maneuver. Keeping his eyes open, Jon proceeded and felt as though he was trudging through murky water. Jon swam through the blackness, uncertain of what lay ahead or behind him. Jon shivered. He wasn't cold. The setting was humid. It stank of perfume and alcohol. The hairs on Jon's neck pricked up and his prosthetic felt heavy.

At any moment, something could happen. At any moment, Jon could lose.

Journeying toward the center of the floor, so far it was all clear. No sign of the Fallen Sons.

"*Nothing on the dance floor*," said Danix.

"Need to make our way to the next level. Search there."

"*Roger that.*"

"Stand by," added Jon. He pivoted around a dancing couple and made his way to the perimeter. Jon shuffled and continued to scope and continued to feel the same ominous assaults burdening his body. When Jon moved, he stopped and was off-guarded by a thumping, encompassing roar. Gazing at all the screaming faces, the raised phones, and all the numbing shrieks from the excited patrons, Jon stepped as Restitute emerged in all his glory. Surrounded by his entourage, he carried a microphone and blasted his loud, scratching voice into the speaker.

"Aw yeah, Conquistador, let's make some noise!"

The entire room exploded as a thundering applause rampaged the setting. Jon was struck by the sheer force of a hundred faces shouting a hundred different words. While still wearing his *Shades*, the light shining on the rap star was difficult to see through.

Jon gawked up to the second-floor balcony.

Although Restitute was with his security unit, a few club patrons were recording him as well as themselves. They took whatever footage they could and continued to relish in the star's presence.

Restitute was now performing. He was in his zone, so to speak.

"Restitute is on the floor, moving," Jon's finger was pressed to his ear. He acknowledged his fellow bouncers and waited for their reply.

"*I see,*" said Li. "*He's going to the stage. We should clear a path, just in case.*"

"*We could,*" replied Danix, "*but that's not part of the plan. We need to stay in position!*"

Danix raised his voice and Jon pulled his finger away from his ear. "Damn it."

Danix was right.

All Jon had was a feeling. He only *felt* like the Fallen Sons were in the club. There was no evidence to support it, however. No, Jon was acting primarily on instinct. This did not justify any of the Doormen leaving their current position, however. It was bad planning, and it was irresponsible too. Jon was neither.

Restitute trekked across the dance floor but his security stayed close. Jon didn't pay much attention to Michael Irons. He was part of the team the same as the others, and though the stage wasn't far, the people were still crowded too closely to the rap star.

Jon's heart raced.

A lot depended on Restitute's safety. Since the club's opening, The Conquistador hosted many performers. All of these performances went well. There were no accidents or problems, but then Jon thought: *what if there were some tonight?*

Restitute was now on the club's stage. He was fully absorbed in all his magnificence and attention, the way all musicians behave when among fans. He rallied the crowd, and everyone present was enamored by the superstar. While everything seemed to be going as planned, Jon stayed on guard.

He was ready even though nothing had happened.

In Jon's mind, this threat was real, even if it had not taken effect.

Jon treated it this way until the full hour finished and the rapper concluded his performance.

"Aw, yeah, Conquistador!" Restitute kept rousing the crowd and Jon kept his back pressed to the nearest pillar. He watched everything and everyone. The Fallen Sons were not present, but at least nothing happened to Restitute that hindered his performance.

Everything went exactly as planned.

Once the rapper was done spitting lyrics, he was escorted to the VIP section along with his security as well as an entire lineup of waitresses and hot club promoters. Jon stood and kept a close eye. What he expected to happen had not happened. And so Jon was relieved. There were no Fallen Sons, no fights, and barely any incidences at all. Most importantly, the show was going well. Restitute's performance was well received. The people were happy and Jon could see a giant smile on Addison's face.

Now began the autographs and photo opportunities.

Those who paid an additional two hundred were given the opportunity to meet the famous rapper, take a selfie, and get a signature. All of this was standard practice. There was much security. It was to take place in the VIP booth in the next ten minutes. Jon didn't have to stand guard. His place was on the floor, where he was supposed to monitor all activity. Kya and the bottle girls moved along with a giant ice bucket as well as a fat bottle of champagne. They held sparklers while Kya led the way. She looked at Jon and waved, but he played it cool.

Jon stepped away so he could let Kya pass. She walked up the steps and handed Restitute his bottle, to which he smiled and gave her a sweet kiss on the cheek. Despite his status, Jon thought Restitute seemed cool but bold. He was polite, and without sunglasses, he was almost unrecognizable.

Restitute uncorked his bottle of champagne and the liquid fizzed and bubbled all around until it poured all over the star's booth. Waitresses scurried to assist and tried to fill as many glasses as they could. Soon, Restitute and his friends were toasting to the good show. Yet suddenly, the feeling of fear emerged in Jon's belly. He didn't know why it did, only that when it did surface, it festered and felt much, much worse.

"Shit," Jon uttered. He hoped none were close enough to hear him.

As Restitute downed his glass, his face afterward was unexpected and weird.

The rap star grimaced and twitched. Looking sour, his cheeks had sucked back into his face and he coughed. Immediately making note of this, Jon was the first to see but he was not the last. Restitute heaved and suddenly, he was coughing so much his face had completely changed. All the veins bulged and his neck muscles were strained, like he was being strangled to death.

"Yo, boss? You good?" Someone in Restitute's entourage snapped to and motioned after the notorious rapper.

"Bro, you good?" Restitute's friend was wearing a red jacket. He placed the coat on Restitute's shoulders. Obviously concerned, Jon was too. Yet, Jon's concern increased when he noticed that Restitute's coughing was not letting up. Going on and on, Restitute wheezed and fought to catch his breath.

Soon after this happened, Jon saw Michael Irons and his security detail blitzing toward their hurting client. Michael and his detail surrounded Restitute. By now, Addison had taken care of all the fans. He guided them to a separate section and made sure they were away from Restitute's booth. The rapper continued his violent coughing while his complexion had altered to show variegated pockets of red.

Jon had no place here now. He was not in charge of protecting the rap star. Still, he was formulating all the reasons regarding what was happening and why. Whether Restitute drank too fast or was suffering from an allergy, maybe he was tripping out as a result of some drugs he'd taken.

All these reasons were incomprehensible.

―――――

Michael moved in and worked with Restitute and his staff. Seeing Michael in action appealed to Jon. He was a professional bodyguard, so protection was his game, whereas Jon's focus was only on people and the club.

"Jesus Christ, he's ingested a toxin. He must have!" Michael shouted. "Son of a bitch!"

"What?"

"Fucking don't drink anything!" Michael snapped.

At this time, Addison had moved in to help too. Restitute's complexion was now maroon. His arms were shaking and his coughs turned to convulsions. His attempts to try and catch his breath were replaced with vehement, bursting thrashes.

"9-1-1!" Michael yelled.

Addison stood with Michael. Jon could see that he was also beginning to change color. His skin was white, and his fingers twitched. Jon could see he was doing his best to keep calm.

But the situation was out of control.

"Don't drink a goddamn thing!" Michael yelled again.

―――――

When Michael screamed for someone to call 911, Jon pulled out his phone and dialed.

"*9-1-1 emergency response?*"

"Need an ambulance at The Conquistador right away," Jon's voice was sharp as glass. "A guest is going into cardiac arrest!"

Jon didn't know if this was the truth but said it despite the fact.

"Need an ambulance right away."

"*Emergency response team is on their way, sir. Please remain calm.*"

Jon hung up the phone and raced after Michael and Addison. He wasn't there to interfere or to hover over anyone. No, as Jon leaned in closer, he made room for Addison and Michael Irons. Being a friend, Michael was aware that Jon was here to help if necessary.

"Called an ambulance," said Jon. He looked down at Restitute. "They should be here soon."

"Thanks," said Addison. He could barely speak the words necessary to calm his friend.

"What the hell did he drink?" Michael Irons barked at whoever was close enough to hear.

Restitute's head bobbed and he fell forward and back.

"Just the champagne," said one of Restitute's boys. "Just the fucking champagne."

"The champagne?" snapped Jon. His eyes opened wide as he began to think about the reasons that pertained to this attack.

"The champagne," said Addison. He spoke slower and, like Jon, was piecing together the reasons surrounding this situation. He was looking deeper and was only just starting to accept it as truth.

"Fucking champagne. *Our alcohol,*" added Addison.

"Did anyone else drink it?"

"No," Michael Irons said to Jon. "Thank God."

"But what about..."

Jon looked at the bottle, grabbed its neck, and yanked it from the bucket of ice. Rubbing the rim with his thumb, everything felt the way it should. Whoever tampered with Restitute's drink knew how to take out a cork but also how to put one back in the exact same way.

The very idea of doing this was a set of skills baffling to the Marine known as Jon Haze.

It was a professional attempt at sabotage. When Jon thought of this, his heart pounded in his chest. It compromised his vision. He felt like he was about to faint.

"We have to get him out of here. We have to..." Jon was sputtering words like he was inebriated. He was thinking too much too fast. The more he thought, the less cohesive and sensical everything began to appear.

Jon steadied. He waited for Restitute and his entourage to clear the booth.

The rap star continued to gag and vomit as he was taken upstairs to the ambulance.

Jon focused on the famous rapper and more commotion surfaced from all around.

What started as a fun night had taken an abrupt and rough turn.

Jon gazed at all the chaos. The situation began to fully dawn on him. He once thought he understood how the club worked. He did, but he didn't know exactly how someone could hurt The Conquistador, and maybe not just The Conquistador. You can rebel against it. You can refuse to follow its rules and cause fights and problems.

You could do this, but then you would just be bounced.

This could cause problems but not significant ones like the those Jon and the other staff were facing down at this moment. If you really wanted to hurt a club, you take away what it needs most.

And it needs only two things: people, music, and drinks.

In one fell swoop, the Fallen Sons had taken all of this away.

They hurt the club in a way only former employees could, and it hurt...a lot.

———

When the ambulance arrived to help the famous rap star, Jon gazed at the dance floor. Although most of the crowd had been clearing out, one person seemed to stay in place.

He stood among the crowd of panic-stricken clubgoers.

This man did nothing except leer at the floor above.

Rex Macintosh, leader of the Fallen Sons, looked at Jon and grinned.

Like a mad clown, he was precisely as Jon remembered. With rage coursing through Jon's veins, he rolled his fingers into a pair of fists. He wanted to leap off the second-floor balcony. He wanted to drop down like a fucking superhero and face off against this ludicrous leader. A move was made, and it was deadly. The

Conquistador's greatest enemy had the upper hand now. They may have won the battle, but there were others ahead. And Jon knew one fact above all others: the war was far from over.

No, the Doormen were just getting started.

CHAPTER 8
FIGHT BACK

AFTER THE NIGHT OF RESTITUTE'S PERFORMANCE and the tampering of the club's alcohol, The Conquistador was faced with an epic backlash. Not even Jon could go online without seeing some story about what had transpired. It was, as Addison said after Restitute was taken to the hospital, a complete and utter disaster.

"New York's legendary nightclub, The Conquistador, is being faced with an investigation..."

Jon tuned into YouTube and searched for The Conquistador. The first result was the Restitute story. He watched it with a close eye. All of it was centered on Restitute. He was taken to a hospital after the incident.

"Apparently, the club's alcoholic beverages were laced with a toxin that induced some kind of vomiting. While no charges have been filed, the club is under investigation by the Division of Alcoholic Beverage Control as well as the Nightclub Oversight Commission. The club's owner, Larry Thomas, did make a statement that he will be working closely with the administration

as well as the NYPD to get to the bottom of what he referred to as a terrible travesty.

"Guests had arrived to watch the performance of famous rapper Restitute, who fell victim to this heinous crime. Although none of his representatives cared to comment, the rap star was taken to a hospital shortly after the incident occurred. No official word has been given regarding his status at this time, though he was last heard to be in critical condition."

Jon stopped watching at this point. The story hit social media as well. With hashtags and stories swarming the scene, Jon couldn't take it. At the same time, Jon couldn't resist going on social media to see more. From what Jon could see, everything was blowing up.

The few hashtags Jon came across were:

#sueTheConquistador and #saveREZ

Jon snickered. No one knew the whole story, and no one really cared to know about it either. Jon couldn't stand the idea that people were calling his club irresponsible when they had no idea it was sabotaged. The Conquistador was attacked by a dangerous group of men who sought to disrupt and destroy it.

Jon texted Owen and Danix.

After Restitute's poisoning, so to speak, all the other Doormen were left shaken. They had to deal with a massive fallout. Patrons were screaming, fights erupted, and people flooded the streets while running amok and not knowing what to do. The police arrived to conduct their own investigation. This included checking with the club's security and looking at a list of its employees. Jon only hoped Restitute wouldn't sue for damages, but how could he not? He was almost killed that night and survived only because of the rapid response of the bouncers and the security detail.

Most of the Doormen were up all night. Kya was overwhelmed.

Jon didn't see her once.

When he reached for his phone, he expected to see messages from Danix, Li, Owen, and Addison. Jon scrolled through the list, and surprisingly, one was out of the ordinary. As it turned out, Kya had messaged Jon.

She was the first to reach out.

> How are you? Are you all right?

It was a simple exchange and nothing other than a simple greeting. Still, normally it was Jon who connected with Kya and not the other way around. Clearly, she wanted an update on Jon and she was concerned about his wellbeing.

To Jon, this couldn't be a clearer sign of affection. He answered Kya right away.

> Fine. Shaken up and lost. I don't know what's going on. The cops? Addison? Mr. Thomas? I mean, have you heard anything?

Jon typed fast. He imagined he wouldn't be hearing back from her for some time. Back in his bedroom, Jon was interrupted when he heard a knock at the door.

"Jon, sweetie, are you up?" Jon's mom didn't usually bother him so late.

Then again, he did work all night. It was now late in the afternoon. If she was to bother him, then it was overdue. Jon looked at the door and answered.

"Yeah. Come in." The door peeled open.

Jon didn't move a muscle. He was wearing only his boxer shorts and no shirt. He didn't care. His mom, during this time, was busy doing the basic things. She'd cook, clean, and she'd read and sometimes she'd do work for her job, which was in marketing. She was also a technical writer for a contracting group based out of Long Island. However, when Jon's mom looked into his room now, she looked like she was wearing makeup.

She was looking done up, pretty. Jon's mom was really pretty.

"Hey," she said, sweeter than usual. "Are you okay? I didn't want to wake you after what happened. Well, I know you don't watch the news, but I'm sure the Internet is having a field day about it."

"No doubt," said Jon. "It's actually bad."

"I'm sorry," replied Jon's mom. "Actually, Michael was telling me all about it."

"Michael?"

"Yeah, he was there too, remember?"

"Right," said Jon. Now, he was remembering the man known as Michael Irons. Yes, he was present. Actually, he was right in the middle of the damn situation, the same as Jon was. What surprised Jon most was the conversation Michael shared with his mom. If they both talked about the incident at The Conquistador, then they were sharing information about Jon's job. And, if they were sharing information about jobs, then that was an indication of just how close the two of them were getting.

For Jon, this level of closeness did not make him feel good.

Now, he admired Michael. Jon thought he did a

good job the night of the sabotage. Still, he was talking to his mom about what happened. Seeing how pretty Jon's mom looked now, something else might be happening too. And it was another detail that did not sit well with Jon.

"He told me everything. He was hired to protect the Res...the Res-ti...you know, the rap star," said Jon's mom.

Jon nodded. "Restitute," he corrected.

"Right," she said. "Anyway, well, apparently he was taken to the hospital and Michael was there with him, you know?" said Jon's mother. "Although, he doesn't think it was your fault, obviously. Someone was doing something at the bar, he thinks. It might be an attack against him, though, maybe a bad fan or something."

Jon wanted to scoff at his mom's theories. They were only slightly appealing, but they were also totally inaccurate.

"Have you had any meetings about it?" asked Jon's mom.

Jon shook his head to answer.

"Not yet," he said. "Addison felt it was best to give everyone some space, y' know. He wants everyone to take some time off so they can recover. He wants to do that before he decides his next move. Besides, there's not much to do while the club is under investigation."

"Investigation?" Jon's mom snapped. She sounded surprised. "Investigated by who?"

Jon didn't exactly know. He provided his mother with the first title that entered his mind.

"Nightclub Oversight Commission."

"Oh my god. What about the police?"

Jon shrugged. "Addison is taking care of the legal

side of things, apparently. As far as we all know, we don't exactly know what went down, so we're still trying to figure it all out too."

"I'm sure you all are."

"Until then," said Jon, "I'm supposed to lay low. Not go yet."

"Well, what about your job?" asked Jon's mom.

"What do you mean?"

"You still have one, right?"

"What, you mean like...am I still a bouncer?"

"Yes." Jon's mother was whispering. He wasn't sure if she was relieved or more frightened for her son's future. He didn't know which was which, and he didn't care.

"For now, I do. Why?"

"It's just that...well, you know I've been talking to Michael. And, well, he thought maybe if things don't quite work out there, he figures you can go and maybe work for him. His agency might be hiring, he said. He told me you did a great job that night. I mean, he told me all about it, and he thinks you can do even better for him. I'll give you the info, in case you're interested."

"Did great," said Jon. He couldn't believe the words he was hearing from his mom's mouth.

First, Jon appreciated a compliment as much as anyone else did. Yet, on the day of The Conquistador's sabotaging, Jon didn't do much. Jon knew when he did something great, something worth mentioning. All he did that night was discover how the back door was opened and Michael didn't know any of that.

Other than that? There was nothing.

"Yeah," Jon's mom said to her boy. "Like I said, he told me all about it. Anyway, his protection agency is very reputable, you know. They have a lot of very impressive clients too that they protect. Michael said with some extra training, he will find you a spot on his team, no problem."

"You do realize being a bodyguard is, like, ten times harder than being a bouncer, right?"

"Sure, but under his watch," said Jon's mom, "he said he'll take care of you. Besides, I think he's a much better leader than that other guy you work for."

"Mom," replied Jon, annoyed by this whole conversation. "You barely know Addison."

"True," she said. "But after what happened, I'm not sure."

"You weren't there, Mom. You weren't there." Jon stood near his bed. Then he hopped toward his closet. He didn't want to talk about this anymore. He was making that clear.

"Right. I know. I don't mean to say that what happened was *your* fault, but—"

"It wasn't anyone's fault," said Jon. "No one's."

"Okay, but look. I just...I just want you to start thinking a little more ahead is all. I know you like where you are now, and I know you're still young, but I would really like to start having serious conversations about the future, alright? I just want you to start having a future."

Jon sighed.

Now completely exhausted, he'd grown tired of having the same talks with his mom over and over again. Jon was tired of having to always explain to her why he wanted to work at the club. He was tired of her thinking too much about his life. Jon was also especially tired of having to hear about this Michael Irons. He was sick of his mom talking about him every chance she got.

Most importantly, Jon was just tired from everything else that came after his job.

"Anyway," Jon's mom said as she stood from the bed and began to make her way toward the door. "I don't want you to think I'm being pushy."

Jon didn't say anything, but that's exactly what his mom was being.

"But I won't be home tonight. Michael's taking me out to dinner, so you'll have to take care of your own meal, if that works?"

"Michael?" Jon replied. "Michael's taking *you* out?"

Betsy Haze was halfway out of Jon's room when she replied. "Yeah, for dinner. Well, first he's going to be taking me out for a little outing," Jon's mom jittered to show her excitement. "You know, squiring me about the town, so to speak."

"The city?"

"Yes."

"And he's not working today?" Jon asked.

"No," said his mom. "He's free. In fact, he did make some money the other night. Says he's good."

"How?" said Jon. "His fucking client was poisoned!"

"Thought you said it wasn't anyone's fault?"

Jon could see where this talk was going. He decided to fold and drop out early. Like he reminded himself already, he was just too damn tired to do anything else.

"Right," said Jon. "Sure."

"Well, get dressed, do whatever, and I'll see you later, yeah?"

Jon nodded. "Yeah."

His mom left, but Jon stayed in his room. He wasn't mad at her or anyone. In fact, he didn't have time to be angry or pissed these days. With his head down in more ways than one, Jon glimpsed at his mother as she left his room.

"Talk soon."

When Jon's mom walked out, the Marine thought of all the people he wanted to talk to. Only one came to mind. He retrieved his phone from the nightstand and skimmed until he saw Kya's name.

He sent her a text while heading to the bathroom. By now, his mother was gone. It was strange how the day is structured when a person works nights. In the Marines, Jon woke at the crack of dawn. Some days he would have only a few hours of sleep. Here, it was different, and sometimes he liked it. Other times, Jon hated it. Today was one of the days whereby he hated it.

Day damn one was a saying Jon heard back in the Marines. He used to say it whenever he dreaded an upcoming day.

The house was empty today, so it was quiet. It was so quiet, to Jon, it felt...scary.

————

When Jon messaged Kya, it wasn't long before he received a response. Still, Jon kept his messages short and somewhat sweet. He said he wanted to meet. He didn't say he missed Kya. Actually, he didn't mention work at all. Jon asked Kya if she was free. She said she was, and they agreed on a place to be.

Jon's phone vibrated as it chimed.

Coffee shop. Same one as last time.
Come.

Jon knew exactly where he was supposed to go. He hurried out the door. Weirdly, Jon's mom's Camry was parked in the driveway. Jon didn't know exactly how she was going to meet with Michael. Jon assumed she was picked up by his car. Such was a nice thought because, due to this fact, Jon had access to his own vehicle, which his mother was letting him use more and more for work. This made his life so much easier for Jon.

For now, it was very nice.

As he rarely had an opportunity to drive, Jon sought to take full advantage of it now.

He snatched his mom's keys from the bowl and sprinted toward the door.

With no pauses in between, Jon jumped into the Camry and drove. He didn't do much driving. Sometimes he forgot how. When this happened, he was sure to take things slow. He brought a coffee with him and ventured through the Queens's suburbs. He wasn't sure what day it was. So often, they came all molded together. He couldn't discern one from the other, and this was always a challenge.

Jon wasn't sure how to do this. Honestly, he didn't care.

He was used to the days blending together. He was used to days turning to weeks and weeks into months. And as a result of this, Jon was starting to see why his mom said what she did. She wanted Jon to think about his future. This is a difficult task to complete. Time passes quickly as you start to get older.

And therefore, Jon wanted everything to slow down as much as it could.

There was only one place whereby time slowed. It happened only when Jon was with the people he cared about. This included his mother, although he was seeing less of her now. It happened with her, and it also happened when Jon was with Kya. Whenever Jon was with Kya, he could remember every hour, every second. Once it ended, all he craved was more.

Jon desired what everyone did: *infinite time.*

Thankfully, where Jon was going now was to obtain more time.

He drove to the coffee shop wearing only a muscle shirt. The weather was scorching. It was one of those hot days in New York where people wore nothing but flip-flops and tank tops. The heat helped Jon to wake up.

As he ventured into the coffee shop, he didn't see Kya there.

It was mid-day, and Jon didn't see a lot of people actually. Despite this, he walked to the counter and ordered something cold and refreshing.

"One mocha Frappuccino, please." Jon didn't drink these too often, but he liked them.

He waited for it to brew and then felt a playful tug on his strap.

"Since when are you a frap drinker?"

Jon scanned Kya up and down. Wearing booty shorts and a tank top, her nipples poked through the fabric of her tight shirt. Jon gulped, a little nervous. "Since I got up late afternoon on a...what day is it again?"

Kya grinned. "No idea," she said. "Absolutely no idea."

Jon smiled at her too. He thought it was cool to see Kya's relationship with time was similar to his own.

"Right," Jon said.

The barista held Jon's dripping cup and Jon took it and felt the cold drops moisten his palm. The woman behind the counter looked at Kya. "Can I get you something there too, hot stuff?"

"Uh..."

Jon watched Kya bite her lip as she considered what she was going to order. Jon couldn't keep his eyes off her the entire time.

"How about a...Frappuccino?" Now Jon was the one smiling. When Kya ordered the same drink as Jon, he looked at her with his head slightly bent. "And you're a frap drinker, are ya'?"

Kya leaned against the counter. "Today, I am."

"Right," said Jon. "Shall we sit?"

He walked to the closest booth. Kya grabbed her drink and paid with her credit card. Jon and she proceeded to sit while Jon sucked on his straw. Jon waited for Kya to sit next to him. He wouldn't start without her.

"So...how you holding up since yesterday?"

"Fuck," she said. Like Jon, she seemed tired. Her eyes were red and Jon could see she hadn't slept much because he didn't sleep much either. "How exactly do you explain what the fuck happened, you know?"

Jon shook his head. "You can't," he said. "You just can't."

Kya nodded.

"I wanted to check in on you," Jon said, "the night

everything went down, but I was...tied up, as you could expect."

"I did expect that," Kya said. "So, no worries."

"But then," added Jon, "I'm sure you were tied up too, no?"

"Most definitely. It was, well, it was rough."

"I'm sure." Jon didn't doubt a word Kya said.

It made perfect sense. Kya was a bartender. Therefore, she was technically in charge of drink distribution. She didn't serve Restitute, though. One of the other bottle girls did. Still, Kya was in the hot seat. After what happened, no one was safe from the ongoing investigation or the criticism. It was awful.

"Well, do you have any ideas?" asked Jon.

"About what?" said Kya.

Jon wanted to tilt his head so it was completely sideways. He was just as perplexed as he was before. "About what happened," said Jon. "Have you heard how it happened?"

"Well, no," said Kya. "I mean, well, Marcy was the one who held the bottle, but we're still not one hundred percent sure that was the drink. After Restitute got sick, Addison came up to us and inspected all the bottles we had."

"Yeah?" said Jon. He was surprised to hear this. He didn't know Addison went to the bar but he should have, no doubt.

"Yeah," confirmed Kya.

"And did he find anything?" asked Jon. He was eager to hear more.

"Not really."

"Really?" asked Jon.

Whenever someone inserts the word *really* into any

part of their conversation, it's usually done to show how something isn't certain. There are some pieces left unresolved or unrevealed. In this case, this *really* signifies to Jon that Addison *did* find something. It might not explain everything, but it could be something big.

"What did he find?" Jon asked again.

"The bottle was still sealed," said Kya, "and the label was still on, but there was a slight detail that Addison thought was weird."

"What?" asked Jon. "What's the detail?"

"Well, apparently," said Kya, "the champagne bottle brought to Restitute's booth was a *different shade of green*."

"What?" said Jon. "You mean, like it wasn't green like all the others were?"

"Well, no," replied Kya, "not exactly. I mean, it was, yeah, but it just happened to be a lighter shade for some reason. Like, it's not totally uncommon. We have served drinks that have looked the same way before and nothing has happened, but it was just a slight detail that Addison felt was interesting, so he put the bottle aside for further inspection."

"I see."

"But what did you see?" asked Kya. "Did you or any of the other Doormen get a look at any of the security footage or was it just the cops? I mean, did Addison say anything about it?"

It was a solid question, Jon thought. He hadn't been told anything about the footage, though he should have been. Jon shook his head. "No."

"Damn," said Kya. "I imagine there might be some answers there too, right?"

"Yeah," said Jon.

With his eyes wide and glassy, Jon felt hypnotized. He was zoned out as he thought about the existence of this footage. He liked thinking about it because it offered direction as well as a potential strategy.

"Definitely." Jon stopped talking as his mind became flooded by new ideas. The footage he was never allowed to view because that technically wasn't Doormen business. No, footage was Addison's territory. It fell within the jurisdiction of the club's head of security, to which he had complete control over.

"What?" asked Kya. When Jon stopped talking, it was clear there was something on his mind. Whatever it was, Kya felt it was something worth mentioning. "What is it?"

"It's just..." Jon removed his hand from the Frappuccino and slid his wet palm across his jaw.

"What you said, about the security cameras..." When Jon articulated his response, he slipped back into thinking more about what Kya said.

"Yeah?" Kya asked as she leaned in and eagerly awaited Jon's reply.

"It's just...it might be a good place to start."

"*A good place to start?*"

"Yes," Jon said to Kya.

"You mean, like we, what...go into Addison's office and like...find footage?"

Jon didn't say yes or no when replying to Kya's question. He didn't do anything to suggest he had an answer. Still, what Kya suggested was exactly what was on Jon's mind now.

"Actually, yes."

"But...that's Addison's job," Kya stated. "He's the

only one who can access The Conquistador's security? It's part of his cooler duties."

Jon nodded. He pretended like he knew the answers, but he really...he did not. All he had was a plan and a slight hunch about whether this footage was accessible or available.

"I don't know. Maybe." Jon shrugged. "To be honest, I really don't know."

Jon took a deep breath in. What he was about to say next was big. He hoped Kya would agree.

"We need to go," said Jon. "We need to go and have a look around."

"Have a look around?" Kya was flabbergasted by Jon's statement. "What do you mean?"

Jon's eyes shot down to the floor. He was thinking about what he meant. Mostly, he was thinking about how to explain this to Kya thoroughly and properly. What he wanted to do was far outside his pay grade, his normal tasks, and his duties. It didn't change how Jon felt. "We need to see what's there, what we could not before. We need to investigate this...*together*."

"Investigate!" Kya exclaimed to the point where she was almost hollering. "What are you now, a cop?"

Jon refocused and his eyes narrowed. He wasn't just thinking anymore. Now, he was scheming, planning. "No," said Jon.

"Then leave the investigating to the police, okay? Just lay low, wait for what happened to clear up, and then we'll be back to normal."

"No," Jon replied. "Not while they're still out there."

"They?" asked Kya. "Did you say...*they*?"

"I did," said Jon.

"You mean, like, you know who's behind what happened? You know who fucked with The Conquistador's supply?"

"Maybe," said Jon. "But I'm not really sure."

"Whoa, whoa," said Kya. "How do you know anything?"

Jon's lips parted and he adjusted himself while sitting in his chair. He was about to say more, but he was hesitant. He wasn't sure he should tell Kya the truth, that is the truth about The Fallen Sons. If Jon shared this with Kya, then he would also be talking about The Conquistador's legacy, its past, and maybe its secrets. So, when Jon opened his mouth to speak again, he looked at Kya while displaying a stern, shrill expression.

"You asked me a long time ago, how much do I know about the place I work? You remember that, don't you?"

"Yeah," Kya said to Jon. "I remember."

"Well, I think I know a little more than I thought," said Jon.

"What do you mean?"

Jon was about to tell Kya everything he knew, but before he could, he realized that the disclosing of these Fallen Sons should wait. It needed to wait because Jon's priorities had changed.

"I don't think now's the best time to explain," said Jon. "I do think, though, the situation we're in—that we're all in—is serious. It's a brutal time and we need to think about how we're going to handle it going forward."

Jon stared at Kya. He was trying to see if she looked nervous. It was at this point Jon would know just how close he and Kya were. If she was going to follow him into this next endeavor, then he'd know for sure she cared about him.

Jon would be one hundred percent certain of the truth.

"We need to look for answers," Jon said. "The cops...they won't provide anything to us. And to be honest, I really don't trust them, not right now."

Kya sneered, and Jon understood why. What he was saying was crazy. He wasn't a cop, but he was—and always would be—a soldier. Nevertheless, Jon did not feel safe at his place of work. Jon couldn't wait for the police to help him or anyone because every time he stepped through the club, he was at risk.

He couldn't tell Kya why or how, but he was. *Everyone was.*

"You don't trust them, huh?" said Kya.

While giving Jon a quizzical look, by now, he had finished his drink. He said all he wanted, so it was time for Jon and Kya to get up and start moving.

"No," Jon said, "I don't." He leaned forward, and his chair screeched until it came out from under the table. It was time to leave, and it was time for Kya to come with him.

"I wish I could explain more, but I can't right now," Jon said. "I can't because, at this moment, we have a job to do. We deserve answers, and until we find them, what happened once will happen again, and I guarantee you, next time, it's gonna be way worse. Now, are you in or out?"

What Jon had provided to Kya was a classic ultimatum. He had yet to give one to anyone in his life, but the benefits of doing so were substantial. By offering this,

Jon was testing Kya's loyalty and knowing exactly where she stood. If she was willing to go with him, then she cared enough about Jon to risk her own safety. If she believed what he said about the club, then she also believed he was a smart, capable, and fearless person.

All of these qualities were attractive for someone like Kya. Jon knew this. More than this, he enjoyed it. Choosing not to say anything after, Jon waited to see what Kya would do. Now he knew exactly what he wanted from her. In his mind, Jon craved it. He couldn't deny his feelings anymore, but then he couldn't force anything to come out either. In the end, all Jon was doing was waiting.

Sometimes, he questioned why he waited and what he was waiting for.

Jon thought about this often, and then he understood why.

Kya was amazing.

She stood just as Jon had seen her stand before, and she looked at Jon the way she did when Frankie and Sam were taken away in handcuffs. She was the same back when it was Jon's choices that led to both justice and truth. Kya stared at Jon with an alluring gaze. Jon believed she didn't doubt him.

No, in truth, he believed she trusted him. And it was this trust that kept Jon and Kya united and strong. When she touched Jon's hand, she held it tightly and longer than Jon had expected.

Jon held hers just the same while also staring into her sultry eyes.

"Yes," Kya said. "Hell yes, I'm in."

CHAPTER 9
BEHIND CLOSED DOORS

The Conquistador was closed just as Addison said it would be.

However, when the doors to a club are closed, it doesn't necessarily mean no one is inside. During the day, The Conquistador was occupied mostly by its cleaning crew as well as additional bar hands. Notably, it's the lead bartender, Mr. Allen Alvarez, who works closely with the servers was likely present at this time.

Jon knew Allen, as did Kya.

Jon didn't see much of him, however, but he was familiar with what he did. Allen oversaw inventory and distribution. After what happened, Allen was likely with Addison now. They were probably both at odds with each other as they both tried to understand who tampered with The Conquistador's alcohol during Restitute's recent performance. Whether or not Allen had done anything remained unproven. No, Jon's reason for going back to The Conquistador was because of another truth.

In Jon's mind, he was certain it was Rex and the Sons.

Jon actually remembered seeing Rex on the dance floor. His presence was undeniable.

The smug son of a bitch that was the fucking leader stared Jon right in the face.

He raised his slimy finger and placed it over his posh lip to deliver a chilling gesture of silence. Jon could see him perfectly now. Jon could see him, and he loathed him. Jon drove Kya to the club and parked in the visitor's section. At this time, the parking lot was mostly empty. Seeing any club in the middle of the afternoon is always a strange sight to behold. The building was almost abandoned, like a warehouse without workers or a school without students. Jon hadn't come across his place of work too often in this light. It was difficult to accept, given that on any other night, one would expect to see it booming.

It pained Jon to see The Conquistador so lifeless.

Greeted without music, without gyrating bodies, and without any beautiful women, Jon didn't like any of it. The girl thing, however, was different now, because now Jon's heart belonged to Kya. And, even so, the sight made Jon feel good when the girls touched him or winked at him as he stood guard.

Jon was always professional. Yet, the perks of his job were wide and high.

He enjoyed every single one of them.

Jon and Kya trekked toward the back doors like two thieves about to break into an ATM. They were really just two pissed-off people who wanted some goddamn answers. Jon moved to the door first and peered over his shoulder. He was about to head in but stopped when he had the feeling he and Kya weren't alone.

Stopping dead, Kya whispered to Jon. "What's wrong?"

Jon squinted and looked back.

"Just want to make sure we're alone." Jon scanned the street outside the back doorway. He checked all the people walking by. He wasn't paranoid. At least he told himself he wasn't. Kya stared at Jon and was concerned. Her head shook in disbelief.

Why was Jon staring like he actually believed he was being watched and followed?

This was a question Jon asked himself as he stood by and continued to inspect.

He couldn't stare for much longer in fear he was drawing more attention to himself. In doing so, he asked himself another question and this was: how many people stand outside an empty nightclub?

The short answer was: not many.

Those that do are either people passed out from the night before or others trying to break in. Now, Jon couldn't stand to be labeled as either one of those things. He was here against the wishes of his boss. No one was to enter The Conquistador until the issue was solved.

Addison's orders!

And so, Jon was not supposed to go in.

"Is it open or not?" Kya asked.

"I don't know," said Jon. "Hope so." Pushing the door with his shoulder, Jon peeped to see if anyone was actually there. Kya stood directly behind him. She and Jon crept into the dark space like they were trespassing.

In a way, they were.

Jon eased his hand in through the door and glimpsed at the club's back ballroom.

As empty as a funeral parlor, Jon didn't hesitate. He slid his feet along the thin carpet. He ventured into another section of The Conquistador, and then Jon walked to the stairs that led up to the second floor and to Addison's office. Jon had been in Addison's place for many occasions in the past and so he knew where and how to access it.

Jon was curious if Kya had ever been there before. He imagined she had. Later, Jon heard some tinkering by the bar and some slight commotion near the club's west wing. He didn't recognize anyone there, so Jon walked on like he was supposed to be there, and he was.

"This way," Jon uttered to Kya.

There were other rooms in the hallway. To avoid being noticed, even if Jon didn't think they would be, he slowed as he passed by other rooms. At the end of the hall was Addison's office. Jon knew it well. When he came to it, he placed his hand on the door handle while Kya followed Jon like she was his shadow. Jon couldn't express just how much he enjoyed this.

He liked not being by himself.

When Jon turned the handle, he did as at a millimeter per second. He listened closely. Addison could be in his office. What Jon was doing was not opening the door. No, he was testing it to see if it *was* opened. If it was locked, then that meant there was no one there. And, if it was unlocked, then Jon could only assume Addison was waiting.

And if Addison was waiting, then both he and Kya were busted clean.

Jon hoped to feel locks. Contrary to what Kya

thought, Jon Haze wanted the door to be locked. Turning the handle, Jon felt the hard brace of a door that would not open. He heard the soft, barely present sound of a clicking lock and a metal hinge. It was then Jon had his answer about whether or not the door had been opened.

"Damn," Kya muttered. "It's locked."

Jon let go and grinned. "Exactly," he said.

"Exactly?" asked Kya. "What do you mean, exactly?"

"If it's locked," replied Jon, "then I know *exactly* how to get in."

"What?"

Until now, Jon hadn't mentioned how he was someone allowed to enter Addison's office. Above the door handle was a ten-digit keypad. The only way the door could be opened was with the entry of four numbers. Jon, however, already knew the combination. He knew it not because he was told by Addison, no. The only reason why Jon knew how to get inside Addison's office was because he watched his boss enter these numbers before.

Always, Addison punched in the numbers without pause or care. When he did this, Jon was curious about why Addison did it so openly. He thought maybe people wouldn't notice him entering the correct numbers. However, Addison Krowe was too smart to assume this.

But Jon *did* notice the numbers. He knew exactly what they were and how to get inside.

"Wait," said Kya. She watched as Jon entered the code. "You know?"

Jon punched the numbers in slowly. The digits

were simple: 4334.

"Yeah," said Jon. He turned the handle and listened to the locks shifting and sliding. "I know."

There was a beep and Jon closed his eyes.

Just because it was locked did not mean no one was on the other side. For all Jon knew, Addison could be there. He could easily be at his desk and could have easily heard Jon entering the codes. Addison could be there, but then there might be someone else there too.

Maybe it was Larry. Maybe it was Allen.

Maybe it was any number of other people Jon didn't know. It could also be Addison's wife. Jon hadn't met her yet. He had heard stories but had never spoken to her directly. For all Jon knew, she could be behind this door. Thankfully, she wasn't.

What Jon saw was an empty office.

He breathed a sigh of relief and motioned toward Addison's desk.

"We have to be quick," Jon said. "Do you want to keep an eye on the door?"

"Yeah." Kya stopped by the desk but made sure to keep an eye on the entrance to Addison Krowe's office.

Jon wanted Kya to stay close. She stayed where she was, which was fine for now.

Jon had some knowledge regarding Addison's computer. Oddly, it wasn't password protected. Jon found this to be quite strange. Yet sometimes Jon left his laptop open. He didn't care whether people saw what was on there. He had nothing to hide, and evidently, Addison didn't either.

Jon was only here to look at the security cameras and nothing more.

"Are you in yet?" Kya asked Jon.

Jon peered over at Kya, who was still watching the door.

"Not yet. Soon," said Jon.

His hand was on the mouse and Jon continued to battle the idea regarding why Addison would leave his computer open, especially now. Also, why didn't Addison have cameras in his office? Jon looked around in search of any but found none. It was a strange detail. They could be hidden, no doubt, but then Jon didn't have time to consider these particular details. He had a job to do and to get done.

When he opened Addison's desktop, Jon quickly scrolled through the applications and looked for anything that pointed to security footage. Jon even tried the word *camera* in the search bar. When typing this word, Jon eventually came across an application that fit the description. Clicking rapidly, Jon must have browsed through at least ten applications in a matter of seconds. Not long after he looked for one, eventually Jon was given access to The Conquistador's security system.

It was easy to navigate, at least it was for Jon. He skimmed the dates until he found the one he wanted. Once he acquired the correct date and time, Jon clicked the screen that captured the rear of The Conquistador. This was where Jon saw where the door was opened, so he had assumed it was the right footage. It was at this point Kya stopped watching the door and decided to snuggle up to Jon. Together, they leaned over Addison's desk and perused the footage.

"Shit, you did it." Now seated on the armrest of Addison's chair, Kya was so close Jon could feel her breast. He didn't say anything and instead kept his attention on the surveillance footage.

"Yeah, I did."

"So this is from the other night, yeah?"

Jon nodded. "It is, back when I found that door was opened."

Jon leaned in so his face became closer to the screen. Both he and Kya continued to watch the video.

"Wow," said Kya, impressed by Jon's skills.

The surveillance footage played on, but Jon was fast-forwarding through most of it. As the video sped up, Jon squinted and waited for the exact moment when he would see just who opened the back door.

"Wait," said Kya. "Go back."

Jon noticed another small detail, so he did what Kya told him to do.

Jon pressed rewind and returned to the part Kya was pointing out. It was taken almost two hours before Restitute took the stage. There were two men, both dressed in black. They looked like run-of-the-mills thugs who walked with slovenly gaits. Both marched toward the door, which was at the corner of the screen, and they weren't wearing masks or anything. While the camera was sharp, it didn't exactly bring faces into focus. Still, Jon recognized them.

"Fuck me."

"What?" said Kya. "You know these guys?"

"I do," Jon said. He swallowed down all his booming feelings of shock, dismay, and rage.

"Who are they?" Kya asked.

Jon was focused as he folded his hands next to Addison's keyboard.

"It's them," said Jon. "It's the fucking Fallen Sons."

Jon didn't share with Kya exactly who the Fallen Sons were. There was an entire back story she hadn't been told, and frankly, Jon was glad she wasn't.

"Brutus Watson and Cole fucking Hausen," Jon said to himself.

Clear as day, both of these men were moving in. They opened the door with the lights and Jon had to assume they also tampered with The Conquistador's supply. They were responsible for the investigation. Worst of all, they were responsible for what happened to The Conquistador's big night. After Jon found what he wanted, he fell back in Addison's chair. The footage provided Jon with some semblance of truth, which was as undeniable as it was terrifying.

"Who?"

"You've worked at The Conquistador longer than I have, haven't you?"

"Yeah."

"Do you remember any of the other bouncers, you know, before you started?" Jon asked Kya.

She shook her head and answered. "No."

"Then you don't know about the ones who worked here but who were let go, the ones who were fired," said Jon. "See, there were other bouncers, other Doormen who fought but who apparently disobeyed and disrespected The Conquistador. And for that, they were dismissed, *exiled*..."

"Right," said Kya, like she wasn't all too taken by this piece of information. "So?"

"Well, the way they were let go, see," said Jon, "it wasn't exactly...nice."

"What do you mean?" Kya asked again. "Not nice?"

"Their crest was taken, torn away."

"What?"

Jon didn't provide Kya with any more details. As of now, the facts remained as they were. The Conquistador was infiltrated and the Doormen were attacked. Their reputation was tarnished and they were compromised. They were weakened, and Jon could barely hold back his rage.

"It doesn't matter," Jon replied to Kya's previous inquiry. "All you need to know is they're back and they need to be stopped."

"But, don't we have, like, what...*any proof?*" asked Kya. "Proof that they were here?"

Kya's question was solid. Yes, they did have proof.

"All we have proof of," said Jon, "is two people used the back door instead of the front."

"Still," said Kya.

Jon sat straight and glanced at Kya.

"You're right," Jon said to Kya. "We do have something, maybe. It's a start, and it's definitely something we can talk to Addison about, no doubt."

"How do you know Addison hasn't done that already?"

Jon stood up from the chair and looked at Kya. "We don't know that he hasn't. I'm sure he has. Come on..." Jon scurried toward the door. He expected Kya to come with him, and she did later. Now that Jon uncovered some security footage, he felt validated. He felt assured. Therefore, Jon's choice, he knew, was the right one. He had come here to achieve a goal, and he did. Stepping back, Jon Haze was reminded of where he was.

"We need to get out of here before he sees."

And, as soon as Jon finished saying these words, someone immediately answered. "Too late." When Jon heard Addison, his body froze like he was being injected with wood. For a second, Jon wasn't looking where he should. And, because he didn't, he was caught.

Busted.

Addison stood before Jon and Kya, and with a glower, his posture was scarier than his expression. His fists were clenched and his feet were spread. Jon bowed his head. He couldn't hide the shame, so he refused to even try. And Jon never lied to Addison...*not once, not ever*.

"Shit," Kya uttered to Jon. "Addison?"

"What?" said Addison. "Did I surprise you?"

Always upfront and truthful, Jon didn't want to start anything, even if he did technically break into his boss's office. Jon had nothing to say except what was already known.

He said it like he meant it, because he did.

"Yes," said Jon. "You absolutely did."

CHAPTER 10
UNTOLD TRUTHS

Once it became apparent to Addison that Jon and Kya had broken into his office, the staunch cooler abruptly asked them both a generic yet obvious question. "What? You think I didn't have any cameras in my office?"

Jon felt like a misbehaved child being reprimanded by a teacher. He thought Addison would have cameras, yes, but then Jon didn't think his boss would check them now. Jon hoped he was busy doing something else. Evidently, he wasn't.

"Didn't think you'd be checking," Jon replied. He hoped his answer would work. It didn't.

"I got an app on my phone," said Addison. "I always check it."

"Even though the door's locked?" asked Kya.

Jon's shoulders twitched. This made sense. Why check what's inside one's office if you've already locked the door behind you?

"Yes," Addison motioned around his desk so he could take a seat. "Based on what we're dealing with, no one is safe, not really. There's no passage that can't be accessed and no commodity that can't be exploited, as you know."

Addison didn't seem upset. He spoke to Jon and Kya in a normal voice and had yet to call them what they were. In this case, they were *trespassers*. They were bad employees. Now, though all of this was true, Addison hadn't spoken about any of it.

He just sat back and continued to speak. "My office isn't any different."

"Look," said Jon. "We're sorry. I know we shouldn't have snuck in, it's just—"

"Never mind," Addison said, waving his hand. "How the hell did you even get in?"

Silence and tension both emerged between Addison and Jon. The cooler asked the Marine a simple question he wasn't prepared to answer.

"Uh..." At this point, Jon was done, no matter what he said, and he didn't want to lie, so he felt it was best just to be straight. Now might be Jon's last opportunity to do so. "I know the combination."

"You what?" Addison raised his voice. He wasn't angry but intrigued. A smile peeked as Addison barked in his chair.

"I know the combination," said Jon.

"And just how the hell do you know that?" Addison snapped.

Jon glanced at Kya. She was smiling too.

"I've seen...you enter...it before?" Jon said all of this very slowly.

He was careful about how he phrased his reply. He shouldn't know the combination to Addison's office to begin with. However, Addison did enter it quite openly.

He didn't hide the numbers. Anyone would see, and Jon often took the lack of secrecy as just how much Addison cared to keep it hidden.

Jon thought he didn't care too much, so he memorized it. He did this with the intention of using it, which he did.

"You have?"

"Yeah," Jon said to Addison.

"Shit," said Addison. "Guess I have to do a better job keeping that a secret, huh?"

"Not really," said Jon. He was relieved to see Addison not angry but fascinated by the Marine's memorization skills as well as his observational power. Then again, that was Jon's duty now. He saw and recorded the minute details for further use. "I'm just, maybe a bit too nosy."

"Clearly," said Addison. Now at his desk, Addison sat astutely in his chair.

"So, it is them?" asked Jon. He ended the silence so he could get back to talking business. "It is the Fallen Sons?"

Hearing this, Addison Krowe nodded.

"They were the ones who broke into the club, tampered with our supply, and sabotaged us."

Addison's chin barely moved. Still, he nodded to confirm. "Yes."

"Shit," said Kya. She was now on the same page as Jon and Addison. "How did they do it?"

The *it* Kya was referring to was the Sons' access into the club's supply vault. Jon was wondering the same thing, in fact.

"Not here," said Addison. "We checked the footage and looked at our vault. The only one in there was

Allen. He had the key. I saw it clearly. He didn't open a single bottle."

"Well, maybe he didn't need to," said Jon.

"What do you mean?"

"It's just," said Jon. He was looking at Addison. "Okay, it didn't happen here, like you said. But maybe the Sons went to our supplier, got on a truck somehow, opened a case, and then fucked with it there."

"To do that," said Addison, "they would need to know *who* our supplier is..."

"Or maybe they don't have to," said Jon. "Maybe the supplier was in on it too."

"Hmm," said Kya.

"Yes," said Jon. He had another look around. He did this whenever he was thinking about something big. "Who's the only contact between the club and the supplier?"

"Everything still goes through Allen," Addison said. Jon didn't know this exactly. He did now.

"Right," replied Jon. "And you spoke to him already?"

"More than that," said Addison. "I was with him. He checked every bottle. Nothing changed that night."

"Nothing we could see, that is."

"See?" said Addison. "What are you driving at, Jon? What are you trying to say?"

Jon closed his eyes and thought about what he did mean—the logistics behind his thoughts and words. Jon believed he was onto something, as he said. He was pursuing a truth, but then he might also be talking out of his ass. Jon wasn't a detective. He was a soldier and he was a bouncer. He didn't follow leads and he didn't ask questions—other than ID, name, and age. Then again, he was here and he was thinking. He had some ideas, yes, and some Jon believed were worth more than others.

"Maybe nothing happened to the bottles that Allen *inspected*, but maybe something else happened to them at some point, though."

"If you're thinking about accusing Allen, you better think again," said Addison. "I checked the cameras. He picked up the box, dished out the bottles, and poured nothing inside. Trust me, they were *untouched*."

"Exactly," said Jon. As Jon began to piece together his theory, his heart raced and his hands began to twitch.

"Exactly *what*?" asked Kya.

"Nothing did happen to the bottles," Jon said. His head shifted from side to side. Jon was thinking too quickly. He needed a minute to let his mind settle. Again, Jon Haze was no detective. He was, however, starting to feel like he was one. "Nothing happened to the bottles because no one opened them *except* for Allen."

"Like I said," stated Addison, his hands folded in front of his face.

Although Addison appeared inquisitive, Jon was surprised that his boss hadn't come across the same theory. It was almost as though Addison wasn't thinking. He was too occupied being a lawyer and not a cop, which was what Jon was.

He was because he needed to be.

"But what if the bottles weren't tampered with because someone poured poison inside of them?" Jon asked the group. "What if the bottles that were opened were *already* tampered with?"

"Meaning?" asked Kya.

Jon glimpsed at Addison. A twinkle flickered in his eyes as Jon fell into a chair.

"*A switch*," Addison said. A lightbulb flicked on.

Jon knew this exact feeling. It was the same moment of revelation that he had experienced only seconds earlier. Jon nodded. "Yes."

"Someone switched the bottles during shipment? How?" asked Addison. "We received delivery the same as we always do. Same truck, same company."

"Maybe the Fallen Sons grabbed the truck, took control, switched the shipments, and then arranged the delivery?" Jon suggested, following a hard line between this notion and the possible truth.

"Son of a bitch," said Addison. He embraced Jon's theory with a cold, dead hand. "Son of a fucking bitch."

"No one ever looks at who's fucking supplying," said Kya. "In fact, I'm pretty sure Allen was too busy thinking about the night that he didn't give a shit who was dropping off the stuff, though he should have. I mean, he was taking inventory, making sure he had enough."

"Exactly," said Jon. "Truck comes, Allen takes inventory, he signs, replies, and then moves on."

"He had one hell of a load that night too," said Addison. "I'm sure he just wanted to get it all unloaded and get it to the bar as quickly as possible."

"Does he know anything about these Fallen Sons?" Kya asked Addison. "Is he aware of them, aware of what's happening?"

Jon eyed Addison and waited to hear his response. He knew that the existence of these enemies was a best-kept secret. Addison didn't move. He placed his hands on his waist and stared ahead, regret filling his gaze like sand gradually spilling through an hourglass.

"No one knows about them," Jon said. He knew this was Addison's answer despite not being asked the question. "They're hidden."

"Not anymore," said Addison.

"Well, should we still tell the police?" said Kya. "What they did was fucking illegal. They poisoned our alcohol and almost killed a huge rap star! We have enough to put them away for fifteen to twenty! It's attempted murder, for chrissake!"

Everything Kya said was the truth, and Jon was glad to hear it. Until now, he thought it would come to this, the Fallen Sons being arrested and punished for their actions. Undoubtedly, it was growing and getting worse by the day, but still, Jon didn't know what the outcome would be.

"Right?" barked Kya. "Am I right?"

For a time, Jon didn't know why Addison refused to take any of this to the cops. He considered the reasons, and there were many.

"What you did to them, the Fallen Sons," said Jon. "How they were let go and banished from the club, I'm guessing that wasn't exactly *legal* too?"

Addison snorted and began to turn around very slowly. Jon received a glare from his boss yet stayed focused and strong. Jon was bold. He was also courageous and had broached a serious subject: the origins of The Conquistador's new enemies. Jon knew all their faces. He knew what they wanted, but what Jon didn't know was how. He didn't know the methods used during their firing or how their crests were taken from them. Jon didn't know any of the details because

Addison never mentioned it, only hinted at it. And yet, Jon didn't care to know, at least he didn't when he was first told the story. He didn't then, but now he was beginning to consider.

Addison didn't talk about the banishing because it was likely too messy.

It was likely very ugly. Maybe it was horrifying.

"We have to get to our supplier."

Like with the forbidden room Jon stumbled across six months ago, Addison refused to provide an answer. Addison roamed to the chair at the corner of his office. It was located between two bookshelves and beneath three framed photographs. Addison grabbed his jacket, which was leather and with a pointed collar. He pulled it off the armrest and threw it over his shoulders.

"I know where it is. Not far from here. We can go and hopefully find another lead. If they somehow managed to get to our truck, then someone there might be willing to help us. Cops take too long, so it's up to us to see this thing through. It's always been up to us."

Addison stood still and exhaled. Jon and Kya were beside each other, unsure of the other's expectations. Jon wanted to go with his boss. He hated Addison's insistence on keeping things secret, but then what could Jon do? He wasn't owed the truth about anything. Even if he was, Addison wasn't going to give it, not now.

While Addison waited by the door, Jon took a big step forward.

"Well," said Addison. "You coming or not?"

Immediately after asking this, Addison stomped out of his office. He marched down the hall, even hurried to the point where he was almost running. As Addison moved, he didn't look back at Kya or Jon. The offer was made and either Jon was going to accept or refuse it. Neither he nor Kya would walk away because both were waiting to see which one would go first.

Jon was normally comfortable waiting for Kya. He wasn't in this case. No, he skulked along and hoped Kya would go with him. If she cared as much as Jon did, she'd come too. After he passed through the door, Kya did so as well. They were so close to each other and Jon wanted to hold her hand.

He wanted this, but instead, he just turned and smiled.

Kya smiled back. Together, they followed Addison out to the parking lot, into his car, and back...back onto the road.

CHAPTER 11
CHANGE OF PLANS

Jon had no idea what car Addison drove. In his mind, Jon was expecting him to own a luxury vehicle. Jon thought maybe a Benz or a BMW. But Addison didn't drive these cars at all. In fact, the car Addison had was one Jon had never seen before.

He did, however, recognize the name.

"DeLorean."

Jon gazed at this fascinating vehicle. The DeLorean was a four-seater luxury car painted a sparkling shade of hot red. When Jon saw the name DeLorean, he obviously thought of *Back To The Future*.

How could anyone not when hearing the name? Such was practically synonymous with the make and yet, it did look like it was from the future. Ultra-sleek and sparkling clean, Kya jumped into the car, but Jon didn't. He was hypnotized and drawn to this DeLorean but was also unsure of how it opened.

Jon touched the handle and pulled. The door flipped up and Jon leered at the car's shiny interior. It was leather, with red highlights, and its controls made

Jon feel like he was in a starship. He absolutely loved it.

"What are you doing?" asked Addison. By now, he'd taken the driver's seat. One hand was on the wheel and he was looking like a rockstar. "Get in."

"Right," said Jon. He gave his head a bit of a shake.

Jon hopped into Addison's DeLorean and pulled down the door. He looked at Kya. She was seated in the center and didn't seem as impressed as Jon about Addison's car. The Marine didn't know what to make of this. The DeLorean gallantly zipped out of the parking lot and swerved into the street.

Jon didn't speak initially. He was still too infatuated with Addison's choice of vehicle.

"Wow, this is, like...what kind of car is this?" Jon had seen a DeLorean before, but none of them looked like this.

"DeLorean Alpha 5."

"Shit," Jon said to Addison. Even the name sounded sweet. "Never seen it before."

"Yeah, it's part of DeLorean's comeback, you know? I got a hook-up. Early access. Not supposed to be out yet, but...when you're affiliated with a top nightclub, you meet people and those people know people who can give you things other people don't have."

Jon still didn't have anything to say. He did not know about this at all.

"Comeback?" Jon asked.

"Yeah," replied Addison. "New company buyer, new motor vehicle. All electric and cool as fuck."

"Looks pretty sick, brother," said Kya.

"Can't believe you own one of these," said Jon. "Especially so ahead of time."

Addison held the DeLorean's wheel with both hands. "Yeah, well," said Addison, "rich wife, rich father-in-law, makes life easier, yeah?"

Jon looked at Addison, who looked almost melancholic.

Kya laughed. She and Addison shared a moment that was too long for Jon to count. It was like Addison said an inside joke that only Kya understood.

It was odd.

"Yeah," said Kya.

Addison's mouth had curved into a partial frown. He wasn't sad, though he looked like he was feeling shame. Jon didn't know much about Addison's marriage. He knew Larry Thomas. The man was old and rich, but also tough. Jon imagined being his son-in-law came with certain difficulties.

Jon could see this was one of them.

Addison was the toughest bastard Jon knew. He had the kind of mental toughness Jon had only observed in the military. Addison didn't serve, yet he acted like a soldier. He was calm, cool, always effective. Addison would have made a great spy had he chosen that as a career path. He was a lawyer, so Jon imagined this was all part of his lawyerly ways.

Jon watched Addison drive. No one said anything inside. Jon hated uncomfortable silences. "So bouncers making investigations? Since when is this part of our job?" Jon's sarcasm was palpable. He could hear Kya giggling in the back seat.

"We're just going to ask a few questions, nothing else, nothing more."

"Yeah, that's exactly what a cop would say," Jon said to Addison.

Addison smiled. "Well, security, bouncing, all of it is part of the same totem pole, if you ask me."

"What totem pole is that?" said Jon, tapping his fingers against the window. He had no idea where Addison was taking him and Kya. Still, Jon liked the drive.

"The totem pole for making things safe."

"We work in the club industry," said Jon. "We're not cops."

Addison was quiet.

Jon was right. Everything he was doing was far outside his job description and way above his pay grade. And yet, Jon was here. He was following Addison to a place he'd never been before.

He felt like a cop. More than this, he felt like a soldier.

———

Jon and Kya had driven with Addison for twenty minutes before reaching their destination. When Addison turned his DeLorean Alpha 5 down onto a new street, Jon gazed through the window. He noticed there were fewer buildings than before. Now, in a more rural setting, they were among seemingly endless stretches of land. Here, Jon was far from home, and all he could see was a cubic white structure lingering in the distance.

"Shit. Where are we?" asked Jon. He checked again for signs. He found none.

"You asked for our supplier," Addison said. "Well, this is our supplier."

"So far outside the city," said Kya.

"Where did you think an alcohol supplier capable of stocking shelves of booze would be?" Addison replied.

"Clearly, not in its limits," said Jon.

"Exactly," said Addison, and he drove down yet another narrow street.

It was rocky and covered in gravel and Jon could hear the DeLorean's wheels grinding the pebbled surface. Now driving toward a warehouse, on approach, Jon was reminded of how he was embarking on a question so outside his job parameters. Again, he wasn't a cop.

"When we get there," said Jon, "what are we supposed to do?"

"You?" said Addison. "Nothing."

"What, what do you mean?" asked Jon, perplexed.

"Oh, I'm sorry. Did you expect me to put two of my employees in a situation so risky?"

"Risky?" said Kya, frightened. "What do you mean, *risky*?"

"We don't know what happened, and we don't know what *could* happen," said Addison. "Either way, I always plan for the worst."

"Well, why did you agree to let us come then?" Jon asked Addison.

"Could I have convinced you otherwise?" Addison asked Jon.

Jon grinned. No, he could not.

"What are you going to do?" Kya asked Addison.

"I'm going to be a lawyer," Addison said to Kya. "I'm representing our club. Plus, do you honestly think this will be the first time I've ever talked to our supplier? I got a title while you two have nothing, so it's best if you both just let me do the talking, yeah?"

"Talking?" said Jon, still as confused as he was before.

"Yes," confirmed Addison. "I do the talking while you stand there and do nothing."

"Sure," said Jon, "but then, why did you bring us here in the first place if we're not going to do anything to help you?"

Jon, now visibly frustrated, clenched his fists. His knuckles cracked.

"Oh, you will be helping me," said Addison.

"How?" asked Kya.

"By doing exactly what you're paid to do at the club," Addison replied. "You're going to watch and you're going to observe. You're going to tell me anything you see when I'm in there."

"From here?" Kya asked again.

"No," Addison said to Kya. "You come with me, but hang back, see?" Addison reached for the door handle and yanked. "Don't get too close, and just...keep your eyes open."

"All right," said Jon. "I'll keep both eyes wide open."

"Good."

Addison stepped out of his futuristic electric car and Kya did the same. Addison buttoned his jacket and Jon could see his friend had now fully transitioned from cooler to lawyer. Therefore, it was important he keep the image of a sophisticated man for as long as he could.

Kya and Jon were each dressed casually. It was gloomy now. There were gray skies and the air was humid. It stunk of something foul.

Once Jon stepped out of the car, he followed Addison to the doorway of the hulking warehouse.

He wasn't sure about the time. Maybe it was six, possibly seven.

He'd forgotten he was up later. He spoke with Kya and spent a lot of time with her before going to The Conquistador. So much time had passed since then and Jon was feeling hungry. He was sure wherever his mom was, she was probably full. Michael was supposed to take her out for a fancy dinner somewhere, apparently.

Jon thought about her and then he saw Addison standing by the door.

"Is this far back enough?" asked Kya, with equal parts sass and dismay. Kya and Jon were far from Addison, but not far enough.

———

The warehouse had a name.

PRESTO SUPPLY AND DISTRIBUTION.

How it worked, from Jon's perspective, was companies sold their alcohol to various businesses. Then, Presto took care of the packaging and shipping. Now, this made sense to Jon.

What didn't make sense to Jon was how quiet the place had been since they arrived. Jon did as he was told, and his orders came from Addison. Jon was only watching and only observing, but this was the first detail he had noticed.

Why was it so bloody quiet?

Addison reached for the door handle and Jon glimpsed over his shoulder. So far as he could tell, it was just them standing outside a warehouse. They were alone in this isolated landscape, with no visible cars or noises anywhere.

Jon, Addison, and Kya were positioned in only one section of the warehouse. There was an entire other side located beyond the doors. It was far from where Jon was, so he couldn't actually see what was there. There could be other cars and other people, but right now, Jon wasn't sure what was going on.

Addison pulled the handle so he could step into this unknown space. As soon as the door opened even a smidge, the Marine was struck with an array of lights and loud—very loud—music.

"Shit." Before Addison opened the door, Jon was hit hard by vibrations. Now, he assumed it was the sound of a forklift or other machines moving pallets and boxes of booze. However, once the door opened, the sensations felt did not coincide with any of Jon's assumptions. No, what was heard was actually the sound of ferociously loud, ear thumping music.

It was so intense all three of The Conquistador's employees were suddenly thrust back. Addison shuffled away from the doorway and looked back at Jon. This location was supposed to be a place of business and yet it did not appear this way.

"What's going on in there?" inquired Kya. And Addison looked at her with the same puzzled look as Jon. All were shocked by this change.

Jon had his ideas about what might be happening. Inside the warehouse could be employees listening to loud music as they worked. However, this would only explain *some* noise. It would not explain the lighting or the vicious vibrations now coursing through the space.

Everything here was different. Everything here was wrong.

"What's happening?" Kya asked Addison. He scoffed and glanced at Jon.

"You've got to be shitting me," Addison said. He pulled the door open and let Jon and Kya both see what was happening inside this "warehouse".

Once the door was opened, Jon glared at the black space.

The music was louder and the lights were brighter. It slammed and beat in a way he recognized instantly. Suddenly, Jon didn't feel like he was in a warehouse in the middle of nowhere, he felt like he was actually going back to work. He felt like he was back working the club exactly as he always had.

"What the hell is this?" Jon asked. Standing by Addison, they both stared into this occupied warehouse.

"Looks like a..." Addison trailed off.

Jon didn't hear the rest of his boss's reply. Jon stopped hearing Addison once he could see what was happening. This once innocuous warehouse had been converted into a full-blown, all-out rave akin to the block parties frequented by high school students.

"A party," said Jon. "Looks like a party."

Within this massive space, every quadrant and crevasse was occupied with hundreds of roaring teens, all of whom treated the section as if it were an actual club and not something used solely for business.

Waving glowsticks, the many patrons sat in makeshift chairs and rubbed against one another without knowing who was watching. To witness such a sight left Jon speechless.

This was the very last thing he expected to encounter. And yet here it was, clear as day.

With his jaw dropped, Jon's eyes shifted to Addison. "How the fuck is this even possible?"

Addison's head shook. "Only professionals could arrange for something like this to take place," he said.

"Is this a party?" yelped Kya.

"It is," said Addison.

"Isn't this the location of your supplier?" Kya was now curious. Jon was too.

"It is," Addison replied, still stunned. "At least, it was."

"And now it's a—"

"A fucking club," answered Jon. He stared at the assembly of sweaty, glowing bodies.

"No," Addison said, his voice getting louder. "It's not a club! What this is...*is a game.*"

"A game!" Kya shouted over the music.

"More than this!" Addison shouted back. "It's a trap! A fucking trap!"

He crept into the darkness and moved into the sea of silhouettes like he didn't give a damn. The questions Jon had were high and many. He couldn't think straight and he was wrestling with the sheer logic of what was unfolding now. The Fallen Sons had taken a warehouse and converted it into a nightclub...but *why?*

Why this? Why now?

Jon couldn't comprehend any of the queries he had,

so he treated this change the only way he knew how. He was a Doorman first and this was just another day working the door. Jon followed Addison but kept his eyes open like he was told to do.

His eyes were open, but his fists were ready.

Always...they were ready.

CHAPTER 12
BELLY OF THE BEAST

THE ORIGINAL PLAN WAS FOR JON TO GO WITH Addison, question the club's alcohol supplier, and find out exactly what was tampered with the night Restitute was hospitalized.

All of this was supposed to be the job of the police, but as Addison advised, everyone except for him was allowed to ask the questions. Jon and Kya were supposed to stay in the car. Then, Addison would rely on his expertise as an attorney and question those in charge.

This was Jon's *initial* plan of action.

It was also something Jon wanted to see. And, though they were now in a place that was unexpected, none of it was unfamiliar. It was surprising, but it was not something Jon wasn't used to. Instead of being in a warehouse full of workers, he was now in a converted club—a setting where Jon thrived.

"What are we supposed to do?" asked Jon.

"Spread out," said Addison. "Look for Rex, if you

can. This place has the Sons written all over it. I bet they're around here, somewhere. Keep your eyes and your ears open."

"Okay," said Jon. He struggled to hear Addison somewhat. Yet, given how close he was standing, the exchange was suitable. "And if we find them? What do we do?"

"Come and find me," said Addison. Jon was struggling to hear Addison. To him, the music was getting louder. If Jon could barely hear Addison here; then he would not be able to hear him or a ringing phone.

"There's no way you're gonna hear in this mess," said Jon. He was standing next to Addison.

"You will," replied Addison, "if you have *these*."

Addison reached into his jacket pocket and removed a hidden object of some kind. Until now, Jon had forgotten how jackets like Addison's actually have pockets. And, once Addison's hand was inside, the man in charge quickly removed two earpieces stashed there.

Jon found it odd that Addison had these.

Addison insisted on bringing them with him because he expected more from Jon. Maybe Addison really was depending on the Marine to make a move and to do more than just stand idle by.

"Here," said Addison. "They're hooked up already. Test them out, see if they work."

Jon looped the piece around his ear. Hearing static, soon Jon was able to hear Addison almost perfectly.

"Test, one, two, test. You good?"

Jon nodded at Addison. Yes, he was good.

"Okay," said Addison. "Split up. You go west and circle the perimeter. Try to find a high vantage point.

We're looking for adults on the floor, anyone you may or may not recognize."

Jon nodded again. He understood exactly what he was supposed to do. Jon did as he was told. He veered off to the side and began marching farther into the crowd. Calm and cool, Jon acquired a stoic demeanor and was back to being a Doorman.

It was a different club, different rules, but same game. *It was Jon's game.*

"Moving west now," Jon said to Addison.

Now in full bouncer mode, Jon didn't see any security so far as he could see.

Although mostly teenagers, Jon studied the appearances of these *kids*. How this rave was set up at such a time was strange to Jon. The Fallen Sons and their leader, Rex MacIntosh, were both capable. So far, they had all proven themselves to be immensely dangerous. Jon couldn't believe they were able to transform a once-working warehouse into a full-fledged party.

From what Jon could see, that's exactly what it looked like.

Jon checked his watch. It was too early for a party.

To create one such as this, Rex and the other Sons must've started early. They would have to summon hundreds of young people and bring them here somehow. Logistically, it wasn't adding up for Jon.

However, Addison did say it could be a trap.

All of this could be one massive setup designed to bring Addison and the others down here. It could be all of this, and yet none at the same time.

Despite Jon's question, what could he do other than go forward?

What could he do other than his job?

"*See anything yet?*" Jon heard Addison's voice in his mic.

"No."

"*Stay on it,*" said Addison. "*You see anyone who's too old, point them out.*"

"Roger that," said Jon. "Where's Kya?"

Since Addison gave Jon his earpiece, he hadn't been looking out for his girl. He assumed Kya was close, but she wasn't. She must be on the floor along with the rest of the strung-out teens. Jon looked around for Kya. Hopefully, she was closer. The teens were many. They bobbed their heads and flailed their glowsticks about wildly. Jon, back in high school, heard about parties like this. He didn't attend any of them. He remembered they were held out in the middle of nowhere, in secluded, abandoned places. This warehouse was *not* abandoned. It was owned and occupied. Jon continued to try to convince himself that this was true. It would be more believable if the location was empty. Jon had simply been led to a place in the middle of nowhere.

This could still be true.

It could be, but it was unlikely. While Jon surveyed, he had not yet seen any of the Fallen Sons. There was no sign of Brutus, Cole, or the others who worked alongside the leader, Rex. No, Jon didn't see any of these men, only teenagers.

————

After searching for a time too long to consider, Jon did see Kya. She was down by a stack of bottles, chatting with two boys. From what Jon could see, she seemed okay. She was smiling and flirtatiously touching the boys on their shoulders. Jon knew when Kya was turning on the charm. As an attractive female who had much experience talking with men, she was familiar with how to create instant sparks.

If that's what she was doing now then this made Jon cringe.

Jon hustled after her. He veered around two teenage boys, all of whom were a group of chatting idiots in football jerseys. Jon bumped into one and knocked him forward. Jon didn't care. He wasn't technically working so he wasn't technically required to follow the same tactics as back in The Conquistador.

He didn't need to keep the peace. He didn't even need to remain calm or be nice.

"What the fuck, man!" Jon overheard one of the teens shout in his direction.

Suddenly, it was déjà vu all over again for Jon. High schoolers were just earlier versions of the punks Jon dealt with at the club. The only difference was they were smaller, weaker, and much easier to break. Jon didn't bother to look back. He was aware it was a bad idea to give his back to his enemy. In this case, however, Jon couldn't care less.

What could they really do to someone like him?

"Hey, asshole!" yelled another. "What the fuck's your problem, man?!"

Jon continued to ignore the call of the knuckleheads. He walked on ahead like he didn't care. In all honesty, Jon really didn't. What Jon needed to do was get to Kya, and that's exactly what he planned on doing.

"Kya!" Jon called to Kya but could barely hear the sound of his own voice.

The music was louder in this section of the warehouse/rave. Here, Jon garnered glowers from everyone standing close. He shuffled to reach Kya. Soon after he increased speed, two more guys in football uniforms stepped directly into Jon's path.

They gave Jon looks so dirty he could practically smell shit coming off their faces.

"Hey, motherfucker! I'm talking to you." Jon stopped and turned.

Now he had no choice but to look back. So, when Jon turned, he stared at the person who called out to him. It was the voice of the one who said *"What the fuck, man"* when he first started walking.

"Just who the fuck do you think you are?" Jon ignored the belligerent idiot talking behind his back.

He wasn't here for a fight, but then he also wasn't going to apologize if one occurred.

The goal was to find the Sons, and that's all.

"You fucking bumped me, asshole. You bumped me hard!"

"Hmm," said Jon, his hands pressed to his side. This is how he would normally approach a hostile situation at The Conquistador. He waited and he assessed. Jon already knew the intentions of this main guy, whom he called *Captain*. His boys were squaring off and trying to surround Jon in typical attack formation.

Again, Jon was familiar with all of this. It was textbook, standard, and also...beatable.

"You should say you're goddamn sorry, son," snapped one kid.

Jon continued to stay silent. The day he apologized to a fucking clown like this was the day he became a goddamn chipmunk.

"Did you hear me, asshole?!" yelled the dimwitted captain. "I said you owe me a fucking apology."

Again, Jon did hear him but he didn't care. Jon wasn't always looking for a fight. Rarely was he ever looking for one. Jon was irritable. He was tired, hungry, and frustrated. He hated being in this place and he hated having to look for the goons known as the Fallen Sons. And Jon absolutely loathed not seeing Kya. He still had no idea about what was happening here, in this shithole of a warehouse.

"Yeah, did you hear him, asshole?!" Another goon spoke as he inched closer to Jon.

Whoever this second guy was, he had on a baseball cap and had a mullet. Based on what Jon could see, the boys' body languages and stances, were all so amateur. They were already done. They just didn't know it yet.

"Hey, look at this fucking guy!" said another idiot. "He's got a fake leg! Check it!"

"What?!" The Captain grinned.

At this time, more people were gathered and Jon had drawn more attention to himself than he had anticipated. Although everything was so silly and dumb, as soon as these jerks mentioned Jon's leg, the Marine tightened up to the point where his body ached.

"Holy fuck, he's got one leg! Do you see this shit? Motherfucker is missing a fucking leg!"

Jon twitched. He didn't have many triggers, but there were a few he could name offhand. The one Jon felt now was one which made him feel lesser, like he was only half full. Jon was capable and had everything he needed right here.

"Who the fuck are you anyway?" goaded the Captain.

Jon grinned. At last, he was asked a question he understood. Jon liked it so much, he wanted the football leader to ask it again. "I'm a Marine."

"What?" snapped the mullet idiot who poked fun at Jon's physical difference.

Before anything happened, Jon learned what he did from Danix. Actually, Jon wished Danix was here right now. Danix would fucking pull these clowns apart like freshly baked bread. However, with Danix's absence, Jon gawked. Then he didn't hesitate. He struck hard and fast. He cracked the Captain's windpipe exactly where he wanted, then stepped back and glowered. The Captain's hands fastened around his throat. His eyes went from white to red in a matter of seconds. Unable to catch his breath, none of this mattered to Jon. After he hit the Captain, he unloaded completely on him and the rest of his dirtbag friends.

Jon kicked the Captain's knee and then struck again with an open palm hit straight to the face. Jon plowed the fool in the nose and squished it like a pancake. The Captain was then left to choke, bleed, and possibly cry.

Jon finished him with a push into a table filled with flip cups.

"Ah!"

Once the Captain was out of the picture, his four hooligans stampeded. All were shaken from the attack and Jon had handled their leader only with a few solid, well-timed strikes. The Captain was now on the floor, trembling. Still, Jon wasn't done. On the contrary, he was fired up and ready for more.

"What the f-f-f-fuck, man?" the mullet dude stammered.

Jon observed the man's quivering lip as well as his quaking shoulders.

"What?" said Jon. "You didn't expect a real fight from a guy who's missing some of his leg?"

From here, Jon clobbered the mullet with a hard back kick and socked the fool in the stomach. Mullet came forward clutching his gut, and Jon followed with a swift roundhouse. He connected with mullet's face and knocked him down to the dirty floor.

With this mullet guy now handled, the remaining three squared off.

Each displayed their own fearful yet petrified looks. Jon could smell their terror. He could strike them all one at a time, but doing that would be too easy. No, Jon needed to work on his defense and what better way for him to defend than now? The first fool lunged for a punch and Jon dipped, blocked, and locked the dummy's wrist. As the dummy exclaimed, Jon ended with a merciless elbow to the jaw.

"Ah!" The dummy fell and the other two just kept swinging like the amateurs that they were. What they tried to hit, they barely could. And so Jon had his work cut out for him now. He veered left, kept both his feet in motion, and avoided everything in his path. While it was easy, Jon couldn't just move.

He needed more. He didn't want to punch. No, punching was too easy. Once given a clear path, Jon did respond. His hands clapped back with a series of quick wrist-driving slaps. A blow like this was both derogatory and degrading. To slap a man is to basically step on his ability to defend himself and to attack his strength.

Then again, these weren't men. They were boys, little, tiny boys. They were undisciplined and arrogant and deserved a good spanking. Jon slapped the boys one at a time, pushed them aside, and watched them fall. At the fight's conclusion, Jon heard a ruckus growing from within the crowd. There was something stirring and there was a change in lighting. Jon blinked and gradually rose so he could stand straight. The slow rise made Jon look all the more formidable and terrifying. From within this vast gathering, a tall man with blonde hair marched through the crowd. Jon listened. The music stopped, and in its place was the faint, nuanced sound of pitiful applause.

"Well done," said the man with the blonde hair. "Well done, indeed."

While Jon was fatigued, the man standing before him was older than everyone else. This wasn't surprising for Jon. The average age of those attending the rave was between sixteen and nineteen. Jon was convinced the boys he just pummeled were seniors. Some of them might have been older. Now that this new man had revealed himself, Jon clenched and readied himself for another bout. Fortunately, this man didn't come to fight. No, he was smiling and laughing after watching Jon beat the shit out of five guys who started something they shouldn't.

He also wasn't a stranger, not in the traditional sense.

And, as the man leered, Jon knew exactly what he was. He didn't like that he recognized him, but then this man was the *exact* person Jon was searching for.

"Cole Hausen?" said Jon.

Cole smirked. As one of the Fallen Sons, Jon knew his face so well he could sketch it.

"In the flesh," added Cole. He raised his hands and

tried to appear flattered. "See you found our little hideout here, followed our map, yeah?"

Map and hideout flashed in Jon's mind. The map Cole was referring to was the one that linked the alcohol supplier to the contamination. This was Jon's idea. And the hideout was where Jon was at this moment, in a converted warehouse. Jon was in a new club where the patrons were far younger and based on what he saw from the boys he beat up, far more stupid.

In the company of this one Fallen Son, Jon raised his hands and backed away.

It was one challenge to fight a bunch of hoodlums in football jackets, but it was another to fight someone like Cole. And their plan was not to fight. Their plan was to talk and to reason. Jon hoped that's what Cole wanted to do.

"Where's Addison?" Jon asked Cole.

The Fallen Son smirked and steadied back into the crowd.

"He's in the back waiting for you. Look, why don't you drop the whole Doorman shtick now and come with me so we can talk, yeah? I mean, that is why you've come all this way, right? You want to talk?"

Although Jon wanted to know, to confirm what Cole asked, he did not. The Fallen Son was correct in what he said, and Jon saw no need to speak about it at all. He stepped along the grimy floor and proceeded to go with this Son. When Jon walked, he glimpsed at Kya.

Almost hand in hand and arm in arm, Jon and Kya motioned along. Looking at the back of Cole Hausen's head, Jon thought about driving a knife straight through it. It would be so easy now, but Jon remembered who he was. He was no cop and he was no murderer. He was an enforcer and he was a friend. He had come here for answers. He had come for the truth. Maybe this was the only way to get it.

When Jon followed Cole, Kya stood there next to him. He was glad she was close. Jon hoped she would continue to be, because right now, he needed her.

Jon hoped she needed him too.

CHAPTER 13
SO MUCH HISTORY

THROUGH THE CROWD AND PAST A HIGH STACK OF boxes, Jon listened to the hard blasting of bad house music. While doing this, Jon also fell victim to the glowers from nearby patrons. Jon ignored all these disdainful looks. Jon moved toward the leader of the Sons and did exactly what he said he would. He chose to stay with Kya, but so far, he hadn't seen Addison.

Jon didn't know where he was or what he was doing.

More than this, Jon Haze did not know where he was being taken to.

He assumed it was someone's office. Maybe it was the exact office used when this warehouse was occupied by workers and not partygoers. Nevertheless, Jon noticed that the stack of boxes was higher in this section than it was anywhere else. Jon glanced up at this pile. Soon, he was brought to a spot whereby all of these boxes were fashioned into the shape of a square.

Two men stood outside of it. They were guards who could have easily been mistaken for regular security.

Jon found the design of this region familiar. It was as though Cole, Brutus, and Rex had set this section as a copy of a club office.

In many ways, that's what this place *really* was.

It was not a rave. It was a pitiful replica of a crummy club. If that was the case, then the Fallen Sons were the bouncers, and Jon, Kya, and Addison were the intruders. And, as Cole led Jon and Kya into this makeshift office, both men outside extended their arms and blocked the doorway.

"Hold up, y'all. No one's going anywhere."

Jon and Kya halted. Jon didn't even want to enter this space. He wasn't sure what Kya wanted, but Jon imagined she felt the same way.

"Relax," Cole said to one guard. "These two are with me."

"Yeah?" asked one door person. He glared at Jon. The reason for this man's hostility, Jon believed, was because of the fight. Word gets around fast in this place. Evidently, that's exactly what happened.

"Yeah," said Cole. "Step aside."

The man did what Cole said to do. He moved aside and made way for Cole, Jon, and Kya. Jon and Kya entered this office constructed out of boxes. Who was there was exactly who Jon had expected. He was sitting behind a wooden desk, with nothing there besides a light and heaps of hundred-dollar bills. It was Rex, present and gleeful. Jon looked at the leader of the Fallen Sons like he was transparent. The longer he stared, the more Jon Haze could see into him. But what Jon saw was nothing.

"Welcome to our new palace. Do you like it?'

"Palace," said Addison. When Jon first stepped into

this section, he didn't know Addison was there. He was seated to Jon's right, in a flip out chair, and with his legs crossed. To Jon, Addison seemed comfortable and unafraid. How he found this place, Jon imagined, was because he had been escorted here by one of the Fallen Sons. Maybe it was Brutus or maybe Rex himself.

"Is that what you call it?"

"Well, you know, we gotta earn," said Rex. "And the only work we wanted was club work...but then, you put an end to all that, remember? After we were disbanded from The Conquistador, we were all blacklisted. No other club would hire us. You know of your club's reputation, its impact on this world. With our crests taken, we were fucking lepers—*diseased*—and with no plans to give it back to us, well...we had to make our lives work in other ways."

Rex extended his arms and frowned.

The lack of employment and work made Jon feel somewhat sad. In that moment, he expressed a small degree of sympathy for each of his enemies. He didn't know precisely what the Sons did that forced them into exile. Jon imagined it was something bad. All Jon knew for sure was they broke the rules and were now not able to find work, employment, or for that matter, happiness.

Jon knew some Marines who wanted work but couldn't find it.

This hurt them and burned most people down to their core. Maybe Rex had fallen into a similar hole and it was eating him up from the inside. Maybe that's why he hated Addison so much, why he hated The Conquistador and the Doormen.

Whatever happened, Jon was here to learn more. He waited for Rex to speak again.

"Is that what's happening here?" Addison asked Rex.

"It is," the leader confirmed.

"So," said Addison, "does our supplier know what you lease his space for? And, to do what, host fucking high schoolers and sell liquor to minors?"

Rex hissed at Addison's cutting comment. The hatred between them still burned. The animosity Rex had toward the club cooler hadn't changed since his exile. Jon could feel the tension, but rather than wanting to escape it, he wanted to bask in it. The more hate Rex felt, the more he might slip and reveal more about the Sons' true intentions.

Jon had to ask himself what did they really want? What was their endgame?

"Everyone has a way. Oh, and your supplier," said Rex, "ain't that great either. Turns out he doesn't care much for your club. He says he doesn't like your contract, and well, we told him we might have a proposition for him, if he's interested."

"Oh, you did, did you?" beckoned Addison.

A ghoulish grin spread along Rex's clown face. "Yeah. Told him we'd give him a new, better contract once our own club opens, but before we do that, we need to conduct some tests and build up our clientele."

"And this is what you had in mind?" asked Addison. "Using his business space and selling alcohol to minors?"

"Well," said Rex, "when he heard we were going to fuck *you* over, he agreed, no questions asked. As long as everything is put back to normal by morning, he has no problem with it. Besides, not like anyone's gonna call the cops and, so far as I know, there ain't no minors here, ain't that right, baby?"

Next to Rex sat a tiny girl. To Jon, she looked too young to even look at. She was acting the part of a vixen who *might* be eighteen yet was easily blurring the line between legal and illegal. The girl's hair was a hard shade of maroon, and she had a nose ring. She stayed next to Rex like she was his own personal lap dog. After Rex addressed her using a stereotypical pronoun, this girl smiled and had another drink.

"That's right," she said.

Jon flinched. There was nothing more disgusting than an older man flirting with a younger girl. Also, the notion only proved just how dirty a man like Rex was. Younger girls are so much easier to manipulate. Rex was showing how he, an older guy, couldn't engage with women his own age, so he had to lower his bar until he found someone who lacked depth and emotional experience. This was what he selected.

"And our supply?" asked Addison. "You admit you spiked the alcohol that night."

"I admit nothing," said Rex. "What?" He cackled as he leaned forward. "Do you think you're going to get me to admit to anything here and now?"

Rex snorted and then he looked at Addison with tight lips and open eyes.

"You forget, I know how you operate," said Rex. "I know every which way you're going to come at me, and I know how to plan around these tactics."

Jon glanced at Addison, who stoically sat before Rex with his hands folded.

"If you think you're going to get a confession out of me like you did that Castellani kid, you're fucking dreaming. Worse than that, you're fucking dumb as shit."

Jon scowled. When Rex MacIntosh, the leader of the rogue bouncer group, mentioned Frankie, Jon shuddered. He didn't know how famous this story was. It was online, but when Rex spoke of it, Jon remembered that night and how he hated every second of it.

"You ain't going to hear anything from me. Yeah, I don't know who fucked with your supply or poisoned your fucking rapper, that dumb blackie whatever his fucking name is."

The other Sons laughed and Jon's sickened stare only deepened. Anyone who refers to a Black person as a *blackie* is either dumb, racist, or both. Yet, Jon knew Rex wasn't dumb. Brutus and Cole stood behind Rex. They were on either side of their leader like typical henchmen.

How any of these assholes were allowed to be bouncers? Jon had no idea.

Then they were fired and reprimanded in the worst ways. Jon once thought this to be a harsh punishment. Now he was starting to think otherwise.

"But then I guess you wouldn't be here if you didn't know the truth already. Does it really matter who's responsible? Does it really matter who did what?"

Jon wanted to say it was. He wanted to make it clear that yes, this did matter.

Short of jumping from his chair, Jon wanted to scream at the top of his lungs. What Rex and his boys did was not only illegal, it tarnished The Conquistador's reputation. Although the Marine's impulse was to stand and shout, Jon inadvertently yelled the first thought that came to mind. Fortunately, it wasn't one that incited violence. On the contrary, all it did was grab the attention of Rex, the Fallen Son's allegedly fearless leader.

"Just tell us what you want?" When Jon snapped at Rex, peripherally, he could see Addison Krowe starting to turn. Now was not Jon's time to speak.

Addison was the one who spoke for The Conquistador and he was the one here to do the talking, not Jon. But once Jon barked, he showed he wasn't afraid of Rex or anyone. The leader of the Sons turned.

"Oh," he said. "Looks like someone is tired of waiting?"

Jon glared and said nothing.

He eyed Rex with his chest up and his head held high. No, Jon was not afraid of anything this man had to say. However, Jon may have also made the situation worse. Addison continued to look at Jon, but it wasn't a deep or disapproving look. Rex grinned at Jon, and then he rotated his chair so he could face Jon as he answered.

"Just tell us what this is about," demanded Jon.

"I thought you already knew that," said Rex, the same clownish grin still visible on his slick face. "This is all about revenge."

"And you had that already?" said Jon. "How much more of it do you want?"

"Oh, what?" asked Rex. "You think what happened to you makes us even, makes us the same?"

"No," said Jon. He hijacked the conversation and was again doing what Addison had come to do. Jon would never dream of stepping on Addison's toes or being bold enough to speak for him or the club.

Jon never could fulfill Addison's role, but at this moment, he couldn't help himself.

Jon was so enraged he wanted to leap across the desk and punch Rex hard in the face. Jon wanted to unleash all hell because it was Rex who might put Jon out of his job. Worse, Jon might lose the only family he had. Although this situation was tense, Jon still believed it was under control. Things were said that could not be taken back. Then again, Jon had no intention of taking anything back. He meant what he said. He stood by everything he did and wanted to do.

"Is that what this about, getting even?" Addison finally took the liberty of saying more.

When he did speak, Jon froze. He wasn't sure if this was his boss taking back the conversation and returning to his assigned role as a *superior*. Nevertheless, he was especially happy to hear this question.

"No, it's about the truth," said Rex.

"The truth?" asked Addison. "The truth as you see it, or the truth as it is, as it was meant to be?"

Addison leered. His question was both condescending and daunting. Yet, Jon loved how Addison said it.

"No," Rex grunted. "It's about the *only* truth. It's about letting everyone know what The Conquistador really is, what it does, who it hurts, as well as its secrets and its hypocrisy."

The mentioning of the word hypocrisy hurt Jon deeply. Jon hated it because the code among the Doormen was all about honor. And, from what Jon could see, there was nothing honorable about the man sitting in front of him. This didn't change the fact that Rex wanted, as he said, *vengeance*. He also wanted to see the club fall. He wanted it to end at the hands of those who were already fallen, which was him and his fellow brothers.

"I want The Conquistador to see that it cast out the wrong people. It fucked with the wrong warriors."

"Warriors?" Addison beckoned. "Is that what you think you are?"

"We fight for what we believe in," Rex replied. Sitting in his chair, he looked only at Addison. "If that's not the definition of a warrior," Rex said, "then I'm afraid I don't know what is."

Jon was silent now. In his mind, this was the true definition of a warrior.

"But," said Rex, his chair squeaked. "If you require further proof..." Rex stood and his hands slid down to his chest so he could unbutton his shirt. The other Fallen Sons stepped back. "And you want to know what a warrior really is," Rex continued, "then you have to look at his scars."

Rex aggressively pulled his shirt to reveal his bare chest. He was muscular and lean and had a few tattoos drawn along his torso. Rex had other markings too, but none of them were as big or as disturbing as the one in the center.

"You remember the scars, don't you, Addison?" Rex asked his former employer. "I would say...you have to remember them."

Jon gazed at the scar Rex referred to. Even if he wanted to look elsewhere, he couldn't.

The mark was massive and grotesque. The fat circle looked like it once contained an image. Now it was nothing more than a mutilated web of dead skin. Its shade was darker than the rest of Rex's body. Jon could only imagine how painful it was to endure something like this. Rex held his shirt open and made sure everyone saw what was done to him.

Everyone did.

Jon looked at Kya. Her hand was cupped over her mouth. Even she was disturbed by the sight.

"You remember, don't you, Addison? Please tell me you remember." Rex glowered at Addison, who stared at the scar like it was nothing.

"Look at it!" Rex's yells sent chills down Jon's spine. Such madness was seen as very disturbing to him.

"I see it," said Addison. "I see it, and I remember."

"Oh yeah?" said Rex. "You do, do you?"

"I do," admitted Addison, still unfazed. "I remember you fought without honor and without a cause," said Addison. He and Rex glared at one another like they were about to get into a knife fight. "I know you wanted to take something that wasn't yours and you have done nothing but poison and run away."

"We never ran," Rex barked back at Addison, still enraged. Jon gazed at this fearless leader. Rex's once prideful and glorious expression was now broken. His lips curled and the sulk Jon had once observed had returned. What Addison said hurt Rex, and Jon was reminded of what made The Conquistador such a lethal entity. Addison's words were strong and power-ful. He could cut people right down to their core, which was exactly what he was doing now.

"Oh no?" Addison questioned. "Last time I checked, every time you've made a move against us, it's been from the shadows. You pounce, you hide, and then you disappear. And you do that because you don't have the guts to stand in the light, where you know you won't be feared."

Addison lifted his hands and gestured to Jon and Kya.

"What we do," Addison said, "isn't in the shadows. No, where we operate is in plain sight, son. We stand and we guard. We protect, we do not run, and we definitely do *not* hide. The people who break the rules, the cowards and the fools, they're the ones that run, and they're the ones that hide."

Jon's head tilted.

Everything Addison said sounded spectacular. It was exhilarating. This is exactly what he and the other Doormen did. They never ran and they never hid. Always, they were where everyone could see. The Fallen Sons were different. They were where none could see them. They were as Addison had described— *cowards*.

"Just like you have, the way you did, or did you not remember how you attacked the bouncing trade? Do you remember that?"

Jon examined Rex's now pouting face. Once again, Addison knew exactly what to say. Rex's mouth swayed like he was nibbling on his tongue. It was clear Addison had offended him, and like always, Jon imagined what his boss was referring to.

"I think you do," said Addison. "See, you look at that mark on your chest like some sort of battle scar, but it isn't. No, what you see there is a fucking reminder of what you are, what you stand for, and it doesn't just come from me or The Conquistador. It comes from the way of life that goes well beyond what we do. You were right when you said warriors fight for what they believe in, but it's *what* they believe in that matters most. And real warriors don't believe in the inglorious victory that comes with revenge or pain or suffering."

Rex glared, and Addison did the same. Their rivalry remained just as strong as it always had been. They still looked like they were going to fight. Although they chose not to, Jon could not escape the animosity or the tension that continued to fill the space.

"You're right," Rex said. His eyes slowly turned upward, and he gawked at Addison. "They don't. You asked me before, where do I think all of this is going? How will it all end?"

Addison nodded. "I did."

"Well," Rex replied, "since you asked that, I now have an answer for you."

"And I'm here to listen," said Addison. "It's actually the only reason why I'm still here."

"Why we're *both* still here." Jon's add-on wasn't necessary. However, it did feel like a good thing to say. Rex, Cole, Brutus, and everyone else who was here needed to know that Addison wasn't the only one present. He also wasn't the only one with agency or authority.

"Then you know what I'm going to say next, don't you? You know there's only one way for this to end. What I'm talking about is so old, it's almost ancient," said Rex. "It goes back, way back to when these clubs were first founded."

"And that is?" asked Addison.

Jon watched his boss's glare intensify to the point where Addison's head began to tilt. Jon recognized the look. It was one of impatience as well as intolerance. Jon was familiar with this expression because he had seen it before. In fact, he had observed it often from Addison.

"You know...*a Showdown*," Rex declared. He spoke with ferocity and enthusiasm. The word *showdown* packed quite a punch. It was a word everyone loved to speak because of what it signified. It was a battle—a duel—and a time whereby two superpowers battled for supremacy. Yet, the Showdown Rex had referred to felt much more specific. It possessed more meaning and, consequently, more purpose.

"A Bouncer Showdown."

More chills crept, now prickling along Jon's forearms and later crawling down to his stomach. They trickled across Jon's chest and soon consumed the rest of his body. Suddenly, Jon couldn't move. He felt thrilled and amped. Now was the time whereby he usually hit a bag or lifted some steel. Still, Jon listened to Addison scoff at the suggestion. Truthfully, Jon had absolutely no idea what Rex was referring to, but he was serious about it. Rex hadn't blinked once while staring at Addison after he spoke those words.

"Are you serious right now?" Addison asked.

He was unimpressed with the suggestion.

"It's the only way to settle it," replied Rex. "You know the rules, you know the game, and if we do this thing the old-fashioned way, if I lose, I'll walk away, and you can consider our rivalry finished and done for. No more need for games or revenge. All that dies."

Addison's jaw slacked, and Jon watched closely. Rex's proposal sounded legitimate but also intriguing. Again, Jon was lost. He tried to figure out what a Bouncer Showdown was. There was only one way for him to know for sure.

Jon grunted to clear his throat, then he turned to look at Addison.

"What's a Bouncer Showdown?"

All that came after was silence. Addison said nothing, and neither did Rex. This silence was broken when Kya decided to speak before Rex. She had said only a little while in Rex's *office.*

"Yeah," said Kya. "What, we like...create a club and see who can run it better?"

Kya's thoughts somewhat aligned with Jon's. All of this did seem logical.

"No," said Addison. "That's not what it is." His response was cold.

"Oh, what?" barked the leader of the Fallen Sons. "They don't know, huh? Jesus Christ," said Rex, "I guess the days of being totally honest with your employees ended with us, yeah?"

Jon's stomach was knotted. It felt like it was being stretched. Another accusation was being made about Addison and The Conquistador that left a bad taste in the Marine's mouth. Jon loathed what Rex was doing. It bothered Jon but there was no time to address this now.

All Jon wanted to know about was the Showdown.

"You two ain't never heard of a Showdown, have you?" Rex addressed Jon and Kya.

He hadn't given either of them his attention since the two sat down. Jon liked how Rex was speaking to him and to Kya. To Jon, this meant they mattered as much as Addison mattered.

"No," replied Jon. "Sounds like a...*a battle.*"

"It is," confirmed Rex. "I guess you could say that, but what it really is is more of a test."

"A test?" asked Jon.

"Yes," answered Rex.

Now, Jon had been tested many times before. He remembered when he was first hired to be a Doorman. Danix took Jon to another room in The Conquistador. It was the Green Room, a *tactical training center*. The room was filled with mannequins and also included a digital scoreboard. It provided various scenarios for Jon to react to. And if Jon failed, then he was hit with a green substance that burned his eyes and stung like a motherfucker.

Jon remembered this day well. Therefore, when he thought about the idea of a *test*, this was what entered his mind.

"What kind of test?"

After asking Rex this question, the leader displayed the same smug and devilish grin.

"Call it...*the ultimate test*." Rex paused for a moment and then kept talking. "It's a lot like a game of Capture The Flag, but it's a lot more intense and way more dangerous."

Jon gulped. Jon had played Capture The Flag back in elementary school. He tried to recall the rules of the game. From what he could assemble, there were two teams, boundaries, and, of course, there was also a flag. The way it worked was there was a line dividing the two teams' sides, and somewhere beyond the lines was the flag. The teams crossed the boundaries and tried to find the flag before they were tagged. Such was easier said than done. It was a deathly struggle to try to cross the threshold. Most people got caught up before they could get the chance to find the flag let alone capture it.

While it was difficult, Jon did remember it being fun. He hadn't played it in years and had no plans to return until now. Nevertheless, Jon thought about the possibility of doing it again. Under these circumstances, it was compelling indeed. It was also quite strange to think about.

"Sounds like it," said Jon. "And the rules of this... game, this Showdown?"

Addison glimpsed at Jon with sunken eyes. Biting his lips, Addison was now impatient if not also pissed off at Jon for asking what he did. Jon didn't care. He wanted to know as much as he could when he could.

"Addison?" said Rex. He diverted the question to The Conquistador cooler. Obviously, Rex understood the rules of this game.

He wanted Addison to answer it as a means of humiliation. Afterward, Addison accepted the offer. He leaned forward and folded his hands.

"There are two teams, one location, one setup, I guess you could say."

Jon watched as Rex's shit-eating grin expanded across his protruding jawline. He was really enjoying hearing this.

"And there are rules," said Addison. "Certain rules."

"Exactly," said Rex. "You see, we pick a spot, a zone, if you will."

"Right," said Jon. His attention level piqued. His ears twitched. He wanted to hear more.

"We choose a zone, mark it, and then we set up a kind of trophy, and we see which one can get to it first."

"That's it?" After explaining how a Showdown worked, Jon thought it sounded silly. It was not nearly as dangerous as Rex had implied, at least not from Jon's point of view. Then again, maybe he was just being naïve.

"No," Addison said later. "That's *not* it."

"Well, what else is there then?" asked Jon.

"Well, see," said Rex, "we set up the game at the club, any club so long as there're guests and shit in it. The bouncers, well, they have to sneak by and try to get the flag while another team of bouncers tries to stop them."

"Wow," said Jon.

"And what happens sometimes," Rex went on, "in fact, maybe all the time, is shit goes down. Problems arise, fights happen, and the bouncers have to deal with this while also protecting their trophy. It's almost fucking impossible and asks a lot of the bouncers working the floor. It's the ultimate test of competition, strategy, force, and stealth. You're not a real bouncer until you've survived a fucking good old fashioned Showdown, ain't that right there, Krowe?"

Rex was referring to Addison by his last name, which to Jon was the utmost sign of disrespect. Few did this because few had the balls to do it. Rex was again being an asshole, but goddamn, he was good at it. Addison eased back and unfolded his hands. He rubbed his fingertips together and then massaged his neck.

"And...how many per team?" asked Jon.

"Usually, it's about five," said Rex. "Five of your best bouncers versus five of ours."

"Okay," said Jon. Now, he was starting to understand exactly how the game worked. "And...how do you get tagged out?"

It was after this question Rex cackled. He was basking in the truth surrounding this game.

"Depends."

"On what?" asked Jon.

"On whoever's club it is," said Rex. "You could touch to tag out, pull them out, but something tells me we're going to go old school for this game."

"Old school," said Jon.

"*Way* old school," added Rex.

"What does that mean?"

Rex grinned at Jon and continued to savor the joy of the game he was now proposing.

"When another bouncer crosses the boundaries," said Rex, "the only way for them to be taken out is to be taken out the old-fashioned way. You remember that, don't you, Addison?"

The cooler gave no response. Addison glared at Rex, and Jon abruptly turned back toward the audacious fool.

"How?" Jon asked Rex.

"He steps too far, and another bouncer can only take him out of the game in a fight."

"But fighting will alert the guests, won't it?"

"Depends on how skilled you are," Rex replied.

Jon knew well that keeping a fight contained was not only difficult, it was damn well impossible. He sighed and tried grasping the reasoning behind this challenge. However, both were adding up quicker than Jon cared to count. He couldn't think about the rules, only the consequences. He couldn't consider the logistics, only the strategy.

It was possible. It could be done.

"It also depends," Rex said again, "on how far you're willing to go."

"We're willing to go all the way," said Jon. He took on the role of leader, which wasn't his to hold. And yet, he decided to anyway.

For some reason, Addison was quiet.

Jon believed it was because Addison couldn't stand to be in Rex's company. To this, Jon sympathized. He hated Rex's personality. He was a racist, a bigot, and a piece of shit liar. Whether Addison or anyone liked it, they needed to participate in this Showdown.

Jon was never much of a leader. He would never describe himself as one. In high school, he barely played sports and couldn't dream of being called a team captain. He rode the bench most of the time, saw only limited playing time, and was neither popular nor cool. In the Marines, all Jon did was follow orders and it's where he discovered his fighting skills and other talents. Now, he was taking on a new role as well as a new identity.

He was speaking as if he was in charge.

He wasn't overriding Addison's authority, or at least he wasn't trying to.

He was just being calm and assertive and exactly what he needed to be. When he asked the question, Rex looked at him with his classic signature smile.

"As far as we have to go."

"That's a good attitude, sport," said Rex. Jon despised being referred to as such. Sport was a nickname for a kid, not a man and Jon was most assuredly the man here. "It's a good attitude and you're going to need a good attitude. You want to see the world change, now is the way in which it is changing. You wanna take them out of the game, then you have to beat them in a fight. No other way around it."

"And it's a fight none of the guests can be aware of?"

"Ideally," Rex said to Jon.

"So, we take it somewhere quiet, still within the boundaries, but away from everything?"

When Jon said this, he was looking at Kya. He wanted her approval. The fact that Kya was silent indicated maybe Jon's mouth was writing checks his body couldn't cash.

"If that's what you want to do," said Rex. He pulled out a cigar and had a match blinking in front of his mouth. He lit the tip and then puckered his lips. Jon didn't think it was possible for him to appear like more of an asshole, but he was wrong.

"Then those are the rules of the game." Rex nibbled on his cigar and glimpsed at Jon, who nodded.

"We can do it," Jon said. "We can get it done."

Jon's focus then shifted to Addison. The cooler was uncharacteristically quiet at the moment. Now leaning forward, Jon pressed his elbows against his knees. Now pensive, Jon was likely thinking about how the Doormen were going to win this fight—this contest—with their greatest rivals. It would be difficult, Jon said to himself, but not impossible.

"Good. But, of course, you don't have the final say…"

Rex looked at Addison, who had yet to acknowledge anything said. So far, it was Jon who was doing most of the talking.

"It's up to the boss to decide what's real and what's a go."

Jon observed all of Addison's mannerisms. Biting the inside of his cheek, he seemed annoyed and just as fed up with Rex's games as before. Not much had changed and nothing mattered until Addison said it did.

"So, what's it gonna be, boss?" Rex asked, all smug and riddled with delight. "Are you down for a little...*duel*?"

With the game set and the pieces now all on the board, Jon eagerly awaited Addison's reply. He didn't want to make his excitement seem obvious, but it was. Jon was ready to throw down right here, right now.

"That depends," said Addison.

"On what?" barked Rex.

"On whether or not you agree to stay out of our way until the time arrives for us to begin. That means no more fucking around with our supply, no more sneaking in through our doors, and definitely no more maps or games, do you understand?"

Rex threw his hands up and eased back.

"You hold a moratorium until the day of the Showdown, and you stay the hell out of our way," said Addison, "until then, yeah?"

"Unquestionably," added Rex. "Assuming you will do the same for us."

"Unquestionably," retorted Addison. His hands slid across his thighs and he flattened his pants. He was done talking too.

"Then it's settled. All we need now is a date."

Addison wanted to say nothing and held out for as long as he could, but Jon couldn't resist. He had the perfect day in mind.

"July fourth," said Jon.

He had everyone's attention. Kya, Addison, Rex, even Brutus and Cole were all eyeing Jon like he was the man in charge. Jon supposed, at this moment, he was.

"What?" asked Rex.

"Independence Day," said Jon. "The Conquistador is having a huge bash, lots of guests, and lots of ways to play with this Showdown."

"That's soon," said Rex, surprised.

"Yes," said Jon. "Not far away, no." Jon was so astute he was almost obtuse, but not quite. He meant what he said and was willing to defend it. He wanted to win.

"And are you sure you'll be ready by then?" asked Rex. "I imagine you'll all have your hands quite filled, planning and organizing your bash."

Jon could feel Addison's stare and whether it was one of fury or pride, he didn't know. What he did know was Jon had set the terms. He chose the day despite not having the power to do so, but still, he had taken control and taken a stand.

"We'll be ready." Jon stood next to Kya, and she looked at the Marine.

Jon remained close to Kya because it made him feel like he had her support. Maybe he did and maybe he didn't. Maybe he didn't care.

"Okay. You'll be ready, Addison, will you?"

Addison stood and buttoned his jacket. "Have no choice now, date's been set."

Jon gulped. Addison did not seem too enthused about the selected date. He didn't look at Jon as he responded to Rex. To Jon, while familiar with various instances before, Addison felt cold. It wasn't because he was angry or upset. Addison kept his distance when he was either. It was a sign of disappointment, and he was passive because he preferred to be callous instead of angry.

He was exactly this way now.

"We'll be ready," Addison declared.

"Good," said Rex. "Then let's make it official, shall we? And let us do that...the old-fashioned way too?"

Rex removed a wilted book with torn pages and plopped it down on his *desk*. Kya flinched. This book had aged into a wilted collection of crinkled papers. Jon gazed at this new book and felt a tickling near his ear. He knew what this was.

"The first edition of The Conquistador Codex," said Jon. "Whoa."

This book looked different than the one he was given when he was hired.

"Correct," said Rex. "A first edition, like you said. You know what, this boy over here is pretty sharp, and he's got some pretty serious balls too. You should keep him around for as long as you can, Krowe. Boy's got a real future in this business."

Shocked by Rex's compliment, Jon was flattered but at the same time afraid. To receive such a comment made by such a bad man, Jon should have felt a boost in self-confidence, but he didn't. Unless Addison felt the same as Jon did, there was not much else to say other than thank you.

Jon didn't say this, not now.

As Rex lifted the hefty cover of this old codex, Jon gazed at the pages. While he already knew how worn everything was, he continued to marvel at this ancient text. Some of its writing was still in cursive. It looked like it was done with an ink and quill. Seeing this in front of him, Jon felt like he stepped back in time.

The Conquistador Codex, according to what Danix said, was a book given to the Doormen when they were first formed. It outlined the rules, the code, as well as the consequences of the world of elite bouncing and nightclub security. Rex flipped to a section where there appeared to be an empty chart. When Jon saw this, Rex removed a pen and scribbled his name. He handed the pen over to Addison.

"Your turn." Addison gawked and was as reluctant as he always had been.

"Name and date, yeah?" asked Rex.

Jon watched Addison sign his name the same as Rex did. Addison's signature, however, was sloppier. It was done in a way that demonstrated just how little he cared, and when he was done, he handed the pen back over to Rex.

"Now," said Rex, "make it official."

Jon squinted. "It's not official?" he asked.

Afterward, Rex leered, and his pupils twinkled amid the faint orange light.

"Not yet."

Jon watched Rex reach into his pocket, and in an instant, withdrew his fist. It was wrapped around something Jon couldn't see, but as Rex uncoiled his fingers, he ejected a blade.

Jon immediately raised his hand.

"Relax," Rex said to Jon. "Not what you think."

Addison glared and Jon looked at Rex. Blade out, the leader of the Fallen Sons opened his hand and pressed the steel deep into his palm. Jon gasped. It was not because he was disturbed or bothered. No, he was only surprised that the agreement needed to be sealed in blood. When he thought he knew everything about his place of work, Jon came to understand a little more. Rex cut his hand and blood dripped onto the page like a ledger. Now blotching the space, a few drops struck the surface, and Rex spun the switchblade before offering it to Addison.

"Your turn." While the exchange was clear, it disgraced Addison.

He took the weapon from Rex and Jon waited for Addison to cut his hand too.

But rather than dragging the blade across his flesh, Addison opted to do something different. He squeezed the blade as a more unpleasant and painful way of drawing blood. Addison didn't take his eyes off of Rex. No, he kept holding until blood wet the full page. This reminded Jon of the instances whereby people, usually soldiers and other tough guys, would hold their hand over a burning flame. The first to move was the loser. In this case, Addison shed more blood than Rex. Jon read this as an indication that Addison was prepared to go all the way when the time came. The Doormen can take more and will do whatever they need to in order to win this Showdown.

Addison returned the weapon to Rex later.

"It is done," said Rex.

Addison nodded. "It is."

Addison pivoted and gave his back to the Fallen Sons. Before Jon, Addison, and Kya could vacate Rex's office, a chair screeched, and everyone stopped.

Rex had risen. "Ah, one more moment there, Mr. Krowe!"

Jon peered over his shoulder. Addison and Kya did the same. Addison sighed and rotated around very slowly.

"You spoke about holding a moratorium before the Showdown. Do you remember that?"

Addison's hands stayed in his pockets. He nodded. "I do remember."

"Then, you also remember saying that you need a lot of practice, eh?" asked Rex.

"He never said that," declared Jon. "I did. Well, I sort of did."

"Right," Rex said to Jon. The leader of the Fallen Sons eyed the Marine with a look of intrigue. "Sure, but there was something else I didn't tell you, but I think you might benefit from it, at least you might in the long run."

"What is it?" Addison glowered.

"Oh, just a little clarification."

"We know the date of the Showdown," Kya said to Rex. As it turned out, she was getting a little tired of Rex's bullshit too. The asshole was the most obnoxious and smug son of a bitch that Jon had ever laid eyes on.

"I know you know that," said Rex, "but do you also know where you are?"

"I'm in a shithole," said Addison. "And I'm staring at a piece of shit."

Hearing this insult, Rex grinned. "Sure, but what you don't know...is why?"

"Why?" asked Jon.

Rex's fingers slipped under his tongue and he whistled. The howling shrieked through the setting and Jon shivered. He hated this sound. The music stopped, and the people at the party all stilled in the darkness. While it was a baffling sight for Jon, it wasn't as baffling as the expressions being displayed by all the teens standing around.

"Why you were brought here," continued Rex, from behind his desk. "You came here looking for answers, and now you got them. However, I let you come here because I wanted to see, see how good you really are. If the Doormen are still the best bouncers in the game."

"Oh yeah?" asked Addison. He eyed the brooding teenagers poised outside Rex's office.

"Yeah," said Rex. "Let's see if you can get yourselves out of a good old-fashioned trap. Seeing as how you're going to need practice for the Showdown, what better way to do that than here and now?"

Jon gawked. "So much for a moratorium."

"Meh," said Rex. "Technically, you're trespassing, so technically, you should get what you deserve. So..let's see what you can do."

Jon counted heads and thought of a plan.

Before entering Rex's space, he counted how many people were present and estimated at least one hundred guests, which was not that many but was still enough. As of now, Jon was staring down at seven boys in particular. One of them was the same boy who Jon beat not too long ago. They stomped toward Jon and Addison, who stayed tight while Kya stood behind them.

"I see you haven't stopped paying dogs to do your dirty work?" Addison snapped at Rex.

"Oh, never underestimate a good dog," said Rex. "Besides, these boys you're looking at now got to come to a free party. The least they can do is repay the owner with a little no-holds-barred action *boom, boom, boom.* Gentlemen," Rex said this as he began to fall back into his chair. Jon listened to his chair squeak while these teens crept in closer. "Don't let these guys get to the door."

Jon knew then that the encounter was not only on, it would be messy and brutal.

The teens were like the hooligans from eighties films, all looking for trouble.

"Back off, boys. You don't want to do this." Jon was calm and relaxed.

This was nothing more than a simple altercation. Jon had faced and endured many of these types of encounters before. Always, he knew exactly what to do. Here, it was different. The people he was staring at were underage. They were not like The Conquistador's customers. They were kids, and yes, Jon did just throw some kids a beating, but that was different. They attacked him and then there were only a handful. Now, that number was higher. Jon wasn't alone, however. Addison stood with Jon like he was his partner. Kya was too, but she was also a target in this forthcoming assault, the same as Jon and Addison. Jon questioned what Kya's skills would be like in this kind of situation. He honestly didn't know, and when Jon glanced at Addison, he pressed his fingers hard into his palm.

"Addison." More teens joined the enclosing circle. "What should we do?" asked Jon.

"Exactly what we always do whenever we find ourselves backed into a corner to which there's no way out," said Addison. "We fight."

"Against them?" asked Jon. "It's gonna be messy."

"Yeah, well," replied Addison. "We could use the practice."

Jon's sigh turned to a chuckle before taking a step back. *Ready.*

"Should you go first, or should I?" asked Jon.

"Let's see who makes the first move, shall we?"

"All right," said Jon. "Let's do this."

CHAPTER 14
MESSY MESS MESS

Jon wasn't enraged after being thrown into an escalating storm. He wasn't furious or broken down by this sea of people now engulfing him from all sides. No, Jon was intrigued. He knew his opponents were going to be easier when compared to those faced before. But that wasn't the point.

The point was Rex wanted the Doormen to suffer. He wanted to see them hurt.

As the attackers closed in, Jon watched Addison drop and roll. Suddenly, Addison looped his leg around a boy's calf and pulled him down. Once the boy was on the ground, Addison chopped him in the neck.

He cracked the fool right in the throat and the fool coughed to catch his breath. Yet, Addison wasn't finished with this guy. After he knocked the kid's Adam's apple, Addison jammed his thumbs into the eyes and pressed until the teen began to squeal. When he was done yelping like a baby, his friend stomped in to help. The idiot raised his leg to kick, but Addison caught him by the ankle. The kicking teen then hopped to find his footing. During his attempt to try to stay balanced, Addison pummeled his opponent right in the balls with a solid uppercut and then once more in the chest.

"Ah!" The hopping teen dropped to his back and sobbed.

This attack did warrant the attention of so many others, all of whom stood there petrified. They listened to their friend coughing like he was trying to throw up.

Jon, however, enjoyed the sight. Despite the fact that he was standing back, he could smell the alcohol exuding from their messy bodies.

It was going to be sloppy, like he said.

"All right," Jon said. "Let's get to the second course, shall we?"

Jon clocked another attacker and knocked him down. Jon then contorted his body, lifted his foot, and clocked the first idiot in the jaw.

Jon watched as yet another jackass fell.

Now down, the guy bled from his mouth, and, looking ahead, Jon spotted a second attacker. Staying low, Jon waited for the second idiot to come forward— feral as an uncaged animal. He attacked without direction or strategy, swarmed Jon with fists, and grunted as he tried to hit the Marine.

Jon focused on the boy's knees. He shoved his feet into the teen's thighs and worked on the leverage. In jiu-jitsu, an opponent striking from close proximity is an advantage. So, when this boy struck, he did so with a weak punch that surrendered his arm. This gifted Jon with a notable gift. With the boy's wrist now in the Marine's hand, Jon kicked and shoved until the boy was on the ground. Then, Jon secured the boy's arm again, then bent down to add pressure to the boy's muscles.

Once done, Jon had the armbar nice and tight.

While Jon and Addison were handling themselves well, more came later.

Like insects, they approached in big bunches, but both Doormen continued to hold their positions. The fact remained that Jon, Addison, and Kya could be injured under these circumstances and they needed a way out, fast!

"We need to move!" Jon shouted. He struck another fool with his elbow and kicked him in the groin. Afterward, there was an opening that led to the back of the warehouse. Jon and Addison hurried, but none checked on Kya. Jon's pace slowed when he thought of her.

Where was she? Why wasn't she with them?

"Wait," Jon said to Addison.

"What?" Addison asked.

"Kya? Where's Kya?"

Addison's eyebrows furrowed. It began to dawn on him that Kya was not present at this time.

"Kya!" Jon looked around to see where she was but had little time to navigate. Jon's head whipped in different directions as he scoured the warehouse for his girl. However, Jon's search for Kya ended when he heard a squeal not far from where he was standing.

"Kya?" Jon followed the sound.

The incessant sound soon led Jon to a section in the warehouse where two pallets of tall bottles were stacked. Jon saw Kya standing between them. When Jon saw Kya, he also saw three other people standing with her. Through the darkness, Jon could hear Kya's aggressive shouts. Jon noticed the three women standing in front of Kya, all of whom were in this fight the same as the guys, only the girls were smaller in size. Their hair was long and greasy. The main difference was Kya was taller. He was definitely more put together than the girls she was standing toe-to-toe with.

Right now, Kya was wrestling with two of them.

Gripping one by the hair, Kya pulled the other one by the neck. The girls squirmed to break free from Kya's hold. Jon could see the girls fuming as Kya tossed them around like rag dolls. Until this moment, Jon had never seen Kya in a fight. Part of him was glad he hadn't seen this, and yet, what Jon was seeing now was not a ratchet girl who slapped and scratched.

No, what Jon saw was not a girl but a woman—a strong, deadly, capable woman.

Jon wasn't witnessing some catfight he saw often at the club. Instead, he was seeing a solid sparring match whereby one fighter was skilled, and the other was just in the way.

Kya loaded her fists and punched like she had experience in a ring. Jon knew technique when he saw it. Kya was literate in the art of jabbing and hooking. Her fist cut into this one girl's chest. Kya pounded her like she was hitting a bag. Jon hated seeing a girl get punched. He loathed whenever girls scrapped at the club. It was almost always ugly and quite difficult to reduce. They clawed, pulled, and sometimes bit. It was sloppy and strenuous. Jon also struggled to grab them. He never knew exactly what he was grabbing. Girls in that situation will say almost anything. They would accuse men of touching them where they shouldn't. Often, when you pulled two girls apart, their boyfriends were usually close by. When they see one of their women being grabbed, they have their own thoughts.

Usually, the altercations escalated.

But here, Kya was facing off against two girls. She knocked one idiot out with a clean shot to the face. Kya held the next one by the hair. While the girl's nose bled, her eyes appeared black from bruising. Kya was throwing these girls around like they were toys, and she was almost done playing.

She hit the last girl in the face and kicked her to the ground.

"Kya," Jon said. He held Kya and began to guide her away from the scene. "We have to go." Soon after he held Kya's arm, she acknowledged him with a fixed, focused stare.

"Please." She looked at Jon and then back at the crowd. The teens were now regrouped.

Each one acquired the same glare as the three Doormen after they hammered the fools into the pavement. While all of this was Rex's idea of a *test*, it was a trap set so Jon and Addison could be injured. No, Rex wanted them worn and torn before the Showdown. Even if Rex was relying on teens to do his bidding, all of them were lousy fighters.

Still, it hurt. Fights, no matter what, always hurt.

"Let's go!" Jon yelled. He followed Addison toward a light in the distance.

When arriving at the warehouse, it was almost evening. However, now it was practically night. Whatever was bright enough to guide all three of them away they followed and Jon raced after the faint twinkle like he was running in a dream.

"Look out!" Another teen popped out of nowhere and tried to take Addison to the floor.

Fortunately, Addison veered and smacked the approaching teen. Upon hitting the boy, Addison hopped over him and kept running. Jon looked up but kept his eyes open and his body ready. Approaching the middle of the warehouse, in this region of the massive facility, the dancing teens assembled. Bouncing to the sporadic beats, those that Jon had encountered were so strung out. They didn't notice him or Addison. Their quick escape soon ground to a halt. Jon and Addison were forced to navigate another obstacle.

"Shit," said Addison.

Jon stood beside him. Looking back for find Kya, fortunately, she was there. She was actually close to Jon's shoulder, with her head almost resting on his body.

"Gotta go through 'em," said Jon. "No other way."

"Goddamn it," Addison snapped. He stepped in first.

For Jon, the people here reminded Jon of cattle crossing in the middle of the road.

He had seen this once, a long time ago, back when Jon visited the state of Montana. At the time, the cowboys were herding animals across the road. Some were peeved about such interference. Jon, however, didn't mind.

He found the entire spectacle to be both calming and beautiful.

Nature roams, and sometimes, things just get in the way. You can either embrace it or fight it. And yet, the fight against nature is never a good one. In the end, nature is the ultimate opponent. No matter what you do, nature always wins.

In this section of the warehouse, the music was loud and the space was dark. Jon slid back and guided Kya so she was standing right in front of him. Here Jon could keep his eye on Kya and stop any incoming attacks. As Jon marched along, he followed Addison like he always did. The music pounded Jon's ears and he looked at the nearest exit.

When they first entered the warehouse that was transformed into a rave, this space was nearly clear. Now Jon wasn't sure if it was or wasn't. He could see slightly beyond the crowd, but even what he could grasp was only a little. Jon could barely see anything. When Addison and Jon hopped along, they pushed through the crowd without apology. Jon continued to hear the sounds of the pursuing teens, all drawing in. Although they had reached Addison's car, ominous forces continued to echo from all around. They were not surrendering. They were not stopping.

And Jon shook his head. Who the hell were these assholes?

Jon slid across the hood and hopped into the car. Addison started the engine. Kya was in the back seat, all buckled up and secured.

Addison shifted the DeLorean into gear and powered up his electric vehicle. While it was no Ferrari, the DeLorean definitely had some get-up-and-go. It accelerated from the warehouse, but that didn't stop a few more idiots who decided to pursue.

They threw what they had at the blitzing vehicle. The miscellaneous items bounced over the car's roof and nicked one of the windows. Jon looked back and counted five silhouettes standing where the car was once parked. These people threw their hands into the air and continued to scream expletives at Addison, Jon, and Kya.

Jon closed his eyes and took a moment. What he and his friends had just faced was a story for the ages. Jon needed time to actually process what had happened.

"Jesus Christ," Jon muttered to himself. "I mean, Jesus fucking Christ."

Addison said nothing. Instead, he kept both hands gripped on the steering wheel. The DeLorean slowed and Jon glanced at the rear-view mirror to check on Kya. Rubbing her neck, her jaw slacked.

"Are you okay?" asked Jon.

"Yeah," said Kya. Her neck cracked. She swayed her jaw like she was trying to straighten it. "I'm just peachy."

"Right," said Jon, detecting her sarcasm.

Jon knew exactly how she was feeling. It was not good.

"Goddamn," Jon said to Addison. "I didn't think we'd get out of there. Fucking Rex. That was one helluva a test if you ask me."

Addison gazed ahead. His expression sent shivers down Jon's back. Whenever he fucked up, went too far, or did something he was not supposed to do, Jon's mother would shoot him a look like this. It was cold, and you could see the venom simmering in her eyes. Jon could also see claws drawing from her fingers, and although Jon's mom didn't have claws, she might as well have when she looked like this.

Right now, Addison was epically pissed off.

CHAPTER 15
SHOWDOWN

"ADDISON?" ASKED JON, CONCERNED AND ALSO uncomfortable. He repeatedly scratched his thighs even though they weren't itchy. "What is it?"

Addison sighed and his head shook. Again, the cooler's attitude toward the Marine was palpable. Jon could smell the disappointment and he hated every second of it.

"Why don't you tell me what the hell you did back there?" Addison asked Jon.

Jon bowed his head.

"What?" Kya asked. "What did he do?"

Although she didn't know what Addison was referring to, Jon did. Such was clear from the beginning of Addison's observably furious expression.

"He set the terms, and agreed to a Showdown," Addison said to Jon.

"Well, yeah," said Kya. "I mean, we have to stop those Fallen Sons bastards, and that's the only way to do it. What? Are you angry? 'Cause you sound angry."

Kya was clearly bolder than Jon was in this situation. She was defending and making it clear to Addison that she was on Jon's side. Jon, however, saw things differently. Addison seemed easy on Kya. She spoke harshly to him and sometimes didn't respect his authority as much Jon and the other bouncers, which was odd given her position. Now, Jon was bold too, and he did speak for Addison and the club, which was not his job. In essence, Jon crossed a line. In this case, it was a big and long line comprised of professionalism and duty.

"I'm sorry, Addison," Jon said, "if you felt I went too far, but we do need to stop these guys, and if that means working harder and doing more, well then..." Addison continued to stay silent.

At this point, Jon didn't know what his thoughts were about what happened. He was shrill. His glare was visible in the moonlight. In fact, the light only enhanced his look of fury.

"Look, I don't know what's going to happen, but whatever it is, it's happening."

Addison scoffed.

"You really don't know what we have to do," Addison barked at Jon. "Showdowns are brutal. Anything can go wrong at any time. And why the hell did you pick Fourth of July weekend? Do you have any idea how difficult that's going to be?"

Jon recalled why he selected this date. He knew the reasons but had yet to elaborate on them. Now might be the perfect time for Jon to do so.

"Do you have any idea how busy the club is going to be?" Addison asked. "How swamped and how crowded. You couldn't have picked a worse time."

"No," said Jon. "See, I couldn't have picked a *better* time."

Jon was confident in his decision but Addison clearly wasn't. He looked at Jon, dumbfounded and disappointed. Jon stared at his boss with a firm look because, truthfully, he regretted nothing.

"What?"

"Look," said Jon, "no doubt the club will be busy. No doubt we're going to have our hands full, but then... that's the point."

"What do you mean?" Addison asked, his patience at a standstill.

"Well," replied Jon, "we can use the crowd, see? We can use the numbers and we can blend in. Tradecraft and stealth, we activate those skills when facing off against Rex and the rest of his Sons. You see, their plan will be to take us out as hard and as fast as possible. They'll be fueled by their revenge, by their anger and not by skill, which is exactly what bouncers are not supposed to rely on *ever*. They'll want to get even as quickly as possible, so they'll be careless and they'll get sloppy. But we won't be. Such high numbers of people will provide us with a lot of cover, a lot to use to our advantage."

"But not a single person at the club can see anything," said Kya. "If they do, the whole Showdown will blow up in our faces."

Jon grinned at Kya. Evidently, she was as much involved in this contest as the Doormen. Her investment in this conflict proved she was not just a bartender. No, she was so much more.

"We'll be patient," Jon said. "We know the club,

know its secrets. The Conquistador will guide us the rest of the way. It will give us exactly what we need."

"And what's that?" asked Kya.

Addison had said nothing. Still, Jon answered like he was the one who asked the question.

"Access," said Jon. "*Unlimited* access."

Jon glanced at Kya, who gazed ahead with a coy smile. She blinked with a little flirtation, and the more Jon asserted himself, the more strength he was displaying. And the stronger Jon appeared, the more this appealed to Kya, the more her eyes began to gleam with infatuation and delight.

Despite having Kya's attention, Jon wasn't saying anything to impress her. The Doormen were the best bouncers around, and the Showdown would prove why this was true.

"We use the numbers," Jon continued. "We channel all our skills and we show these assholes what we're really made of. We put this rivalry to bed and we beat the Fallen Sons at their own game. Whatta y' say, Addison? You down...for this *Showdown?*"

Addison's head shook. Reluctant as he may be, there was little Addison could say now. Jon was calling him out. He was demanding his boss's loyalty and his courage and Addison was not someone to run in the face of a challenge. No, like everyone else who worked at the club, Addison refused to surrender. He stood with Jon, because they were more than just an employer and employee. No, they were friends. They were brothers, and with Kya in the mix, they were almost like family.

"We're going to need time to train," Addison said as he accepted this new reality. "We're going to have to train every day until the Fourth of July. We're going to have to practice at work and outside of it too. We'll need to learn better tradecraft and how to move without being seen at all. We might be Doormen, but for this test, we're going to have to transform into something else."

"And what's that, Addison?" Kya asked. The cooler's gaze narrowed.

The next word caused goose bumps to scatter along Jon's arms. Addison was a solid boss, no doubt, but now he was also a badass carved straight from the pages of pulp fiction. Jon adored it when Addison activated this side of his personality. Jon rarely saw it, but when he did, he absolutely couldn't get enough of it.

"Ghosts," said Addison. "We have to become... *ghosts.*"

CHAPTER 16
BRING THE BAD GUYS

JON'S IMMINENT RETURN TO THE CONQUISTADOR was everything but normal.

Having escaped the rave at the warehouse, and having accepted a new club challenge, there was too much to explain and not enough time to explain it. When calling the meeting, Addison summarized the situation to everyone present as easily as he could.

Showdown. Contest. Rules. *Winner takes all.*

With all the Doormen in The Conquisitador's conference room, once everyone was informed of what was ahead, the elite bouncers, in their usual and glorious fashion, had only one response.

"When do we start?"

The answer to said question was just as straightforward but more encouraging.

"Right now."

Once Addison made this clear, the meeting was adjourned. All that was on the horizon was a war and the training needed to win it.

This Showdown was an attack on the entire club, not just its security.

It demanded the focus of everyone who worked in the business and dated back to the early days of the nightclub industry. Despite this, everyone got in line and agreed to the Showdown's parameters. All understood what was expected of them now, and as Addison stood at the head of the table and explained the rules and the regulations, he touched on what everyone had to work with, what everyone needed to do.

"Since you know the rules," said Addison, "now we can discuss strategy."

Jon was sitting beside Owen at the time. The Doormen were all on the same page, but what Owen struggled with most were the logistics of this game. He was just asking too many questions.

"So, what?" asked Owen. "We're in a contest or something?"

Owen whispered this to Jon, who was staring straight ahead. While waiting for Addison to introduce the primary plan, all Jon wanted to know was the best way to go forward. Jon remembered that he was the one who agreed to this situation in the first place.

Jon wanted to have a Showdown and he wanted to have it now. He wanted to know how he was going to win. He wanted to divide and conquer like he said he would.

"More than that," Jon said to Owen. "We're in a fight for our lives."

Owen's eyes popped.

Addison stood at the front of the room. Everyone was focused on the cooler, yet those sitting the closest to Addison were Danix and Li. Being the oldest Doormen, their knowledge of the Showdown traced back to the earliest days of The Conquistador. They knew of its history and its traditions, and Jon hoped they had some tricks up their sleeves too.

"The way in which we're going to combat this situation," Addison said, "and how we're going to win is we're going to focus on three specific areas in order to prepare for it. Stealth, communication, and *necessary* aggression."

Jon smirked. He liked this strategy so far. All of it was vital. It was a crucial place for the Doormen to begin.

"Evasion?" Owen whispered in Jon's ear. However, what Jon didn't know was if an evasion was even possible. Then again, not everyone who worked at The Conquistador had an extensive knowledge of this craft. It was wrong to assume everyone did.

"Escaping," clarified Addison after hearing Owen whisper. "To beat the Sons, we're going to have not only channel all the skills we've learned so far, but we're going to have to refine them in ways we never have before. The Showdown is a game of Capture The Flag, so whoever obtains the flag wins, and we have to do everything we can to stop the Sons from getting a hold of them. Those are the rules of the game, and that's how we're going to play. Since it's happening here, at our club, we'll have home field advantage, but that won't be enough. Rex and the Sons are going to have a few tricks up their sleeves too, no doubt about that, and they won't be fighting fair."

"Isn't playing fair part of the game?" asked Li.

"Traditionally speaking, yes," said Addison, "but this is a Showdown. The only rules that are enforced are to guard your side, make sure no one gets your trophy, and make sure no guests are hurt or made aware. It's gonna be tough, but not impossible."

"We're going to be exhausted too, though," said Owen.

"Yes, we will," said Addison. "But thankfully, what I see in front of me are workers, and real workers don't tire easily. All of you are the best bouncers in this business, which means if we ever had a chance at winning this thing and beating these assholes, the people I see now are the only ones who can do that."

"Well, when is the Showdown?" asked Danix.

Jon was pleased to hear Danix say something now. In fact, Jon wanted to hear from as many bouncers as he could. Everyone needed to have their own say as well as to heed their own advice. They were a team, and a good team is measured by everyone participating and contributing equally.

Jon was fully prepared to do his part.

"Fourth of July," Addison stated as if the date meant little to him now.

"What?" asked Li.

"July Fourth, did you say?" Owen piped in now as well.

After that, the room erupted. Everyone reacted the same way to the date announcement. Clearly, this was not the date any of them wanted. Not even Danix was impressed by it.

"That's our busiest day, Addison. We'll have a lot of guests to manage," Danix said. "A lot of distractions, a lot of things that can go wrong. Did they pick that day?"

"No," said Addison. Jon detected hints of regret as

his boss answered. Now was Addison's opportunity to point the finger at Jon.

Being the one who selected the day, Jon gulped while Addison stood tall and nibbled on his lips. Jon could see Addison preparing his response. He could already hear him saying the words that Jon feared. He was going to admit it was all Jon's fault.

Jon picked the day, not me. It's all Jon's fault we have the Showdown on the Fourth of July, our club's busiest day.

"I picked it." Jon's eyes opened wide and he exhaled. "I chose the Fourth of July. Me."

Jon gasped while Addison chose to spare the Marine from possible criticism. Maybe it was because Addison didn't want Jon to take the heat for choosing such a day. Maybe it was also because Addison saw Jon as something more than just another bouncer.

"Addison, that date is a killer," said Danix. "We gotta get it moved."

"No," said Addison. "Once a date is set, a date is set, and we have no choice but to honor it."

Jon heard Li muttering something in Chinese. However, his tone was not encouraging to Jon. No, Li sounded pissed. Clearly, The Fourth of July was a bad day in his opinion too.

"Well, like I said," Danix said, "that night, we're going to have our hands full."

"Exactly," Addison replied, forceful yet also assertive. He gazed sternly at Jon like he was the only one in the room. "The more bodies we have in this place the day of the Showdown," said Addison, "the more of an advantage we're going to have."

"What?" asked Owen, unable to grasp the logic behind Addison's statement.

"Yeah, how so?" added Danix. "We attack, someone's going to notice, and the Showdown ends. With all the guests around, they're going to react."

"How can they react to something...that they cannot see?" Addison's question silenced everyone in the room.

Jon thought about this concept of seeing and not seeing. Often, the Doormen moved through the club without anyone noticing or reacting to them. This was their primary advantage, but the Doormen never intentionally tried to keep themselves hidden. There were some instances, yes, that Jon could recall from memory. He remembered how he would emerge from the shadows and surprise guests .

Often, they never saw Jon coming.

Maybe this was what Addison Krowe was referring to now. In Addison's mind, this was the Doormen's primary strategy going forward. The Conquistador's head of security had to get everyone else to believe it too.

"And what *can't* they see?" Jon asked.

"If we want to protect this club and win this game," replied Addison, "then the guests are going to be our best assets. We don't fight, we strike hard and fast like cobras. We move in and we move out. We're going to have to neutralize in a matter of seconds and then disappear seconds after."

"Disappear...into the crowd," Jon confirmed.

"Yes, they're not guests," said Addison. "They're cover. *Tradecraft*."

Jon smirked. Tradecraft, as he knew, was a military

term. Now, Jon's Marines didn't specialize in tradecraft, but the Navy SEALs and Delta operators certainly did. In Jon's mind, the Doormen of the Conquistador were the Navy SEALs of the bouncing world. And, as Addison was keen on reminding everyone here, they were and always would be...*the best of the best.*

"Still," said Danix, "we should map out a perimeter and decide on our primary striking areas, close to the speakers, the stage, and near all other hidden sections as well. We hit them where there's the smallest chance of them hearing or seeing anything, and that's how we win."

"*Use* the club," said Li. "*Use* The Conquistador."

"Like I said," Addison said. He stood tall and continued to look only at Jon. "We have home field advantage because the Fallen Sons don't have access to an official club, and so, we'll be the ones who are in control, mostly."

"Yeah, the prime movers," said Jon. "So to speak."

From across the room, both Jon and Addison were joined in a stare of pure affirmation and agreement. Both were seeing the bigger picture now, and each one understood exactly what needed to be done. And, because they were both responsible for creating this new strategy together, they were joyful. They were joyful because they approved.

"Always," replied Addison. "Now, if we're smart enough and careful like we always are, then we can use our environment. We can rely on each other's movements and skill set."

"So what exactly are the areas we *should* focus on?" This question belonged to Owen.

He was still sitting next to Jon but was now leaning

forward. The areas Addison had referred to—and Jon knew this offhand—were specific regions of the club. They were the parts that would allow for Doormen to attack and continue while being unseen. Jon knew The Conquistador like the back of his hand, but as far as areas most immune to guest activity, Jon scratched his head.

He didn't know.

"For now," said Addison, "we're looking at the spaces that will serve us well when luring in the Sons, our enemies. See, once we get them there, we can take them out of the game."

Addison held a remote while behind him was a solid LED screen. When Addison pressed a button on the control, the screen displayed a three-dimensional map of The Conquistador and showed all its sections and subsections. Some of these regions were labeled. Those that weren't were the obvious *secret rooms* located inside the enigmatic nightclub.

Jon was familiar with only one.

He called it the Room With The Red Door or Secret Room, and Jon knew it well from the last time. However, when Addison said the Doormen were to focus on these primary areas, they were highlighted in yellow. This was a strange color to choose, but then this form of interaction was not new, not to Jon.

In the Marines, he sat in rooms like this all the time, and he listened to men like Addison all the time. This was nothing more than a mission briefing, where Jon and his team were informed of all the variables as well as the overall plan of execution. It always amazed Jon how much The Conquistador reminded him of the military. It was one of the reasons he didn't struggle like the other vets did. In many ways, it was familiar and ironically easy for Jon to forget his pain due to the loss of his former "best" friend, James. Whether it be the briefing, the strategizing, the working, or the timing, Jon never doubted that this was exactly where he belonged and that it did help him to heal. It made Jon stronger.

"First area, *the stage*." Addison clicked the remote and magnified this section of the club. Shown in a three-dimensional schematic, it was a stark image that Jon and the rest of the employees were viewing now. The stage was traced with fine lines and showed nothing other than its bare bones. Still, Jon required this method of viewing. If he didn't see the stage this way, then he wouldn't have noticed the two doors located beneath it.

It was actually quite fascinating.

"Our stage is equipped with two hidden doors," said Addison, "and each one leads into a storage facility down below."

Addison clicked the remote and showed what was beneath this stage. Exactly as Addison said, there was another room there, and it was one Jon hadn't stepped foot into ever.

"And the storage facility leads to a bar room," said Danix, "which will take us right back to the club itself. It's almost like..."

"A hidden tunnel," said Jon. He was fascinated by the reveal of yet another secret part of the club he thought he knew inside and out.

"The club is a castle, old friend," said Addison. "It shifts and it changes, and the more time you spend trying to solve it, the only slightly closer you get to truly understanding it."

This was true on so many levels. The Conquistador was a hub for gathering secrets, but it was also an ancient, compelling place. Although this always made Jon question the truth surrounding the company, here it was their greatest weapon.

"We use the stage too," said Addison. "We hit all the Sons there without any guests noticing and then get back on the floor as soon as possible."

"And who's going to be guarding the stage?" asked Li.

"Well, we have five members on a Showdown team," Addison replied. "Who wants to guard it?"

"I will," said Li. "I'll take the stage."

Li nodded, and so did Addison, who raised his hand and gestured to Li.

"It's your spot now."

"Good." Now, Jon assumed Li had used the doors beneath the stage before. If he didn't, he wouldn't have been so quick to agree to guard it. At least, this was what Jon thought.

"Next location will be the VIP," Addison continued, "and you all know why this section was selected."

No one spoke up to confirm this, but none of them needed to. Jon understood why the VIP section was the best place to do battle with the Sons during the Showdown. The location was comprised of several booths. Jon recalled Kya walking in and behind these booths, handing bottles to guests as well as tending to their every need.

"This area will give us copious amounts of mobility. We will find Rex and the Sons here. We can pull them out and toss them into a booth, if need be. Guests will just think they're seeing someone who's too drunk and who has passed out in the VIP, which, let's be honest, is not exactly a sight worth seeing. It definitely won't be on the Fourth of July, that much I can tell you."

Hearing Addison say this only confirmed Jon's reasoning. The VIP section would be overwhelmed but everyone there would be drowning in the celebration. Not one would notice an altercation in a space so narrow. Now, the VIP section was always booming. Guests there were the pinnacle of distraction. People purchased the VIP so they didn't have to worry about anything. And, thanks to The Conquistador's illustrious reputation, they were accommodated quite well. Therefore, none saw beyond what the section allowed them to see.

"VIPs will be packed that day," said Danix. Everyone already knew this was true. "We'll have to keep them distracted."

"Everyone who purchases a booth during the Fourth of July will be supplied with two bottles instead of one, as well as some extra wait staff. I'll be doubling up our service that night."

"Good," said Danix.

"The goal is to get the section so buzzed they won't notice a goddamn thing. In fact, on the Fourth of July, VIPs will be the primary location. If we keep the fighting away from the guests, we can hit them here."

"Hard to fight in that section," said Li. "Not a lot of space to get hands dirty."

"Exactly," said Addison. "Not a lot of space for us means not a lot of space for them too. All you have to do is ask yourself, who's better with space? Is it the Doormen or the goddamn bouncers who know nothing about stealth or how to beat an enemy like Rex?"

Addison's question was rhetorical. The Doormen were trained on how to operate within a small space as well as how to deal with dangerous men. Confinement, with little room to move or act, was a challenge all the Doormen rose to on many occasions. Now, the VIP section was prime for altercation. Jon felt confident whenever he worked there. And there was another feature about this place not yet mentioned. However, Jon felt the need to do this now.

"The waitstaff," he said, "can they be in on this too?"

Suddenly, there was silence. It was like a bomb had exploded in the dead center of the conference room. Prior to this moment, everyone was present and attentive. Now, everything felt intensified to the point where people seemed angry.

Jon didn't intend to garner this kind of reaction. He was just thinking out loud. He said the first thought that came to his mind and didn't expect himself to be heard. After speaking to Danix, his friend grunted and looked at Addison, pensive as he stared.

"Is...that...allowed?" Danix glibly inquired. It was as if the very idea was too much for him to consider. What Jon believed to only be an idea had now evolved into an actual possibility.

"The rules of the Showdown are clear, only five members per team, and only they can participate."

"Sure," said Danix. "But how will they know? I mean, our servers..." Danix looked to the back, where the waitresses were all sitting, Kya included. "I mean, they'll see and know what we're doing so..."

"But they'll all be working," Li said. Jon could see

that Li was also considering the real possibility behind this innocuous request. "They have to be that night."

"Right," said Danix. "So, they're working, and they might be able to cover for us while we do battle in the Showdown."

"Holy shit," Jon whispered to himself. Such a suggestion provided a loophole as well as a significant advantage.

What Danix presented was yet another advantage the Doormen would have during the game. The servers, bartenders, and bottle girls might not be players, but they could still help.

Until now, this wasn't even considered. Thanks to Danix, it was.

"Provide other distractions," said Addison, eyes wide.

"Yeah," said Danix. "Whenever we move, they move too, just in a different way."

"Yeah, but...won't Rex pick up on all of that?" asked Owen. He was anxious. Jon noticed his right hand squeezing his left. Jon recognized this as a feature of his friend's sometimes nervous personality. Owen had a solid temperament, yet he was one of the Doormen who experienced moments of uncertainty and hesitation.

"How's he gonna prove it?" asked Danix. "And remember, the only rules for Showdowns are boundaries and getting our hands on that flag, *their trophy*. Nothing else matters, and so, we might be able to make this work."

"The main contact security teams have with coworkers is eye contact," said Addison. "If it's too noisy, we won't be able to communicate with each other."

Hearing this now made the Showdown all the more challenging. Jon watched Danix inch his chair closer to Addison. Evidently, the big guy had more to say.

"Okay, so they just have to keep their eyes open is all," said Danix. "Subtly is the name of the game."

"Aye," said Addison, his gaze shifted to the back of the room. "Ladies, do you think this is something you can handle on that night?"

Jon waited for a response but his attention was on the women, as was Addison's.

In fact, at this moment, everyone was looking at the rows of stunning females dressed in short skirts aligned at the back of the conference room. Jon knew most of these girls.

There was Divine, who was Kya's close friend. The other waitresses Jon knew were Marcy, Gabby, Felicia, Stephanie, Rachel, and Amari. All of them were good. Each woman was strong and capable. They had dealt with their fair share of shit and knew how to take it and dish it out just as easy.

All of them were solid girls.

"We got this," said Divine. Jon appreciated her show of confidence, even though she really didn't know what she was agreeing to.

The Showdown was going to be a rough game from start to finish. They would be busy July 4th and buried under a mound of drunken fools with too many hands. Yet, everyone who worked at The Conquistador could multi-task. There was nothing too great for any of them to simply collapse and fail. They wouldn't be the best club in the business if they couldn't handle multiple challenges at once, and they absolutely would.

"Well, if the wait staff are going to be in this as

much as we are," said Jon. He was thinking out loud again but was far less reserved than he was in the past. "Someone will need to keep track. Someone will have to relay and communicate. They'll need to coalesce, just like we'll do if we want to nail this Showdown and keep ourselves out of sight."

"Right," said Addison. He immediately agreed. "All our priorities will be on the Sons and the guests. We won't have time to communicate with every waitress and get word back to them when a fight is going on. That's just too much to do."

"Way too much," Li added in his two cents.

"Well maybe we won't have to contact all of them," suggested Jon. "Maybe all we'll have to do is contact... *one*." Jon was drawn instantly to Kya. "One server who can communicate with all the others." Jon smirked at Kya, who leered back at the Marine. She knew exactly who Jon was talking about.

"And who did you have in mind?"

"No one," Jon said to Addison. "Not up to me."

Kya's eyes sparkled. Jon assumed it was joy she was experiencing. She was pleased by the acknowledgment. She was not only one of the best bartenders employed at the club. No, she was one of its best employees too. Kya knew this was true, but then so did everyone else.

Addison's focus shifted from Jon to Kya. He raised his hand and pointed.

"Well, I guess if we were going to elect one person to take the reins, I guess it would have to be..." Addison didn't say Kya's name out loud, but then he didn't have to.

"Sure," Kya shrugged. "Why not?"

"Yeah," said Jon. He turned to look back at Kya. "Why not?"

"Still haven't decided the location of our flag, though," said Danix. Everyone in the room was suddenly back to talking business.

"Right," said Addison. "The flag is simple, really. We'll choose a plaque, one of ours."

"Well, which one?" asked Li.

Jon didn't care what one it was. The Conquistador was awarded several plaques over the years, each one demonstrating its reputation and its prestige. Jon saw several in Addison's office. He could vaguely recall what they said. Whatever they did say, Jon didn't care. The idea of choosing a plaque as a flag was a good decision.

"The only one," said Addison. He pointed at the back wall.

And the one Addison pointed at was an obvious selection. It was the plaque awarded to The Conquistador for having the *Best Service*. It was an honor gifted by the International Guild of Nightclub Owners, which was separate from the Commission.

Jon had never heard of the International Guild and so, he was skeptical of it being real.

"Okay," said Danix. "We have our flag, so now let's talk about location. Best place to hide would be..." When Danix didn't finish, Addison interceded.

"Well, it can't be hidden anywhere," he said. "All flags have to be visible during any Showdown, as the rules dictate."

"Can't be any place that's easily reachable, though," said Owen. "I mean, right? Obviously?"

"Depends on how you define reachable," added

Danix. "I definitely know a few places where we could put it."

"Where?" asked Addison.

"Exactly where they'll be expecting it to be," Danix said, acting all confident and slick. "Up top...where everyone can see."

"You mean the balcony?" suggested Addison. He nodded to express his approval.

Jon considered the balcony as the chief place to hide this flag. It seemed like a good place, but exactly where it would be on the balcony was unclear.

"Where?" asked Jon. "Where on the balcony?"

Danix's question was identical to Jon's.

In fact, everything Danix said during this briefing was sensible and well-spoken.

Jon always knew Danix to be a stoic fellow. He was not afraid to speak his mind, but rarely did he speak or feel the need to speak to anyone. It was only when things got real and situations escalated that the former Navy SEAL/professional Mixed Martial Artist provided his own thoughts and feelings. Most of what Danix shared was not an opinion, however. It was notable and comprised only of things that needed to be said and what he gained from years of experience in this industry.

Jon wanted to know too.

He wanted to know where the Doormen's flag would be positioned *on* the balcony.

"It has to be within reach, remember," stated Danix. He was aware of the rules of the game the same as Addison.

Hearing this, Addison nodded again. "In the center, where they can see it," Addison said.

"But is that accessible?" asked Li.

Jon reviewed the balcony from memory. He could see it completely now as he pictured its center. In Jon's opinion, this was a good place for their flag to be placed. When Li asked if it was accessible, Jon didn't know.

Maybe, he thought. *Maybe*.

"It'll be near the ledge," said Addison, "and if you make it to the second floor, which they might do, all they'd have to do is make it around a few tables and they could get their hands on it.

"But they won't make it to the second level," Jon interjected. "They'll stay where they need to stay, and we'll guard it for as long as we have to. It all depends on where they put their flag too, doesn't it? That's a factor as well."

It was then Jon was instantly struck by a new thought. He knew everything that they, the Doormen, were planning to do. He was familiar with their strategy, but what Rex had planned was a complex uncertainty. All Jon knew without a doubt was Rex was dirty. He was a tricky bugger. Jon learned this firsthand when he and Addison tracked down the alcohol supplier and found themselves in the middle of a damn rave. Rex knew not just how to break the law but how to protect himself once such a law was broken. Like Jon understood from the onset, Rex was a man who knew how to pivot and how to maneuver. Most importantly, Rex was once a Doorman himself. Jon anticipated that wherever Rex decided to hide his team's flag, it would be in a solid location—a damn good one.

"We will know where it is...ahead of time?" asked Jon. He felt like this was a good question. He didn't know the parameters of the Showdown, how it began and what would happen once it was over.

"The captains meet ahead of time, yes," said Addison. "They'll talk about the location and where the flags will be placed. We will know before the Showdown starts, but only minutes before, no sooner than that."

"Yeah, okay," said Jon, "But...who monitors *us*?" Jon asked. "Who decides on who's out and who's in? Who's the referee?"

The room went quiet. Again, Jon was referencing another facet of this game. What Jon was concerned about was who called the shots? A solid inquiry, no doubt.

"A Keeper will be coming in to monitor and keep track of the Showdown," said Addison.

"A Keeper?" asked Owen. "What the fuck is a Keeper?"

Owen's abrasive tone changed the atmosphere. Keeper, to Jon, sounded like a strange title, almost fantastical and out of place.

"What's a Keeper?"

"Exactly what you think," Addison said to Jon. "Someone who keeps. Keeper is the ref. He's an impartial observer called by the Commission who acts as a third party. Since Rex got us to sign in our own codex, he'll submit the proposal regarding the Showdown to the Commission and they'll send the Keeper down here. He'll be the one monitoring the entire game."

"And what do they look like?"

"Usually, a man in a suit, but I don't know," said Addison. "No one will know until the day, which is what we need to start focusing on."

Jon's plan after this briefing was to return home.

There, he would do as much research as possible. He wanted to know more about this Showdown. He wanted to know the rules as well as the strategies. He thought about all of this, and then he thought of this new person known as the Keeper.

To Jon, they didn't even sound real.

All of it sounded made-up and possibly a slang term for something that was an actual position. Jon wouldn't know, as Addison said, until the day of.

"So...what happens now?" asked Jon. "What do we do?"

"Exactly what you think we're going to do," replied Addison. *"We get ready."*

CHAPTER 17
EMERGENCIES

THE DOORMEN HIT THE GROUND RUNNING AND commenced their training right away.

This started on the first floor among a sea of active guests on a night like any other. Together, the Doormen worked on various forms of egress and evasion. They collaborated heavily on communication and exchange. They watched the stage, the VIP, and all the other places mentioned by Addison during the briefing. These places would be the primary locations for luring the Fallen Sons.

While hard at work, Jon found himself accelerating his process. He would talk fast and work even faster. By doing this, Jon managed to keep most of the club's knuckleheads under control. He and Owen worked the floor while Danix and Li took positions as well. There wasn't a lot of time to test their skills, but they were walking on a tightrope. The rules of the Showdown proved difficult, and the challenges they offered were clear. What Jon wanted now, he wasn't sure he would receive.

Jon believed the only way to win was through cooperation.

However, while Addison and Danix did offer great advice, if Jon wanted to win, he would need to consult as many people as possible. And for Jon, this wasn't just the Doormen, it was other experts outside the club industry too. Now, it had been some time since Jon's mom had met the charming professional bodyguard known as Michael Irons. Jon had intermittent run-ins with Michael. Each time he did, he found himself liking him more and more.

He was interesting and unique. In fact, he reminded Jon a lot of Addison.

To begin, both men were potent and knowledgeable of certain topics. They were topics that captured Jon's interest. No doubt, Jon enjoyed what he saw in Michael. And yet, he hadn't seen much of him or his mother these last few weeks. Jon worked every night in preparation for the Showdown.

Still, Jon asked himself, did Michael know some tricks that the bodyguard profession knew but the bouncers did not? Maybe Michael knew a few things that might help Jon and the Doormen during the Showdown? Yet, if Jon was going to ask Michael questions, then he would also have to tell him about what the Showdown was and why he was consulting an outside party.

So far as Jon was aware, the Showdown was a secret within the nightclub industry.

Showdowns were legendary and were known only by a few.

They also weren't, in the strictest sense of the word, legal. Jon didn't know whether or not he should even tell Michael about it at all. The only way he could was if he answered the primary question surrounding their relationship.

The question was the one Jon had asked himself time and time again.

Did he trust him?

—————

When Jon woke after working a long shift, he found his mother sitting in the backyard. It was a small space with not much other than a garden, a bird feeder, a table and four chairs. Sometimes, Jon would sleep well into the afternoon and other times he'd wake up at a more traditional time.

"Mom?"

"Good morning, sleepy," Jon's mom's was always pleasant and caring. Ever since she began dating Michael, she was in a better mood too.

Jon was happy to see his mom so content, but loathed thinking about the reasons why she might be acting so sprightly. In fact, such was a running joke at The Conquistador. Often, the bouncers would make a few cracks about why Jon's mom was in such a good mood. It was because she was seeing more "action" than Jon was getting. These jokes wouldn't always land for the Marine. Some might hate the idea of hearing their mothers mentioned in such a lewd context. However, for Jon, guys were guys and the other Doormen were like brothers to Jon, and their humor was indicative of their relationship. And yet, all of them did have a point. Granted, Jon was happy for his mother being loved and maybe making a little of it when he wasn't around, but really loved how she was enjoying life and how she was being more energetic. For the longest time, she was alone, with no one to keep her company or help her when Jon wasn't around.

Jon appreciated what Michael was doing for his mom, even without knowing him too well. He was there for Jon's mother, and that was good enough...for now.

"Hey," said Jon. He stumbled onto the porch on what was a bright day. He scuttled along without shoes and without a shirt. He was still fatigued from the long rest he just had. Jon was barely able to see his mother due to the glorious sun.

"Long night?"

Hearing his mom's question, Jon couldn't help but sigh and laugh. "You have no idea."

"I'm sure," said Jon's mom. "Coffee?" She held up her mug as an offering, and Jon saw the cup and shooed it away.

"No, actually, I was wondering if I could talk to Michael?" Jon asked.

"Michael?" said Jon's mother, Betsy. "Like *my* Michael."

If not for the fact that Jon was starting to like Michael, he hated how his mom referred to him as *hers*.

"Yes," Jon said reluctantly. "*Your* Michael."

"What about him?" Betsy asked Jon.

"I need to speak to him about something is all. It's about work."

Jon's mom's face gleamed with enthusiasm. "Sure," she sparkled, and she placed her coffee down on the table. "But may I ask what about work exactly?"

"Nothing," said Jon. "Just...just need his advice about some small things, that's all."

"Advice as in...*job advice?*"

Jon hoped his mom wouldn't say this. What she wanted most was for Jon to find steady employment. This was a subject first introduced by Jon's mother but it was also one supported by Michael. He wanted Jon to come work for his company instead of working as a bouncer at The Conquistador. It was more stable and definitely paid more money. Nevertheless, Jon didn't know much about Michael's business at all.

Yes, Jon knew he was a bodyguard and that his firm was hired to protect Restitute at that event and they were there that one night when everything went up in smoke. They were reputable, efficient. Other than that, Jon didn't really know too much else about Michael but he did have his cell.

"Sure," Jon agreed with his mom. "Job advice."

This wasn't exactly what Jon was inquiring about. It was just easier for his mother to accept if that's what he said. If she could think he was interested in working for Michael, and this made her happy, then Jon was calling about that and only about that.

"Well, you have his number, don't ya'?"

Jon remembered getting Michael's contact info at the club. He did have it despite the fact that he never used it.

Jon nodded at his mom. "Yeah, I just wanted to let you know I'll be talking to him, that's all. You know, I wanted you to know for sure."

"Great," said Jon's mom, "but you don't need my permission to talk to anyone. You know that, right?"

Jon played like he didn't need his mom's approval but still felt good about telling her. However, not needing someone's permission to do something is confusing, especially when it's given by one's parents. Michael was Jon's mom's boyfriend. This was how it was, but it didn't matter here, not in this circumstance. If Michael Irons—head of his own bodyguard agency— could prove useful, then useful he would be.

Jon *would* use him.

"Okay," said Jon. "Thanks."

"And Jon," said Betsy. Jon began to make his way back inside his house.

"Yeah?"

Jon's mom was now grinning ear-to-ear. She puckered her lips and blew her son a soft, corny kiss. "I really like that you're trying to get closer to Michael. Trust me. He's a good guy."

"Yeah, Mom," Jon said. "Sure. Whatever you say."

Jon was never the kind of child to tell his mother exactly what she wanted to hear. He hated lying to her. He didn't like it because he was not very good at it. In fact, no one was. Always, she caught Jon whenever he was lying to her. And so, none of them did lie. Jon walked away from his mother and sent a text to Michael. Jon told Michael he wanted to meet. He said he wanted to ask Michael a few questions.

When?

As soon as possible.

Jon watched the blinking ellipsis. He was surprised at how quickly Michael answered him. He could only assume because of how close he was getting to Jon's mom. Again, Jon wasn't sure what to make of the gesture.

Were he and Michael friends now?
Michael told Jon to meet him at his office.

Headquarters?

Jon sent Michael this text.
Michael sent Jon right back.

Yeah. No good?

Jon stood in his kitchen where he held his phone with two hands. He tapped the screen and continued the conversation.

No. That'll work.

Great. See you then.

———

Their phone conversation was short and sweet. It was exactly as Jon intended it to be. Easy and straight, Jon was in his mom's car, on his way to the address specified by Michael when the two talked about his job way back. The headquarters to Michael's agency was in Manhattan. He told Jon he worked in a glass building with glass windows, which was sleek and very cool to look at. Jon parked on the street, but when he marched toward this elite office, he found Michael waiting for him in the grand lobby.

He smiled at Jon and waved.

"Hey," Michael said. "Thanks for making it."

"Yeah," answered Jon. "Appreciate you meeting

me." Jon played the interaction off as casual, like Michael was only just a contact lending a helping hand. They were not friends, well, not exactly. However, Michael was sure to treat Jon like he was a friend. He placed his hand on the Marine's shoulder and escorted him to a bench next to the store.

"Sure thing, sure thing," added Michael. "Anyway, have a seat. Office is pretty messy, and I have to hightail it out of here soon. I know you wanted this to be short, so...I'm sure you won't mind."

"I don't," said Jon. He sat on a bench outside Michael's place of work. He was appreciative about how Michael was willing to help. Still, Jon would have preferred to stay inside.

"So...what can I do for you?" Michael asked Jon.

"I needed your advice about something," Jon replied.

"Figured as much," Michael Irons smiled while sitting cross-legged on a metal bench next to Jon. In a suit and no tie, Michael's shirt was unbuttoned near his neck. He looked the part of a man who was not only smooth but also professional.

He was wearing some nice cologne too.

"Need to know if there's anything you do to isolate these threats quickly," Jon said, "without anyone knowing about it."

"Isolate?" asked Michael. "I'm not sure what you mean?"

"Are there," said Jon, "like any...tools you might use, you know, day-to-day that are quick to neutralize and take someone down without noticing?"

"Take someone down as in..." said Michael.

"Neutralize," said Jon. "In a way that's non-lethal and legal, obviously."

"I see. Why? Why are you looking for such things? What's this really about, Jon? You know you can tell me...*right*?"

Jon could feel Michael ogling him. He was a kind man. And, from what Jon could gather so far, he was a decent one too. He was adamant about helping Jon, no doubt. He was also paternal, like the father Jon missed but wanted so badly to see again. He wanted to help, but clearly not at the cost of hurting Jon's job or reputation.

"It's just...work-related, you know."

"Work-related?" asked Michael, now skeptical about Jon's claims.

Jon wasn't too surprised to detect doubt in Michael's voice. What Jon was saying wasn't exactly easy to process. Then again, what he was asking Michael about was suspicious. He couldn't tell his mom's boyfriend, a senior bodyguard, the entire story.

For now, half the story would suffice.

"Work-related, huh?" asked Michael.

Jon didn't provide any more detail other than to give just a little more context.

"In case of emergencies," added Jon.

"Right," said Michael. "Guess things are getting pretty rough down there, huh? Ever since what happened to Restitute and all, I imagine Larry has all of you guys on high alert."

"Yes," said Jon. "You could say that."

"Look," said Michael, "if you're on the market for non-lethal tactics to bring down an attacker, there are a number of tools you might be able to use secretively, if you choose to."

"I know," said Jon. He was aware of these kinds of tools.

"But gauging your tone and choice of words," Michael continued, "I think you're looking for something a little extra special, am I right?"

"Yes," Jon replied. "Just so long as it's *legal*."

"And tasers and batons are all out of the question?" questioned Michael.

"Completely," said Jon. "Too much noise and the Doormen don't really care about that kind of stuff. We use our words, remember? It's our best weapon."

"Right," said Michael. "No mace either?"

"Mace?" Jon replied. He almost tsked because he thought the suggestion was ridiculous. "That's for women who get mugged in alleys. I'm looking for something that's more under the radar, something that few people know about except for people who are at the top of this game, people like you."

What Jon delivered was a solid compliment. It was something he didn't plan on saying but felt the moment called for it. No doubt, Michael was good at his job. He was hired to safeguard a well-known rap star. And, according to Jon's mother, his company served a lot of other important men and women. Jon going to him for advice made sense. Jon might have some mixed feelings about Michael as a man, but as a bodyguard and as a professional, he was very good.

"People like me, yeah?"

"Yes," confirmed Jon. "People like you."

"Okay," said Michael, taking in the compliment. "I think I might have something that can help you."

Jon watched as Michael Irons reached into his jacket pocket. When he pulled his hand out, it was wrapped up in a fist. Jon squinted and leaned in to get a closer look. He had no idea what Michael was holding, though it was something small enough to keep hidden inside his hand.

"You a James Bond fan?" Michael asked Jon.

Jon shook his head. He'd seen a few Bond films but wouldn't call himself a fan.

"Well," said Michael, "Pierce Brosnan's my favorite, and *Goldeneye* kicks ass."

"Right," said Jon. He had no idea what Michael Irons was talking about.

"Well, here's something I use in case of emergencies."

Michael splayed his fingers.

On his palm was a banded device that resembled a wristwatch. Its face was square and its strap was leather. The design of this tool was not unique, not in Jon's opinion. Sticking out of the *watch's* face was a thin strip of metal. To Jon, it looked like a needle. Despite recognizing some of what he was seeing, in the end, Jon truly had no idea what Michael was giving him. What Michael Irons had was something Jon had never seen before.

"What is it?" Jon asked.

"Exactly what it looks like," said Michael. Jon didn't like this response. He had no idea what it looked like. "It's a *tranq*."

"A what?"

"You know," said Michael. He assumed Jon was as familiar with said tool as he was. Jon wasn't. "*A tranquilizer*."

"Are you kidding me?" Jon snorted. Suddenly, the James Bond reference made sense.

"You said you wanted something that was fast-acting and legal," replied Michael, "and, well, this is what we use in case of emergencies."

"So...this thing shoots, like what," said Jon, "darts, I'm assuming?"

"Yep, that's exactly what it does," added Michael. "In fact, it fires a low-impact knockout dart. We use it if someone manages to get past us too fast to grab onto or someone gets too close to the asset we're protecting. We hit them with this, they get woozy and lose consciousness before passing out. No one sees it coming, and no one knows how to react once it makes contact. It's easy to hide and even easier to use. Here," said Michael, and he offered the dart to Jon. "Try it on for size."

Jon's head shook because he was in disbelief. He was both enchanted and disturbed at the same time. He wrapped the band around his wrist and made sure it was nice and tight. It felt the same as a wristwatch, only sleeker and definitely mistakable for that very same object.

Jon felt nervous having this on his person. However, Jon believed Michael when he said it worked fast and was exactly what Jon was searching for. He liked its design but felt like he was holding more than just a simple tool for knocking someone out.

"How does it work?" asked Jon. Michael leaned in to inspect this gun.

"Well, first...make sure it's turned," said Michael. "Make sure it's turned and make sure it's set and then you just point and shoot. It's that simple."

"Where's the trigger?"

"There." Michael Irons pointed at a red button at the side. It was quite noticeable, and when Jon saw it, he grazed it with his thumb. He looked at the trigger and felt his heart pick up.

He couldn't shake the feeling that what he had in his possession was something more.

"And you said it's easy, right?"

"Very easy, yes," said Michael.

"Okay, and as far as it being, you know, like..."

"What?" Michael interrupted.

"Like...*legal?*" Jon inquired.

"Oh, right," Mild laughter trailed out of Michael Irons's gleeful face. He looked at Jon again and placed his hand on his shoulder. "Sure. Yeah, all good. It's only a knockout device. Legal, the same as how a mace and a taser are both legal."

"Yeah, but this doesn't feel at all like that," said Jon. He had never seen or heard of this device. The fact that it was not known only made Jon suspect its usage as well as its abilities.

But was it really worth the risk?

"It's fine. Trust me. Just for emergencies," said Michael. "I mean, you trust me, don't you, Jon?"

A waft of air expelled from Jon's face, almost like he was scoffing. He supposed he did trust Michael now, sure. He supposed this because his mother trusted Michael. And Jon did want Michael to be right, but then he was helping him. Michael had taken time to assist Jon, and he didn't have to do this. And so, acting distrustful toward Michael would show how Jon was actually ungrateful and he wasn't.

It would also imply Jon didn't like Michael. Truthfully, Jon wanted to like Michael. More than this, Jon wanted to believe Michael was a good person deserving of his mom's affection and love. And, while this weapon he had lent to him was new and different, maybe it would prove to be as useful as described. Maybe it would prove to be exactly what Jon wanted and needed to send Rex and his boys packing and to beat their sorry asses.

"Yeah," Jon said. He removed the gun from his wrist. "I trust you."

"Good," said Michael. "And look, you don't have to use it if you don't want to. I said only if the situation calls for it, in case of emergencies."

"Right," said Jon. He remembered saying this too. "I understand."

"So, like The Conquistador is on high alert, huh?" said Michael. "Is that why you're packing something like this?"

Jon nodded but continued to keep the idea of the Showdown a secret.

"You could say that,."

"Right," Michael said to Jon. "Well...is there anything else I can help you with, or is that all?"

"No," Jon said right away. "That's it."

"Oh, okay. Sounds good then." Jon stood from the bench and glanced at Michael.

Michael's mouth curved like he was frowning. He looked like he was hurt by Jon's abrupt response. If Jon just came to grab something and that was it, then Jon was technically only using Michael. He didn't really want to see him, and he really didn't want to talk to Michael either. No, Jon just wanted to take something and then move on. Jon didn't think Michael would be so sensitive. Then again, he *had to* be. If he was dating

Jon's mom, then he wasn't just a gruff and skilled body-guard. He had to be more. While sitting with a wounded expression, Jon scanned Michael Irons and observed the man in his hurt state.

"Hey," Jon said. "I just wanted to say, umm, thanks. You know, thanks for helping me out. I...I really appreciate it."

Jon was never good at thanking people. He struggled with the concept of gratitude as a whole. He hated giving it, and he hated receiving it. When he extended such a courtesy to Michael, however, his ears went back and his eyes opened wide. His face lit up and Jon could see he was content by the offering.

He enjoyed being thanked.

"Oh," said Michael. "Yeah, no problem. It's...it's my *pleasure.*"

"No, honestly," admitted Jon. "I really appreciate it, and you know, I'm sorry if I've been maybe a little rude and unappreciative, you know, being with my mother and everything."

"Don't say another word," said Michael. He lifted his hand and waved it at Jon. "I get it. You know, I'm the new guy dating your mom, and well, that'd be hard for anyone to accept, I think. No need to explain."

"Yeah, but," said Jon, "ever since she's met you, she's been happier and smiling more than she ever has, and it's not because of me she's feeling that way. It's because of you," Jon admitted. "You're the one who's making her happy, and well, that's pretty amazing. Actually, it's pretty fucking awesome."

Michael smiled and Jon did the same. Now being sincere toward Michael, Jon was truly appreciative for everything he had done. What Jon said, he meant. His mom was happier and it was all because of him, because of Michael Irons.

"Well," said Michael, after sharing a moment of mutual respect. "Thanks for saying that, Jon, but I don't need to tell you what a special woman your mom really is."

"No," said Jon, still grinning as he looked at Michael. "You don't."

Michael nodded and Jon stepped back. Now that Michael had helped Jon with what he needed, the Marine felt it was time he headed back to the club. The Showdown was going to happen and Jon needed to be ready. While proceeding to his car, Jon stopped. With the dart gun in hand, Jon was struck with the same thought that had plagued him earlier.

"Legal, yes?" Jon said to Michael just before he left. "You're sure?"

Michael smiled and crossed his left leg over to his right.

"Yes," he said. "One hundred percent."

And this was all Jon needed to hear and he was now well on his way. He tried to imagine the night ahead, but Jon struggled to get a clear picture. He didn't know what to imagine because what he was trying to imagine was quite scary.

Actually, it was terrifying.

CHAPTER 18
COIN TOSS

JON DID EXACTLY AS HE SAID HE WAS GOING TO DO. He drove from Michael Irons's office back to The Conquistador. However, Jon was hungry, starved actually. He had some power bars stashed in his pocket and he chugged a fat carton of chocolate milk before he left. Jon gobbled all of it down in just under an hour. When Jon arrived at the club, he parked in the lot and walked in through the front door.

Although he would normally use the back, tonight, he decided to go another way.

But as soon as Jon entered The Conquistador, he was hit instantly with unwavering feelings of tension. All the Doormen were present, as well as all the servers, the bottle girls, all the bartenders, and anyone else who was required. The first person Jon saw was Danix. He saw him and then he saw Jamal too. Jon had not spoken to Jamal since the briefing.

With both standing by the door, Jamal was one of Jon's closest friends. He hadn't spent much time with the Marine these last few weeks. They just didn't see each other as much as they normally did. Jon regretted not speaking to Jamal. He missed him a lot.

When Jon crossed paths with the biggest Doorman on the scene, he offered his hand.

"Nice to see you, Jamal," Jon touched Jamal on the shoulder. "Miss ya."

"Yeah, brother," Jamal replied. "So, you all set for tonight?"

Jon didn't know what to say, so he didn't say anything. He gave Jamal a confident smirk that suggested he was ready. However, this smile was forced and far from sincere. Jon didn't know what he didn't know. And so, after he rolled in, he looked at Danix, whose firm expression heightened the tension.

Everywhere Jon looked, all the faces seemed identical. Everyone looked grim and stoic. Like soldiers on the eve of battle, all were now heading into the eye of the storm. Jon examined the first floor. In addition to Danix, he also spotted Li positioned by one of the pillars. Meditating with his hands folded, Jon watched as Li performed open-handed movements that Jon was familiar with. Li's background was in kung fu. Whatever he was doing now looked like its basic movements. Now practicing his technique before the Showdown, Jon thought it was smart. Jon felt he should do the same if he could.

Jon moved along and came across Addison and Larry, both of whom were on the second floor. Both were standing close and looked to be having an intimate conversation.

Jon thought about what they might be talking about.

He hoped it was about the legalities surrounding this Showdown, what was allowed and what wasn't. Jon looked at the secret dart gun secured around his wrist. To the average onlooker, it was only a wristwatch and nothing more than that. In the dark, no one would even be able to see it. Jon considered telling Addison what he had, but he looked too busy to talk. With enough on his mind already, now was not the time to bombard Addison with more things to worry about. Jon also remembered what Michael said. *"Completely legal."*

Jon didn't doubt Michael.

He was a professional. He was also Jon's friend. Jon looked away from Addison and Larry and turned his attention toward the bar. Before any shift, Jon would stop by and speak with Kya. Considering what the two of them had been through, it was becoming a more common occurrence.

As of now, she was just as busy as everyone else. She loaded bottles and also had a mic looped around her ear. She was going to be overseeing all the wait staff, who had all agreed to provide cover during the Showdown. Tonight was to be her busiest night yet, and Jon didn't want to do anything to disrupt her focus. He'd be a selfish son of a bitch to do something like that. Although Jon refused to do this, he couldn't move on without saying a single word.

The Showdown would be a challenge for everyone involved. It would also be one hell of a risk. Kya meant more to Jon than she realized, so he couldn't embark upon the Showdown without her knowing he was going to look out for her.

Kya needed to know Jon would be there for her no matter what happened.

When Jon stepped to the bar, he leaned over the counter. Kya was so busy she didn't notice Jon standing there. Jon was glad she didn't. What he wanted to say wouldn't take very long.

"Hey." Jon grazed Kya's arm and her hair whipped as she turned.

"Jon, hey." While Kya seemed pleasant, Jon didn't quite know exactly how Kya was feeling. So far as Jon could tell, she seemed happy. Jon supposed that was enough. This was all he needed.

"Look, I know you're busy," Jon said, "and I know things are really hectic right now."

Divine and the other bartenders sprinted around Kya like she wasn't even there. Jon gauged how preoccupied they all were, but then again, Jon reminded himself how he wouldn't be long.

"But I just want you to know that I'll..."

"That you'll what...Jon?" asked Kya, a bottle in her hand.

Jon was suddenly at a loss for words.

He was struck by a new thought that in turn struck him silent. Now thinking about Kya, the kind of position she had put herself in, Jon gulped. If Rex and the other Sons realized what she was doing, then they would do more than just take her out of the game.

No, they would treat her the same as any other player, and this might hurt her badly.

While Kya did manage to hold her own back at the rave, still, there was uncertainty. There was anxiety, and Jon was afraid. Jon had faced war, bombs, explosions, and so much violence, and yet, the same fear clung to him like a damp cloth.

No matter what Jon faced or what he had conquered, fear would always be present. So long as there was someone he cared about, always, Jon would fear losing them.

Always.

"I just wanted you to..." Jon's struggle persisted. Kya could see Jon fighting to find the words. As she saw this, she reached out and touched his lips with her finger.

"Hey," she said. "It's going to be all right. I promise."

Jon swallowed back all the anxiety that had surfaced in his throat. He bucked up as best he could and put on a brave face. After Kya assured Jon of this, he accepted that his time with her was now over. It was time for Jon to return to his business.

"Okay," Jon said. "It's just, if you need anything, I mean, I won't be far, yeah? You know that, right? You know I'm...I'm always close by?"

Kya's eyes twinkled. Jon thought she was touched by his assurances. He meant what he said, and Kya's pleasant demeanor indicated she heard and believed his every word. Jon didn't want to ruin the moment, and seconds later, he didn't have to. Another hand touched Jon's shoulder. This pulled his attention away from Kya and back to the now unfolding situation.

"Hey," said Owen. He guided Jon away from the bar. Jon didn't wish to look at Owen. No, he was still with Kya. Always so confident, Jon was enlivened by Kya's spirit. He also envied how certain she always seemed to be when working.

"Yeah," Jon said to Owen.

"Addison wants to meet with us. A Keeper is here."

"What?" said Jon.

"A *Keeper*. Just come on."

"Right." Jon scurried with Owen and they both paced from one side of the club to the other.

Now headed to a section of booths located just left of the dance floor, these booths weren't the VIPs set for bottle service, they were the tier two booths. They were the kind people purchased when they were rich but not super-rich.

"You got the proper apparel? We all have to be wearing our uniforms because, you know, we're a single team."

"Oh yeah?" said Jon. "Right. I got that."

Until now, he really didn't know what Owen was referring to. The shirt he wore was the one he sometimes did. Thankfully, it was exactly the one required. Jon thanked Lady Luck for such a coincidence.

———

In perfect order, all the Doormen were aligned next to each other like schoolboys ready to be chosen.

Rex MacIntosh, Brutus Watson, and Cole Hausen were exactly as Jon remembered them. They were there, *along with two more men*, and all were wearing matching shirts that were a shade of auburn-red while the Doormen's were indigo. The selections of such threads made the teams look totally opposite—precisely what was intended.

Jon steadied toward Addison and insisted on standing in the middle. There was another individual poised there too. However, Jon did not recognize him.

"Do you have your flags selected?" This man spoke.

This man was an older gentleman dressed in a

tuxedo jacket with golden buttons. Gray strands extended from the back of his neck and led all the way to the center of his back. This man was tall and lanky. He was what Jon would call wiry—strong yet thin at the same time. His wardrobe was old-fashioned and conveyed the image of a door person who guarded the expensive apartments in Manhattan. Maybe that's who he was too. He glanced at the Marine with a crooked eye.

Jon shuddered because he was intimidated.

"Yes," said Addison. "We do."

"Very well," said this older man. He reached out, and Jon watched as Addison provided him with the item chosen to serve as the Doormen's *flag*. While all of them had discussed what it would be, Jon gazed at the plaque now being offered.

All the other Doormen watched as it was submitted.

"Acceptable?" asked Addison.

The old man—*the Keeper*—inspected the plaque while wearing a pair of white gloves. The Keeper's position was a classification within the club that did exactly what the title suggested. He *kept* and he *maintained*. He watched, viewed, and he observed. He also made certain the rules of the Showdown were respected, and right now, his duties were to do all of this before the game officially began.

"This will suffice," replied the Keeper. He twirled the plaque, which was thirty inches in length and around twenty inches in diameter. It was by no means a small item, but Jon felt it was a suitable size fitted for a flag.

Evidently, the Keeper felt this way too.

"And your flag, sirs?" The Keeper was cordial. Jon wanted to know more about his history.

He appeared to be the same age as Larry was, and the two were also almost the same height. How one became a Keeper in the club industry must be a complex and arduous process, Jon thought.

Nevertheless, it was a process that brought this man here, to The Conquistador.

When he asked about the Fallen Sons' flag, Rex stepped in. Unlike the Doormen's, the Sons' flag was covered. Rex slipped off a leather cover and removed what was underneath. There was an object that possessed the same dimensions as the Doormen's flag. At least, it looked this way initially. The Sons' flag was actually a board about one inch thick. It had charcoal strips of what looked like ribbons pinned to the board itself. Jon assumed this was a collection of some kind, and it was. However, what it collected was something so vile it forced Jon to grimace because he could barely stand to look at it. For Jon, it was too gross, too shocking, and far too disturbing to see without having bad images blasting through one's mind.

"What?" asked Rex, seeing everyone's offended expressions.

Every single Doormen, including Addison, became appalled by the sight.

"You didn't think we'd let you just throw them away, did you?"

What they were, Jon knew, were the former crests once worn by the Fallen Sons. They were the badges given to anyone selected to be a guardian at The Conquistador. It was something Jon owned, but also an item he brought only on the rarest occasions.

Now, in the case of Rex, Brutus, and Cole, their charred and scorched badges were pinned to this one plaque. Together, they represented the grotesque symbols of their former lives, of who they *used* to be.

Seen as displays of both honor and shame, how these items were taken after they were burned off was disturbing and unusual. Jon refused to think about any of this now. He didn't approve of what Addison did to Rex or the others. Then again, Jon didn't exactly know why the Fallen Sons were forced into exile. Could've been for something terrible, maybe for something horrifying. Jon glared as the Keeper accepted the plaque from Rex.

"Flag accepted," said the Keeper. "Now, before each team member places their flag in a specific area of the club, the rules of the Showdown need to be explained."

"All ears," said Rex.

"First rule of the Showdown," said the Keeper, "is as follows: one, all teams must stay here, in this location. Showdown is to happen within club grounds, and you must not venture outside, is that understood?"

Jon observed how everyone on the teams nodded in agreement.

"Rule number two," continued the Keeper, "is once a member of the team is put into a submission hold, knocked down, or knocked unconscious, they are then, in effect, out of the game. If they are hit by the laser pointer represented here." The Keeper opened his hand and showed the laser pointer he had referenced. Jon found the using of this device amusing. He hadn't seen a laser pointer since high school. "Once the red dot touches you, you will then be asked to leave the game.

Therefore, you must retreat out of bounds because you are no longer permitted to be inside. Now, is all of this understood so far?"

Again, no one said anything. Jon and his fellow Doormen did understand.

"Next rule is," said the Keeper, "once the other team's flag is recovered, the Showdown is over, and the victor will be whoever is holding the other team's flag. After that, all bouncers on either team will stop what they're doing and return to the center to observe the results. They will surrender and the game will come to an end. If anyone disobeys any of these rules, for whatever reason, then the Showdown is done, and both teams will be asked to stand down immediately. Now those are the rules for a Bouncer Showdown, precisely what we're participating in tonight. Does anyone have any other questions to ask before we begin?"

Jon had no words. He was eager, yes. He was so eager his hands twitched against his thighs and he wanted nothing more than to commence the Showdown as quickly as possible. He eyed Rex, Cole, and Brutus, all of whom looked determined as they stood behind the Keeper. Not one of the Doormen spoke up after the rules were explained.

Jon assumed this was how this interaction would end. It didn't.

"Bring your A-game there, Addy boy," Rex teased. "It's gonna be a rough one."

The name given to Addison was a pejorative one at best. Addison was never spoken to in such a callous way. Receiving this classification, Jon watched as Addison gawked at Rex with a slacked-jawed gape.

"You have no idea."

Both Addison and Rex were now locked in a death stare. Jon could feel his adrenaline starting to surge. He felt like he was in an armored truck approaching a caravan of enemy insurgents.

"Both teams are permitted to hide their flags accordingly. We'll start with The Conquistador Doormen first," said the Keeper. "Mr. Sons, please gather by the bar and turn your heads to give your opponents the privacy they need."

The Fallen Sons turned like the Keeper had told them to do.

"Choose your spots carefully, yeah, Addison?" teased Rex. "You don't wanna give away your position too much, do you? Don't go somewhere to bark up old history, if you know what I mean?"

A battle-hardened, grizzled look became Jon's visage. For once, Jon understood the subtleties in the insults provided to himself as well as to the other Doormen. The location Rex was referencing was the secret section of the nightclub. It was in the place where few were permitted to go. It was the same place where the so-called *special things* were stored.

Jon was not familiar with these things. He loathed thinking of them, though, especially here and now, when he needed to keep his head in the game and stay focused. After Rex MacIntosh provided Addison Krowe with the sly remark, the shunned leader of the fallen caste cackled before fading into the background.

"Doesn't matter whether you know where it is," said Addison, "or you don't. You'll never get to it anyway."

"We'll see," said Rex.

Addison handed Danix the plaque, which the most

lethal bouncer at The Conquistador diligently accepted.

"Go," said Addison. "You know where."

"Aye," said Danix, like the obedient soldier that he was. He scuttled while the Sons disappeared into the dance floor.

Jon didn't bother to look to where the plaque—the Doorman's flag—would be taken to.

He didn't because he already knew.

On the second floor, the balcony was the ideal location due to its many obstacles.

However, right now, Jon wanted a piece of Rex. The two hadn't sparred, not really. In fact, the only time Rex and Jon engaged in any kind of fight was back when the two first met. At The Conquistador at that time, Jon assumed he was dealing with a band of knuckleheads. As it turned out, Jon was facing down The Conquistador's worst enemies. Tonight, Rex was pushing everyone. He was taunting and acting like a fool. Rex was a decent fighter, but he was more effective at manipulation and psychological warfare.

Addison, who had the toughest mind Jon had ever come across, was the ideal opponent for this. He didn't let Rex's comments get under his skin. Still, Jon could feel the hate burning inside. He wanted to play in the Showdown right here, right now.

When Danix departed, he shuffled up to the second level and tied the plaque to the railing. To The Conquistador patrons, the Doormen's flag was nothing more than a piece of weird decoration. It was just a giant crest-shaped piece of varnished wood, which was ironic considering the Sons' choice for flag. Once everything was locked in, Danix moved to the first level and rejoined the team. Now that the Doormen were done with their flag, all of them looked away so the Sons could hide theirs too.

The one who had the flag was Cole. With the *crest display* pressed to his chest, he turned to the stage. Before hiding it, Jon saw Rex grabbing Cole's arm. He pulled him in and whispered something in his ear. Unfortunately, Jon was too far away to hear. Also, their lips were covered so Jon couldn't read them.

The Keeper told everyone to face away. Jon did as instructed. The Sons hid their flag and the Keeper waved at the rest of the Doormen.

"All right," the Keeper said, "now you all know the rules, so now that your flags are all in position, your boundaries are set, and you're all set. So, it's time for the game to begin. A Showdown can last up to three hours, but cannot officially begin until the club's doors have opened. And, since this is your club, Mr. Krowe, you will give the order, sir."

"I understand," said Addison. "And it's not my club."

Addison was no doubt an assertive man. Right now, it was like he wanted his point driven hard into the Keeper's mind. This club did not belong to Addison. In fact, it never did.

"Of course," said the Keeper. "But you are your team's captain, the cooler, and this is your home field, so...ready when you are."

After hearing this, Addison nodded. "Send word out to Jamal," he said. "Everyone is to take their positions and know their spots."

"Right," said Li.

"Now open the doors. We got ourselves a Show-down to win."

CHAPTER 19
A WORLD ON FIRE

THE CONQUISTADOR BECAME PACKED IN A MANNER of minutes but Addison's orders were clear.

Jon was asked to cover the stage with Li as backup. Owen had the dance floor, and Danix was up top. The second bouncing unit, who was not in the Showdown, was told to do their own thing and stay out of the game.

Addison was near the bar while Kya was asked to circulate. Watching all the booths, Kya wasn't officially on the team. She was just another person on the lookout for trouble. The Fallen Sons were here and were spread out among the various sections. Rex stood with Cole. Now dispersed around the club, the remaining bouncers knew of the Showdown, and so did every other member of the staff. However, they were not to participate. Larry was in his office, watching from above.

If the Doormen lost the Showdown, then there was no foretelling of the other consequences. Jon shed himself of any feelings of loss and potential downfalls. He would not lose. The Doormen would beat the Sons here and now and end their rivalry once and for all. The plan was solid and the tactics were tight. Jon had a few tricks up his sleeve but he presumed Rex did too.

Jon began to move and, the entire time, kept his eyes on Kya. She was working with the bottle girls, giving them drinks to serve while also glancing at Jon. Every second was vital. Every movement was critical. Jon stayed tight on guard. He kept a close watch on all the Fallen Sons. They were dressed in their colorful attire, and the Sons appeared as another bouncer unit currently working at The Conquistador.

However, none had crossed any boundaries, not as of yet.

The line in The Conquistador between the two teams was drawn now. Everyone knew where it was, but none had yet to cross. Like wolves trotting toward a fallen prey, Jon flirted with the notion of crossing. But, recalling his days playing Capture the Flag, making the first move was never a good start. According to Addison, as soon as the flag was spotted, any Doorman could go and take it. Jon was the first to spot the flag. The Fallen Sons had chosen the section near the DJ booth, not far from the stage where a train of girls gyrated to the thumping music.

There, however, was an issue with this location.

Unlike the Doormen, who selected a place where their flag would *stand out*, The Fallen Sons' location for their flag was among a cache of other items. It was near portraits, pictures, and other menial decor. And, with their crests being here, it would make taking it all more challenging.

Jon knew this, and yet he was not afraid of it.

No, Jon could see everything all well, and he was

prepared to make his first move. The game of the Showdown was to cross boundaries and capture the flag before the other team captured yours. The rules couldn't be more straightforward and so, all that was left to do now was to see who had the balls to get it done.

And Jon was ready.

He slipped in between two dancing groups and approached the boundary. Jon glimpsed at Addison before going in. While it was his choice to move, Addison was the team's unofficial captain. He commanded and he approved. Still, Jon wanted that flag, and he wanted to play.

When he entered the Sons' territory and approached the stage, the other Sons noticed. Though Jon was subtle, he didn't move too fast or cut too quickly.

He had his target and he had his method for going after it.

He wanted the other members of the Sons to come as well. By focusing on their flag, Jon was also keeping himself cool and calm. He was just another bouncer going about his business. The music amplified and the incessant beats rattled Jon's headspace, which made it harder to focus. The stage was only five feet away, and suddenly, Jon felt another body move in.

He knew from posture and feeling they weren't patrons. They weren't even close.

The first Fallen Son stomped after Jon, who stepped back. Jon could see the rival team member closing in. And, as another nameless guy standing in the wrong place at the wrong time, Jon couldn't let a single dancing fool know what was going on.

No patrons should know either. They certainly couldn't stop what they were doing.

Jon was smart. He was smart and he had a plan. He marched and focused on the Son now in his way. This man was bigger than Jon and so the two were not equal. Yet, Jon's plan for getting this one Son out of the game was simple. He was just going to put him to fucking sleep. With this other Son making a move, Jon liked it. It was standard and predictable. Too easy to be professional, the Son cocked back his fist and lunged in for a straight punch.

Jon handled it right away. He veered to the right and let the Sons' weak blow shoot near his ear. After this, Jon squeezed his opponent's forearm and smacked him in the elbow. This position gave Jon total control. Then, Jon kicked the man in the shins and pushed his shoulder to bring the rival Son down. It was a quick series of subtle yet dangerous moves that Jon had relied on time and time again. The clubgoers didn't stop, and so, they didn't see what had happened.

This all boded well for Jon so far.

Now, this Son was one tough son of a bitch.

Yet, the strike at Jon was only an attempt and nothing more. Jon could see it from a mile away, so he hit back and wrapped the Son into a headlock. Then, he thrust his head into the fucking stage. After this Son was taken out, a red laser touched the unconscious member and the Keeper appeared from the darkness.

Like a specter, the Keeper's black attire granted him excellent camouflage. If he didn't have such a distinguished face, Jon wouldn't have noticed him at all.

"Out," the Keeper said to the beaten Fallen Son. "Proceed out of bounds."

The Fallen Son walked slowly and rubbed his neck. Jon hopped to.

"No patrons informed so far as I can see," said the Keeper. "Continue."

The Keeper vanished as the first member of the Fallen Sons' team was removed from the game. Jon couldn't see Addison or any of the other Doormen now. Wherever they were, Jon hoped they were pleased. Technically, this did put the Doormen in the lead.

It was one down but four more to go.

When the Keeper parted from the dance floor, Jon looked at the stage. The Sons' flag was there, and, until now, it was free. However, things quickly changed. Two Fallen Sons had made their way to the stage and were now guarding the flag. Their position prevented Jon, or any other Doormen, from closing in.

It was too protected now.

Jon scoffed and backed away from the stage. He would return for the flag when he was able to. While he was off the dance floor, Jon could see that the lead his team once had was in jeopardy.

The Fallen Sons were also getting in on the action.

Owen stood by the stairs. His position was to guard the second floor, but his hands were full. Standing before him was the Fallen Son known as Brutus. A tough bastard if there ever was one, he wanted to get to the second level, but Owen refused to let him go.

A face-off quickly ensued.

From what Jon could see, it wasn't in Owen's favor. Brutus was too fast and too strong. He barreled through Owen like he was furniture. Now Owen was tough, but he was also new. He was the newest Doorman currently on the floor. This provided him with a list of disadvantages. What Owen lacked most was fortitude. When he was hit hard, he struggled to recover.

Jon could see that's what was happening from farther away.

Brutus landed a solid chop to Owen's neck, an unconventional method of attack. Still, it worked. Owen tried punching Brutus back, but Brutus answered with a swift elbow to the temple. It was quick and succinct. Brutus had the skills needed to take Owen out of the game.

Jon hustled to get to the fight, but it was too late. Like the Fallen Son, Jon's friend Owen joined the ranks. Owen was gone too.

"Shit." Owen shook his head to recover. He was visibly flustered but not completely inert. Jon knelt next to him and held his hand. "Fuck. Goddamn it, that was me getting tossed in a salad."

"You good?" asked Jon. From his point of view, the question was trivial. Obviously, Owen wasn't good. He had just been punched in the face and his nose was bleeding. No patrons had reacted so far, but Jon could see certain people shifting toward the scene.

Owen spit whatever was in his mouth and Jon offered his hand. "Come on," he said. "Let's go."

A laser pointer danced on Owen's chest and the Keeper was there in the corner. Like a ghost, he nodded at Owen, who read his signal loud and clear. Owen was out of the Showdown.

"Give 'em hell for me!" Owen shouted in Jon's ear.

Jon brought his mouth directly into Owen's ear and yelled back. "You know I will!"

Jon helped Owen to his feet while Brutus scampered after the stairs. On his way up to the second floor, it is where all the other Fallen Sons were...maybe? Honestly, Jon didn't know for sure. He did know where his friends were. One was at the top of the stairs.

Facing down the racing Brutus was Li fucking Huen.

Guarding the top, Jon watched Brutus encounter the most unpredictable bouncer in the game. Not even Jon knew what Li was going to do. When Brutus reached the center of the stairwell, Li stepped down.

Brutus's skills were on point. He was fast and delivered numerous attacks. Executing quick cuts, Brutus struck Li, who was a kung fu master. While Jon and Danix were students of different martial arts, Li focused solely on one. Jon once believed this placed him at a disadvantage. Li's philosophy was to learn as much as you can from one sensei instead of training under a collection of different ones.

Jon believed this to be true despite not subscribing to the rule himself.

At this moment, Jon watched as Li and Brutus chopped each other with swift and open hands. Soft and hard, they tried punching while the person in front did the same. Jon was positioned below the stairwell, where he watched Li and Brutus do battle. Li punched and knocked Brutus back. He then cracked his nose with a swift uppercut.

Lightning fast, Jon could see Brutus's head cocking back and could hear his coughs. Li stood his ground and elbowed Brutus in the ribs. Then he followed that with another punch. After this, a low kick followed. Li pushed Brutus down with two straight hands.

He hit with a cool pop to Brutus's chest, which was clean. Li's strike was like a knife cutting through butter.

Brutus felt the push. He shuffled back and almost lost his balance. Jon caught Brutus before he could fall. Then, Jon wrapped Brutus up but didn't choke him out. Instead, Jon just cradled Brutus. The man was so shaken he grunted while being pulled. Now holding Brutus, Jon was opening himself up to an attack. Still, Jon had no choice. The Keeper was with Jon and Brutus. He tapped the Fallen Son's shoulder and mulled him over with a blank expression.

"You are out," the Keeper said to Brutus. "Proceed out of bounds."

Brutus snorted with derision. Then he pushed Jon away. Jon clapped as Brutus marched off to the side, his head bowed to show his shame. The Doormen had now taken the lead, and two of the Sons were out of the Showdown while only Owen was out on their team.

Jon was pleased with this result. His head was torqued to look back.

Li stayed in position and Danix stood with him. The flag was protected by them now and yet, not one was going after the Sons' flag. Two of them were on the stage, casually walking back and focusing on the dance floor.

Still, Jon continued to scan the floor. Seeing nothing, Jon hurried up the stairs and reunited with Li.

"You good?!" Jon yelled at Li.

The kung fu master nodded and glimpsed at his arm. His forearm bled and Jon shook with disbelief.

"What the hell?! How'd that happen?!" Jon yelled again.

Li shrugged. "I don't know." He was quiet as Jon turned to scan the club a third time.

"I don't see the rest of them!" he yelled.

"Who?!"

"Rex! Do you see him?!" Jon screamed in Li's direction.

Li surveyed the space too. With Rex now out of sight, the Doorman could not see the rival leader at all. Danix hurried to catch up to Li and Jon.

"What?! What is it?!" Danix yelled at Jon.

"No Rex! No Cole!" Yelling again, the three Doormen stood at the top of the staircase.

While they were close to the flag, it wasn't as guarded as it should be. There was room for Fallen Sons to take it, but in the most unconventional way. This was terrifying to Jon. If he couldn't see his enemy, then he was breaking the cardinal rule designed not only for the Showdown but for the entire bouncing profession.

"We have to find them!" Jon yelled at Li.

Danix was keeping watch on the same place as Jon was. The team members who were out of the Showdown were all standing by the bar. Jon looked at this section and his face had brightened. He was overwhelmed by a new thought. They had brought Kya here for a reason. For now, she was in charge of taking care of the booths and everything else in between. And, if the Doormen couldn't find Rex on the dance floor, then he had to be either by the bar, the stage, or the VIP section.

Jon's heart raced. Was he there? And, if so, was he near Kya?

Jon hustled back to Danix and Li. The only way to find Rex was together.

"Any sign of him?!"

"No! If they're not on the floor!" asked Danix, "then where the hell are they?!"

Jon pivoted and shifted back and forth. Reviewing all potential locations, if he couldn't see them here, then they...

Jon's head shook. He couldn't put the pieces together. He wanted to see Rex, but when he considered all locations, there was only one place he could be. And it was the last place anyone looks when they're in a club or when they're in a room, *any room.*

Jon's heart pounded and he felt a surge of anxiety and fear.

Rex was here, yes, and he was close too. He was in the only place he could be.

Above Jon's head, he looked at the ceiling.

Rex and Cole, now both above, crawled across the strobe lights like rodents in the gutter. Unable to see seen by any guests, Jon saw the Fallen Sons moving along the ceiling. Like he said, they were close.

The flag was on the other side of the railing!

Directly beneath the Sons, unaware of what was happening, was Kya.

The Doormen couldn't acknowledge the Sons' current location. They couldn't without notifying Kya as well as the guests. They also couldn't get to them using conventional means. In the end, there was nothing more unconventional than crawling along a ceiling. But that's exactly what Rex was doing.

He was crawling across the fucking ceiling!

"Spread out!" Danix ordered the other Doormen.

Rex crept down the post and Cole was there with him. The two Fallen Sons approached the second floor, now booming. The booths were packed and there were people grinding the railing like pole dancers.

The setting was an explosion for the senses. The

entire room was imbued with new sounds and new faces. All were enhanced to the point where not a single patron noticed anything.

Danix, Li, and Jon were squared off. Now in a triangular position, they approached the post while Rex and Cole hopped down. It was then Jon decided on a strategy. Here, he slid toward Danix and pulled his shirt.

"We just have to stop them!" Jon's voice managed to carry over the music. He was not only yelling as much as he was enticed by a lethal combination of caffeine and rage. What Jon had planned now was far more effective than the alternative.

"What?!" Danix yelled back.

Jon watched Rex leap off the post like a ninja. Staying low, both Rex and Cole shuffled but still none noticed them. It was still too loud and too active but soon, Rex and Cole were now on the other side of this one booth.

It was Kya's booth!

"All we have to do is take Rex and Cole right here, right now and we can get them out of the Showdown! Then we can get their flag and end this thing!" Jon shouted. "We outnumber them! This should have been our plan from the beginning!"

Danix nodded. With all the Doormen assembled, the situation remained tepid. Despite the strung out condition of The Conquistador's guests, the Doormen still had the advantage. They had more men, plus they had Kya too. She was working but still, she was aware and she could help. Jon was ready. He still wanted a piece of Rex and was prepared to face him.

Shuffling toward the railing, Rex and Cole pushed two dancers aside like they were mannequins.

Jon crept up along Cole but Li followed. Danix, however, proceeded around the booths and slid his hand along the steel. He was calm, focused, and unafraid. And yet, this was not the ideal place to have a throwdown.

Then again, they had no other choice. It was, as the saying goes, now or never.

Danix stepped in front of Rex and crossed his arms. This was Danix's usual tactic whenever he caught a guest doing something they shouldn't. Rex, who was not like most guests, stopped and smirked at Danix.

"Hey there, Danix!" Jon could hear Rex over the music.

He and Li were behind Cole Hausen, who was only five steps behind Rex. All of them were closed in. All of them were surrounded. The three-on-two was still happening.

"Found your flag!" Rex shouted at Danix. "Nice hiding place!" Rex knew all the Doormen were gathered here except one.

"So where's Addison?!" Rex raised his voice again. "Not playing like the rest of us, is he?!"

"We got the jump on you, man!" Danix shouted. "There's three of us and only two of you! The Showdown...it's over, Rex! You never had a chance!"

"You think your numbers scare me?" Rex's emphatic reply penetrated the shadows and was so hot it was practically a searing wave of heat. "You think this is about some game? I know you think that's what this is about, the Showdown, and I know you think you've won! No matter what happens, you're still gonna lose! No matter what!"

Rex said this with a big smile showing on his face. Jon unclenched his fists. Cole inched closer to Rex, and Li scuttled to the side. Jon couldn't get Rex's words out of his mind. He listened to Danix respond like he didn't care.

"Then why don't you just go home?!" Danix shouted. "Call it a night and just go home!"

"Oh, I wish I could do that!" said Rex, "but see, I still gotta plan here! I still gotta mission and a long night ahead of me! And you know how it works, don't ya'? You have to stay until the night's over!"

For some reason, Rex was saying this next part very slowly. It was like he was in no hurry to grab the flag, which was a strange occurrence that Jon couldn't comprehend. He watched Rex like a fucking hawk because whatever he said didn't mean a damn thing. No, he was here, and he was in the game, and that game was still not over.

"Then what are you waiting for?" Danix yelled at Rex. "Do it!"

Rex smirked before burping out an obnoxious chuckle. It was the same laugh Jon observed back at the warehouse/rave. Jon hated it then and hated it even more now.

"Not a goddamn thing!" Jon knew what was about to go down between both parties. Danix never punched first and yet, he did now. Delivering a monstrous left hook, Jon had never observed Danix willing to go so far so fast. The men were between three pillars, and there were even a few guests hanging out in this section. After Danix ignited the face-off with a punch, Rex blocked. From there, Jon and Li got in on the action. Li kicked Cole from behind, and Jon jumped across with a flying elbow.

Together, they popped Cole in two regions. It forced the man to stumble but not to drop.

The fight was on and everyone was grabbing their own piece of it. When Kya saw what was happening, she clapped and called out to one of the bottle girls.

"Bring out some champagne! It's someone's birthday today!" While in a fight with Li, Jon could hear Kya screaming at the other servers. She was actually speaking too loudly while also standing too close to Cole.

After being kicked by Li, the Fallen Son stumbled too far from the fight.

The last stand among the Doormen and the Sons was happening near the booths but away from all the guests. This not only kept the Showdown somewhat secret, it also prevented Cole and Rex from getting closer to Kya. She was helping the Doormen with the Showdown, but technically, she wasn't supposed to.

She shouldn't be here, and yet, here she was.

Bottles of champagne and sparklers were all deployed, and the stunning women carrying them naturally drew all the guests' attention. Jon thought this was beneficial until he saw where Cole was standing.

"You!" he yelled. "You called them!"

Spotting Kya, Cole charged at Kya while Jon and Li both kept watch.

"You're not supposed to be playing! Who are you? Why are you here?"

Jon knew from the beginning that Kya said what

she did. She was too close to Cole. He was a perceptive guy. Actually, all the Sons were. And, while Kya's intentions were noble, Jon did need a distraction. It was just Kya's came at precisely the wrong time.

When Cole saw Kya helping the Doorman, he snatched her wrist. "Keeper!" Cole shouted. "Non-player in the game! Non-player in the fucking game!"

"Get your hands off of me!" Kya shouted back at Cole. Jon stomped.

"Fuck you!" Cole yelled in Kya's face. "You cheating little slut! You lying no good—"

"What the hell did you just call me?" Kya proceeded to spit in Cole's face, which drew the attention of more guests. Jon refused to watch Cole put his hands on Kya, so he lunged for his shoulder.

"Get your hands off of her!" Jon screamed before he clamped Cole's deltoid and cocked back his fist.

As soon as Jon made contact with Cole, the infuriated man's elbow shot back. He rammed Jon's mouth. Jon quaked while Cole continued to hold Kya by the hand. After seeing Jon hit, Li rolled in and answered with a furious knee and elbow.

"Gah!" Cole's chin snapped back and his eyes began to roll. Despite being hit this hard, Cole resorted to another unconventional attack. With Kya still in his grip, he tossed her into Li.

"Ah!" Kya's yell was fierce. She was in distress but no longer in the fight. Then again, neither was Li. When he caught Kya, Cole jumped in.

He had Li clear in his sights and was completely unaware of what was to come. Jon watched Li look at Kya. He inspected her to see if she was all right.

"Are you okay?" Li's voice was muddled, but Jon was an expert lipreader. He understood this was what he was asking Kya. With his hands on her shoulders, Li stared at Kya. Jon aggressively made his way to where they were standing.

"I'm fine!" Kya replied, speaking over the music.

"Look out!" Although Jon tried to warn Li, the man was dead set on helping Kya.

Right now, Cole had a direct line straight to her fucking face. He had Li exactly where he wanted him, and Jon knew this.

Worse, he could not stop it.

"Li!" So concerned about what was to come, Jon felt like his friend's single-syllable name took several seconds to speak. Li was fast, but right now, he was incapable of acting at his top speed. No, he pushed Kya, and Cole's fist cut furiously through the air.

The most Li could do was try to block it, but it was too late.

Until now, Jon had only seen Li punch many times. Li's number was so low, so low Jon could count them with only one hand. Yet, that was then, and this was now, and now it was a terrible sight to behold.

Cole rocked Li with a solid jab and connected with the kung fu master's chin. Solid and fierce, once Li was knocked down, his head rotated like it wasn't connected to his neck. The punch should have knocked Li out cold. If it were anyone else, it would have.

Jon could see Li leaning against the railing in a daze. Jon hurried to get after him, but in the end, it was too late. Cole popped Li in the groin with a straight kick. Then, he snagged the Doorman's head and smoked him again, this time into the railing.

Li waddled. The recent attack garnered the attention of Danix too and Rex.

"Shit," Jon uttered.

Still with Kya, Cole marveled at his work. Li was a tough son of a bitch and was so deadly and capable, but now, he was on the floor...*bleeding.*

"Keep your head in the game next time, yeah!" barked Cole. "Rule of bouncing, never let the guests distract you from doing your fucking job!"

Cole straightened his shirt. It was once three on two, but now it was two on two.

Addison was still nowhere to be found.

Where the hell is he? Jon asked himself. *Where the hell is Addison?*

And, with Kya's role in the Showdown now compromised, Jon felt someone tapping his shoulder. When the Keeper man witnessed what Kya was doing, he raised his hand and waved his index finger from side to side. Giving Jon the *uh-uh-uh* gesture of disapproval, the Keeper did this to Jon while scolding Kya as well. "No outside help!" the Keeper yelled. "Penalty!"

"What?" Jon didn't know there even were penalties in a Showdown. Apparently, there were. The Keeper reached under his coat and removed a zip tie. Jon's eyes opened so wide he nearly vomited. If he couldn't use his hands, he was done for!

"Turn around!" the Keeper ordered.

Jon did as he was instructed. He feared making further compromises to his team or to the game itself. Since he was the player, he was being penalized instead of Kya. With no choice, Jon rotated and the Keeper pulled Jon's hand behind his back and connected his wrist to his belt.

"I'm penalizing one of your players instead of disqualifying them!" the Keeper yelled at Danix. "One arm gone!"

"Come on!" Jon tugged his wrist and tried to break the tie.

What he received was the Showdown's equivalent to a warning. This lightened his influence and removed him from the competition, but only for a short time. Yet, time here was critical. It was everything.

"Sir," said the Keeper, "you are hereby removed from this Showdown! Please proceed out of bounds!"

Li rose slowly from the floor. Once the Keeper told Li where to go, the other Doorman walked off. However, here was the worst section of the club. Here was where the fight was happening! Thankfully, it was happening outside the booths. And, thanks to Kya, the sections that were fully occupied were busy with their bottle service and listening to music to really see what was transpiring. Drugs, as Jon learned at this job, were a powerful thing.

"I have to get back!" Jon shouted at Danix. "I have to get back in the game!"

Jon looked on from the stairs and saw another Fallen Son approaching. And, with him now marching at Jon and Danix, this Son would be supremely outnumbered. What was once a two-on-one would transition to a three-on-one.

Even for Danix, this was too much. And yet, that was precisely what was happening. Jon blitzed after Danix and didn't waste a second.

"I'm coming!" When Jon screamed, Cole retrieved a bottle of champagne from a table and pulled the sparkler.

"Hey!" Jon yelled before coming to a full stop. He didn't expect Cole to take this bottle. "What are you doing?!"

Jon looked down at Cole's hand as it squeezed the bottle.

"Improvising!" Cole yelled. Cole looked back at Rex, who was still in a fight with Danix near the banister. "Get the flag!"

Cole smashed the bottle and snatched a drink off one of the tables. The drink he swiped looked like bourbon. Combined with a smashed champagne bottle, everything was flammable and Jon knew what Cole was planning. He had spilled the drink too close to the guests. The bottle girls were assembled around one table and so, they noticed.

The booze spilled, and Cole grinned at Jon. "Ha-ha."

"No!" Jon roared. With the guests' attention now on him, everyone stopped to gawk at Jon.

And what Cole had cleverly created was an incident that happened all the time at nightclubs. Bottles spill often, and though this is unlikely, it is still not impossible. And none could prove this happened because there was a contest happening within the club. To everyone, it was just a bad accident. To the Fallen Sons, however, it was exactly what needed to be done in order to take the Doorman's flag.

The Keeper could not penalize the Sons for this.

Yes, what they did was wrong, but it was *not* against the rules. So, when Danix saw the spilled alcohol, so did Kya and so did everyone else. The remaining Doormen, including Jon, hurried to work with the fuming crowd but, in doing so, left a clear path toward their flag.

While all of this was happening, Rex climbed over the railing and pulled the flag from its place.

"Gotcha."

Everyone's attention was elsewhere and Jon looked at the railing. He saw a cloaked figure positioned there. He squinted to be sure of what he was seeing.

Whoever this was, it wasn't one of the Doormen.

None of what Jon saw had matched any of their descriptions. It wasn't Addison. This figure's body was different. And it wasn't one of the Sons either. This unknown player was on the other side of the railing. There, they pushed through the crowd and made their way toward the middle.

When Jon saw this "other" figure, he screamed again. "Hey! New player! Intruder! Intruder! Cheater! Cheater!"

Jon rushed to Rex as the cloaked figure took the flag and held it up high. Whoever they were, they had to be someone Rex trusted.

Who was this new player? Were they a Son or someone else?

Why didn't the Keeper see them? How could he not?

The rules of the Showdown were being bent and altered. After witnessing such unlawful acts, Jon looked at his wrist. The dart gun given to him by Michael was still set to fire. It was usable but, at this moment, absolutely necessary.

If the Sons wanted to play the Showdown this way, then Jon accepted how it could be played by two people, by both teams. When Jon marched after Rex, he rolled along the ground to force himself directly into the leader's path. Jon then hit Rex with a boot to the gut.

"Gah!" Jon dropped directly between Rex and this new person, whoever they were.

Though not his original plan, it was precisely what needed to be done. Jon had only slightly tangoed with Rex before. But, he was out of his element then, and so he would most definitely be out of it now.

Danix was still in the Showdown, but he was not in this fight.

This fight was between Jon and Rex. No one else.

It was leader versus rookie in a fight to protect The Conquistador. Jon was all that stood in the Fallen Sons' path to victory. He was the only Doorman left, except for Addison, who had clearly abandoned the Showdown for some unknown reason.

This should have infuriated Jon, but he could not think about it now.

Forced to battle the toughest bastard in the game, Jon kept his fists up and flexed his chest and back. He was ready.

Rex did the same. "You got spirit, kid," said Rex, "I'll give you that! But you know you're in a situation you can't control, right? You know you have already lost!"

"And you cheated, asshole!" Jon yelled back at Rex. "You've always been a cheater!"

"Nah!" Rex said to Jon. "I just know my way around the rules, is all! Winners don't break rules, they bend 'em, and that's why they always win, see?! Now, get out of the way! Trust me! You don't want what's coming! You don't know why we did what we did."

"Yeah, well, oldest saying in the club handbook

there, bro!" Jon replied to Rex. "Never trust your opponent, never underestimate them! You never know what tricks they might have up their sleeves! You never know what they're going to do!"

"Good advice!" Rex screamed.

"Not for you!" Jon's reply was unexpected.

It coerced Rex into shutting one eye and scanning the Marine up and down. It looked like Rex was trying to see through Jon. However, Jon didn't care for the small talk. He definitely didn't want this fight to turn into a staring contest. No, he was here for one purpose only. He was here to finish the Showdown. And, as Rex made the first move, Jon found himself making his own.

He snapped his leg and kicked low, hard, and fast. Rex backstepped. Now near the balustrade, the two men traded blows. Rex's were solid. Jon took a few hits, all of them had forced him to stagger but not to fall. Jon's prosthetic provided him with suitable balance and resilience. Jon punched again and Rex blocked again. The cloaked figure was by the stairs, moving surreptitiously through the dark setting.

All Jon wanted to do was knock Rex into next week, and he was more than prepared to do this now.

He tried to kick again but failed for a third time.

Rex snatched Jon's fist, ducked, and moved in for the elbow. After clobbering Jon in the gut, the Marine answered with a furious headbutt. Jon had taken hits like this before but Rex's felt different. He was able to summon more force, more strength, and while Jon did manage to land a few strikes of his own, they were nothing compared to Rex's.

"Jon!" Danix stomped after Jon.

Jon glanced at Danix. He was now off guard, which was exactly what Rex wanted!

Being the chief of distractions, as soon as Jon looked over, Rex chopped him in the neck. Jon flinched and Rex pushed him hard into the railing. Now tripping over his own feet, Jon collided with the cold steel and looked at Rex.

"Too slow there, boy!" Rex shouted. He reached and grabbed a chunk of Jon's hair. "You're just too damn slow!"

Rex pulled Jon to his chest. Jon glowered.

By now, the flames were out and the club was starting to settle. The Showdown was nearing its end. Jon could barely last another second. He was winded and he was injured, and he felt like he was going to puke on his shoes. Jon's head snapped and he gargled blood. He felt dizzy and nauseous. Rex pulled Jon to his feet. Almost unconscious, Jon couldn't resist. He was beaten, and his back was against the wall, *literally*.

Rex was unhinged, and no, Jon could not let him get his hand on that flag. If he did that, then everything the Doormen fought for would have been for nothing. The entire future of The Conquistador was at stake, and Jon had no choice. What he was about to do was not part of the rules, but since the Fallen Sons had already bent their fair share, Jon had to ask himself, *what did he have to lose?*

He also asked another important question:

What other choice did he have?

"You got guts, boy, like I said," continued Rex. He stood with his fists clenched and with the same maddening grin like the one he showed back at the rave.

"But you don't know exactly what you're doing. Best to just step aside while you still can."

"Rule number two of the bouncing world," Jon said, fury burning in his once stoic eyes. "If your voice can't do the job, then you think of a new strategy. And sometimes that new strategy is thinking outside the box."

"Yeah, well," Rex replied, "I've never really been one for rules like I said. It's the reason why I was let go, but then again, The Conquistador has never been one for rules either, so...who cares if you break 'em, right? Still, I did remember one rule more than all the others, and that is always plan ahead! Always cover your ass and make sure you got the right people!" Rex laughed. He was being sarcastic because he didn't honestly think Jon had any tricks up his sleeve, but he was wrong.

Dead wrong.

Rex punched, and Jon stepped aside and then flicked his wrist. From beneath Jon's palm, a dart ejected and Jon didn't know how to aim this device given by his friend, Michael Irons. Therefore, Jon's strategy for using it was to stand as close as possible. He was only two feet from Rex, and so the distance between the two was negligible. Jon aimed for Rex's neck, and due to the proximity, the hit was successful. The dart pegged Rex just below his right ear, and once he was nailed, the leader stopped dead in his tracks. Blinking rapidly, Rex grunted while Jon looked around. No one saw a damn thing, not even the Keeper. Rex grunted again before he lifted his hand to his face. Slowly, he reached for the dart sticking out of his veiny neck.

"What the...what did you..." Jon anticipated that Rex would fall to the ground unconscious. Should this happen, he'd pull the dart out of Rex before the Keeper noticed. Even if it was found, Jon felt it wouldn't matter. Most of the Showdown's rules had gone out the window, and Rex admitted this outrightly a few seconds earlier. And yet, as the Keeper came forward, he raised his hand and waved everyone else in.

"Showdown over! Showdown..." Before the Keeper could utter the same phrase again, Rex fell into Jon and pushed him out of the way. After shoving Jon aside, Rex shuffled to the stairs. He scurried down to the first floor.

Seeing him run away, Jon kipped up from the ground and chased.

"He's getting away! He's moving!" Since Rex was hit with a dart, Jon imagined it wouldn't be long before he passed out. Still, he wasn't going to wait for that to happen. Jon's goal was to stop Rex now, while he still had the chance.

"Jon, wait!" Danix yelled at Jon and urged him not to chase Rex wherever he was going. Yet, when Jon saw where Rex was heading to, he had no choice but to act. Rex waddled down the steps and pushed more guests aside. With his hand pressed to his neck, Rex swayed like he was about to fall.

Still, he was hanging on. Whatever this dart was laced with, it was not strong enough to bring down the leader of the Fallen Sons. It might not be strong enough, or maybe Rex was just really fucking strong. Jon watched him as he headed beneath the stairwell. While he hoped Rex would try to get to the exit, he realized he was approaching the one place he shouldn't go.

The door to the Secret Room or Forbidden Room was only three steps away.

Rex barreled toward it.

The door was locked, but Rex barreled his shoulder into it and it opened. For some reason, the door was opened.

How? Who opened it?

"Son of a..." As a former Doorman, Rex knew where this room was as well as how to access it. But whether he knew what it contained...remained to be seen.

Jon hated how Rex retreated to the same place as Frankie Castellani those months ago.

Still, there was so much more to this one room than Jon understood. When he reached the bottom of the staircase, Jon touched his ear and screamed into his radio. "Addison!" When Jon shouted into his piece, Rex was calling the one person he had yet to see. "Rex...he's heading to the one place he can't! He's there now! Hurry!"

Jon hoped Addison was already made aware of Rex's movements. So far, he had not joined the Showdown and this reminder became very specific. Jon demanded Addison's action. And after calling his boss again, Jon received no response. He couldn't wait for an answer. No, Jon couldn't wait for anyone.

And, when the door did open, Jon had at last arrived at the location.

Struck with déjà vu, he had been in this situation once before. Jon chased Frankie through this space but he hoped he would never step foot inside that room ever again. Jon really didn't want to know what secrets were contained there. The previous instance whereby he was inside, he knew it had glass windows that showed out onto the dance floor. Yet this was only one room. From what Jon could recall, there were others too.

In fact, there were *many* others. With a sigh, Jon looked back and held his breath.

Like he was about to take a plunge into a pool of freezing water, this was exactly what he was about to do. And so, Jon glanced behind him one last time. "Into the unknown," he said to himself. "One last time."

CHAPTER 20
GLORIOUS LIES

SINCE JON EXPLORED THIS SO-CALLED HIDDEN room, he thought he knew what to expect.

He could recall vivid details about the location, including the glass walls and the many rooms and subspaces. Jon also remembered the mirrors and the exotic furniture being stored there. It was like a treasure room in a museum, collecting artifacts from The Conquistador's long and complicated past. Anticipating all of this before stepping in, what Jon saw now, however, was nothing like what he expected.

"What..." As Jon was rendered speechless, what he had come across was a narrow hallway sheathed in shadow. The only region brightened was exactly where he was standing. Still, Jon didn't know what was possible. All he knew for certain was he could hear Rex's heavy footsteps.

Jon didn't spare a second.

He rushed through this room and followed Rex the way he did Frankie Castellani. The only difference now was Rex's *slower* movements. The dart was taking effect, and soon Rex would be out. Then again, that was only the ideal outcome. And yet, once it was revealed that the Sons were out of the game, the Keeper would have to rule in favor of The Conquistador. Then, the rivalry between the Doormen and the Fallen Sons would come to an end and things would go back to normal.

Jon gulped as he considered this as a possibility. Too much had happened and Jon was battling another eerie outcome. Where was Rex going, and why was he there, in this *one* room?

"Rex!" Jon soon found Rex in a room the Marine was familiar with. In fact, Rex was standing in the room Jon feared most of all.

After coming to this location, Jon found Rex slumped in a chair before a glass shelf.

Rex's hand fell off his neck. The serum from Jon's dart was now working and Rex could no longer stand or sit straight. Jon hoped to feel satisfied by this, but he wasn't. Rex might have been defeated, but where he had run off to was an eerie place.

When Rex stumbled into this new room, Jon was now chasing. No, he was trying to reach him before he pushed deeper into this *hidden room*. Now, Jon didn't have time to notice where he was. Where he thought he was happened to be the same room Frankie passed by. While Rex's gait was unbalanced, he swiped *something* off one of the platforms. Why he chose to do this was not known to Jon at this time. In the end, all the lone Doorman wanted to do was grab that dart and bring Rex to the Keeper so the game could end.

Jon leaped. He tried grabbing Rex's shoulders. Then, when preparing for the hit, a leg cut Rex from behind one of the posts and slammed the leader of the Fallen Sons. Soon after this kick was delivered, Jon looked at the attacker.

It came from the one person Jon longed to see but had not yet encountered.

Addison was here. He was alone and glaring. Poised and still, Addison did not appear to be alert or shaken in any way. He gazed at Rex as he lay flat on the floor. Now clutching what he'd stolen from this room, Jon turned to look at Addison.

"Addison," Jon said. "What are you doing here?"

"Protecting," said Addison.

"Protecting what?" asked Jon.

"The only thing *worth* protecting," Addison replied. He marched toward Rex and pulled what was in his hand. Jon couldn't see exactly what it was, but it was small and *shiny*.

While Jon disapproved of Addison's decision to stay out of the Showdown and to be here, in this forbidden place, he refused to hold back his frustration. Biting down on his tongue, Jon's teeth were clamped so much he almost tasted blood.

"Protect what?" asked Jon. "Protect...*this*?"

When Jon heard Addison say he was protecting this one room, it had to be because it was valuable. Yet, in Jon's mind, it was meaningless compared to the priority tonight.

Still, Addison insisted he stay here. *Why*, Jon thought. *Why on Earth would he be here?*

"Enough of this!" Jon screamed. "I'm tired of being

kept in the dark about what's really going on here! So what is it, Addison? Why are you here now instead of with us, out there?!"

Jon pointed at the door. Yet, when inside this one room, Jon began to see what looked like a vault. It was a galvanized section, but in the dead center were these... keys.

Gold keys!

Just like Sam had referenced to Frankie, these keys were shaped in a familiar yet compelling design.

Solid, yes, and golden, yes, but also something else. They were old keys.

"*Key*," Jon said as it finally dawned on him exactly what he was looking at. "What the hell are these things...are these...like keys?"

Before this moment, Jon had turned a blind eye to this section's existence, but no more.

The secrets hiding in The Conquistador were grand and suspicious and yet still, Jon was demanding the truth. When Jon lost his temper, Addison raised his hand and jerked his chin toward the key Jon was holding in his hand.

"Look at it." Jon heard his friend loud and clear. However, the command given was confusing. He had no idea how he was supposed to interpret all this secrecy.

The keys, what do they open? *What do they unlock?*

"Look at what?"

"What's in your hand," Addison specified. "What Rex was trying to take from us." Addison pointed at Rex again. He was still unconscious in his chair. "See for yourself."

"It's a key," said Jon, holding this elegant golden key. It was also heavy. It felt like a train whistle in Jon's hands. *"It's a key."*

"No," informed Addison. "It's *the* key. These are The Conquistador's *keys*, or as it's known in our world...its *ciphers*. Unlimited access to near unlimited doors in every club across the entire world. Exactly what a nightclub promises. It's the key to the one door, *the ultimate door*, Jon."

Addison couldn't have made his point any clearer. Jon would not refuse again.

So desperate to learn of his club's scary truth, the Marine refused to hold back or waste time. Jon raised this one gold key and dropped it down onto the nearest table. The key was too old for Jon to grasp or embrace as it was. There were multiple keys in The Conquistador's vault, and each one looked older, and yet, all had retained its value. For Jon, it had likely grown expo-nentially.

In essence, The Conquistador was a place of access. *It needed its own keys in order to acquire it.*

What it was, truly, was an untapped resource that had coveted and acquired more power over time. It had established a grand reputation and was built into a powerful entity, one that Jon could not fit inside his head. He flinched on second glance. Still, Jon was puzzled as he glanced at this special key. Head tilted, Jon gawked. He was not intrigued only frustrated and irritated to learn and see what he did.

"What is this place?" Jon asked Addison. "What is this club?"

"This," said Addison, "this is what gave The Conquistador its status and its place among the guild of nightclubs. It's all the great treasure owned and earned by Larry and others who built this club. With this, he was able to open this club, and it is because of these ciphers that he is able to keep it open and go anywhere he needs to go. It's a tool part of a story much older than you, much older than even me."

"Does this cipher belong to Larry and his family and you," asked Jon, "which, in effect, is also your family?"

Addison didn't say anything. This was true. The keys *might* belong to Addison.

"Where did they come from?"

"Larry Thomas has a past beyond us, beyond you, but it is his past, nonetheless. The Conquistador is one of the first clubs ever created, and so, it has privileges only a few other clubs possess and these keys ensure the survival of that privilege."

"Son of a bitch," said Jon.

"The Conquistador is not just a club, it's a thriving business connected to powerful people, is part of a much bigger world. It's a world of endless opportunity, and using these keys, one can open, forge, maintain, and grow. See, keys open doors, Jon. They open doors and we are the ones who guard them. The bouncers of *integrity*. We make sure only certain people are let in. This is our purpose, Jon. This is why we are Doormen."

"Well, what did you plan on doing with all these keys?" Jon asked Addison.

"We were interested in keeping them, obviously," replied Addison. "Gold counts for a lot on the market, but these keys are more than just gold. Actually, it is now the most valuable commodity in the clubbing industry. It is exactly what need...if we need it."

"The Conquistador," whispered Jon. At last, the name of the club made complete sense. Conquistadors sought treasure, and these ciphers, apparently, were a treasure in the bouncing world. Jon shook his head to regain his composure and then he asked, "need...*for what?*"

Addison turned to Jon and glared. He refused to answer Jon. *For what,* was not a question he wanted to explain.

"Okay," Jon said after. "So, you've kept all these keys here, inside this secret vault, but isn't that—"

"Illegal," Addison interrupted. "To hoard these materials? Somewhat," said Addison.

"How?" asked Jon.

"No one knows about it and no one can. If anyone discovered the great secrets of our club, it would be a fucking gold rush, literally! Everyone would want to come here, and so far, many have tried, and many have failed, failed because...of *us.* See, Jon, that's why you work here. You protect more than just a club, you protect its future, its principles, and its place in society."

Jon's head shook and he was disenchanted with Addison's logic. He couldn't explain or understand any part of what Addison had just said. For now, he chose not to even try.

"I stop people from finding this and taking things," said Jon. "I'm just a fucking security guard."

"No," Addison snapped back at Jon. "You're a fucking Doorman, and you stop people from going where they're not supposed to go and taking what's not theirs to take. What you see here, Jon, in the wrong hands, could take over this club and use it for everything it stands against. It could be used to open the *wrong* doors, see? The Conquistador was built for everyone. It is based on a specific principle and ideology, and it's one we fight to protect."

Addison was speaking about principles that, while sound, still prevented Jon from fully grasping and understanding. "The Conquistador, like all old clubs, is a place where everyone can be welcomed and be free, and whether you choose to see it that way or not, that part of this club is being threatened. Worse, some people have no place to go other than here. This is their sanctuary, Jon, and the ciphers are all that stands in the way of The Conquistador's reputation, of its future, which is now...your future too."

Jon's head shook again and Addison continued to explain.

"If someone gets a hold of these ciphers, they could start their own club or a business within the Guild with nefarious, possibly dangerous intentions. Nightclubs can be used for all sorts of bad things, but if a club gains these keys, then within the old guild—which is us—they could open any doors they want to, open a new club that could end our own. The Conquistador is an entity that refuses to change or evolve, and that makes us a threat."

Jon's head continued to shake and he was descending deeper into the vast world of the unknown. More words entered his mind he couldn't understand.

Guild? Ciphers? *Old guild?*

Jon gulped as he tried to understand but couldn't because none of it made any sense.

"You're still new to this world, Jon," Addison said. "You still do not know exactly how it works. We use these ciphers to maintain and protect. These ciphers, in the end, help the people who are the closest to us. People like you."

"Like me?"

"People who are in need of guidance and care, Jon," said Addison. "People who need opportunities and purpose and who need a place to go to forget about their problems and pain. That place is...here."

"And that's why you hired me? Because I was some kind of charity case?"

"No," Addison said, "I hired you because you were needed, and that's why you're here now. The Conquistador is part of something great. You just don't know it yet. There's a lot of power in these walls, and with power comes change. Should someone understand how Larry Thomas got these ciphers, then they would all come and try to take it for themselves. See, Larry never trusted anyone, and in order to protect his investment, he needed someone who knew their way around it. He needed a—"

"A lawyer," Now Jon was the one interrupting. Suddenly, it was all becoming clear. "Son of a bitch."

Jon snapped because he should have seen this truth sooner. However, now he began to see that maybe he did and just refused to accept it. Although Jon was perturbed, Addison continued to smirk as if he was enjoying revealing The Conquistador's prized possession.

Even still, Jon could still only somewhat understand.

Still, he was unsure, unfamiliar, and also...*afraid*.

"So...The Conquistador it's—"

"Priceless?" asked Addison. "More than you know. More than you could possibly know. What's stored here, in this room, is a value beyond control. I was hired to be Larry's attorney. I was the lawyer he needed to help protect his club as well as its assets. I agreed to help him but became so much more when I realized how deep the world goes. Like Larry, I became involved too. I became a part of something great, something I feel is worth protecting."

"But this isn't what we do," said Jon. "We're not gatekeepers or guardians. If this was ever found out, then all of us would be—"

"*Dead?*" barked Addison. "Yes, we'd all be dead or invaded, no doubt."

"But who else knows about it?" asked Jon. "Who else knows about these ciphers?"

"Some," Addison said. "Some found out the same way you did, and yet, all of them chose to stay. All of them chose to stay and protect this because they understand the truth. The ciphers cannot fall into the wrong hands."

Jon's legs wobbled and his knees felt weak. He didn't know, and he didn't want to. Suddenly, he was overwhelmed by all the fatigue he'd been battling since the Showdown. Jon couldn't stand the thought of being in a place that was, in so many ways, *no different from war.*

Actually, for Jon, this was worse. War is about saving. This was about owning.

Different.

"So you see," said Addison, "this is what you're *really* protecting. It's why everyone has always been trying to get in. It's what the Sons returned to get and why they were exiled because they wanted to use it. It's also what Frankie Castellani and Sam really wanted that day they were trying to set up their operations."

"I thought that was about dealing drugs?" Jon said to Addison.

"Drugs," replied Addison, "was only the beginning, but building a new club was his endgame. It's what Frankie really wanted to do."

"How much do you know about where you work?"

This one question had spontaneously entered Jon's mind. It was the question once asked by Kya but it was the same question that continued to emerge whenever Jon found himself thinking about his place of employment.

"What?" said Addison. He didn't understand the question.

"It was asked to me once before," said Jon. "Until now, I didn't know what to say," Jon answered. "The place I work is not what it seems," Jon made this declaration with the utmost certainty. It was exactly how Jon would describe The Conquistador now. *"It's filled with secrets."*

"No," said Addison, "The Conquistador is filled with *opportunity*," he corrected. "It's filled with nobility and with honor."

"No," said Jon. "It's filled with things that's putting everyone here at risk. It has placed all of us in a situation that could cost us our lives."

"And how is that different from any other day?" asked Addison. "You were hired to protect, and that's what you're doing."

"I was hired to be a fucking bouncer!" yelled Jon. "Not a guard to gatekeep one person's wealth, his treasure, and something other people want to steal. I'm in the middle of a war and I didn't even know it!"

"Do you want to know why I hired you?" Addison asked Jon. "Why I *really* hired you?"

Jon shook his head. He didn't want to know why. He didn't want to know anything else.

"Because you know the price of victory," Addison said to Jon. "You heal quickly, you know how to bounce back, *and* you know what needs to be done in order to get things done because you are right...you *are* in the middle of a war, Marine. On one side, it's us—it's The Conquistador, its future, and everything it has sworn to protect. And on the other side, it's people who want to rob, steal, and take our ciphers and open new doors within the club industry. It's people who can't be trusted, Jon, and who want to take our club and use it for nefarious, unpredictable purposes. So, now that you know what's really at stake here, there is only one question you have to ask yourself, and do you know what that question is, Jon?"

The Marine was silent. Jon didn't want to engage in what he believed to be a pointless and redundant interrogation. No, Jon couldn't be persuaded. He was too disturbed by what he had been told. He was actually so disgusted he couldn't stand to hear another word.

"What side are you on?" Addison asked. "What side are you on, Jon?"

It was Addison's point of poignance. It was Jon's last opportunity to speak.

"You remind me of what I felt when I left the desert," Jon said, "what led me here, what brought me back home. I got hurt, yeah, but I also stopped knowing what I was fighting for, who was right and who was wrong. I kept my head down too long and too often. And right now, I feel that way too. I thought I was doing the right thing. Now...now I'm not so sure."

"Yes, you are," said Addison. "You know we're on the right side. You just didn't expect it to be so complicated, but I assure you nothing has changed."

"But that's just it," said Jon, "after tonight...*everything's changed*. Me being here, working and knowing the truth...it changes everything, and that's why I can't be a part of it, not anymore."

"What are you saying?" Addison asked Jon.

Jon cleared his throat and he could feel a new strength starting to build. Generally, this feeling was exhilarating and rewarding for him. Now, it was the strength Jon needed to make a decision he never thought he would ever make.

Before Jon could reply, he walked to the door. He couldn't bear the burden and so, his conscience was forcing him to make a very difficult decision. When Jon pushed through, he expected to see people dancing and to hear music playing. And yet, while Jon did hear the music and he did see people, it was not the people he expected.

The people waiting for Jon were the Keeper, his fellow Doormen, and the Fallen Sons.

Now together, the Keeper stood in the center while everyone else stood at attention. No one had recovered the flag.

Did this mean the Showdown was over?

Jon eyed the Keeper, who stood still with his hands behind his back.

"The Showdown has concluded," the Keeper said.

"Teams are required to report back to their respective boundaries."

"Yes," said Jon. "But one member went out of bounds. He was—"

"Cheated!" Addison barked the word as he stood behind Jon. He passed through the same door and was carrying Rex with him. Rex, who was still unconscious after being hit with Jon's secret weapon. "He crossed boundaries, went where he wasn't supposed to go. He should be disqualified," said Addison. "And that means...*we win.*"

While all of what Addison said was true, Keeper stood there unfazed, almost as though he didn't care. "A lot of rules were broken today," said the Keeper. "Not just one."

Jon's head bowed, not out of shame but out of embarrassment. Obviously, the Keeper was aware of what Jon had done.

Still, the Keeper said what he did.

Rules were broken, but who broke them first was the real concern.

"Then who won?" demanded Li. "Who *won* the Showdown?"

The man who was the Keeper shook his head and then answered. "None. There will be no victor tonight."

"What?" barked Danix. "What do you mean?"

"How? We beat their entire team," snapped Owen. "We had them all taken out. We didn't get the flag, but we stayed in the game. Going by the rules of Capture The Flag, we should have another match, so let's do that. That's the rules."

"It is," said the Keeper, "but only if the rules were

adhered to and they weren't. One rule was severely broken compared to all others, which were mostly just bent."

"What rule?" said Owen. "Who broke it?"

The Keeper removed an iPad from under his jacket. Jon didn't know how the man managed to keep this device on his person the whole time, but somehow, he did.

"Every team member must go weaponless. None are to rely on tools of any kind to assist them when engaging with any of the other participants. Now, this rule must be respected, but then one team member decided to break it."

"Who?" asked Danix. "Who brought a weapon to the Showdown?"

Jon could feel his heart plummeting in his throbbing chest as he rubbed his wrist and soothed where the tranq gun used to be. Jon's reason for using this tool was justified. Rex broke the rules first, and Jon needed to stop him!

However, it was still a secret. None knew about it except for Jon. Rex was unconscious. The Keeper wasn't anywhere near Jon when he shot the dart. The only one who was there was that cloaked figure Jon couldn't see.

This, Jon thought might be no one, but he was wrong. It was *someone*.

The Keeper pressed his finger to the tablet and glimpsed at Jon and only at Jon.

"Footage was captured that proves what was suspected all along, the Doormen break rules. They always have, and that they are a corrupt and broken guild of bouncers."

The Keeper showed his tablet while everyone stood around him. And, sure to Jon's regret, the footage was of him and of Rex. It was captured on the club's second level. It showed Jon shooting Rex with the dart before he running away. The Keeper replayed the video again and again. In fact, he transferred the video, somehow, to the plasma screens that surrounded the VIP booths. Everyone could see Jon now, shooting Rex over and over again. And so, the Keeper made sure all the Doormen saw what happened. Once this footage was revealed, all eyes turned to Jon.

He stood among his colleagues in disgrace.

"I had no choice," Jon declared. "He was attacking Kya. He broke the rules first."

"By attacking someone who was not supposed to be in the game," added the Keeper. "As I said, many rules were broken today, but this one requires more examination than what can be done in a Showdown."

"Examination?" Danix glowered. He required more information, more explanation about the examination the Keeper was referring to. Before the Keeper could say more, he gawked at Jon and at Addison.

"A *schism* has been created here at your club now, sir," the Keeper said. "There was a clear break in the code of ethics, and for this, you will require immediate intervention and review."

"Intervention?" said Danix. "From *who*?"

Jon was beginning to ask himself the same question. He wanted to, but then suddenly, his anxiety transformed into a feeling far worse than worry. It was a form of fear only felt when a person comes close to death or when they accept their own demise.

However, Jon wasn't looking at death.

He thought he was looking at humiliation and shame. After all, he was the one who used the gun on Rex. But it was Rex who pushed Kya. And, while she was technically helping the Doormen, Rex still *struck* her.

This was Jon's justification for using this gun. He was clear. Rex broke the rules first!

"Outside agency," clarified the Keeper. "A private organization that has registered with the Commission in case such problems do occur. I will be granting them permission to move in once the Commission approves of their temporary status. I will let them know you have violated the rules and regulations and a new bouncing team must be brought in for the time being."

"Volunteered?" replied Jon. He was almost rendered speechless. "How?"

"Doesn't matter," said the Keeper. "It needs to be done by them, by...a group called the OverTakers."

Jon's chest felt hollow. The title, *OverTaker*, was peculiar and odd but it also had specific meaning. It did because he had heard it before. He couldn't place where or how. He tried tracing back the origins of this title, what it meant and who would give themselves such a name.

He thought about the letters first.

O and T.

But where? Where did he see them before?

The door. In New York. Fancy building.

Jon's mind was rewinding like an old VHS tape. He did see these words O and T. Yes, he did! They were part of a company's logo. In fact, they were indistinguishable from any other company's logo. They were designed to stand out. But the location whereby Jon observed these two pieces was somewhere he had visited of his own volition.

Then, suddenly, it hit the Marine. The truth he was searching for was found.

Michael. Irons.

He was the person who provided Jon with the weapon. He was also the same person who told Jon it was "safe" and "necessary."

He said it was legal. Maybe it was, but then maybe it wasn't.

At the time, Jon didn't know why Michael insisted that Jon take the weapon. He didn't think much of it because he trusted him.

Jon trusted Michael.

OverTaker.

Jon's mom told her son on many occasions what Michael Irons did for a living. He operated an elite protection agency, she said. It was a company comprised of men who were well-trained and who were hired to work as professional bodyguards, but was that even real? Was it true? Was Michael Irons ever a "bodyguard" or was it all just one giant ruse designed to gain Jon's trust and use him to access The Conquistador, its secret and its treasure? Jon didn't know the name of Michael's company then but he never asked about it. Recalling the logo, however, the pieces were beginning to come together for Jon in the most terrifying way possible.

It startled him so much he couldn't catch his breath.

Michael Irons's company had a name. It was a prolific name, so prolific it was almost unforgettable. They were The OverTakers. Jon found this to be a strange name for a protection agency, but then maybe that's not what it was at all.

Maybe that's not what they were ever. Maybe... Michael never was who he claimed to be.

Michael Irons...was a liar.

His team was the one the Keeper had referenced.

They were part of the same world as Jon and he didn't even know it. Then again, how could he? But then, that would also mean...Jon thought this and then he began to consider how Michael was involved.

Did he intend to set up Jon from the very beginning?

Did he ever care about his mother, or was she just a ploy in Irons's game of conquest?

Jon couldn't accept the why or the how. He couldn't understand because if what Jon suspected was true, then he had put his trust in the wrong man *twice*.

By Jon going to Michael, Jon had, in effect, compromised himself and his fellow Doormen. Rolling his fingers into his palm, Jon's nails dug hard into his skin. He trembled as another terrifying thought entered his mind. Now remembering that cloaked figure, at the time, Jon couldn't see who it was. Whoever they were, they were close enough to capture the footage of Jon using his gun. And, if they were there, then they also knew what Jon was going to do from the start.

As Jon understood, there was only one person who could know.

Jon gulped as he looked at the Keeper. With finally the strength to speak, Jon was barely heard but fought to be as clear as possible.

"Who?" asked Jon. "Who was there to see?"

While the Keeper was a humble man, even he had

no answer for Jon. As Jon inquired about the identity of this great orchestrator, the Keeper stepped aside. Strolling in with a walking stick and dressed in a tuxedo, Jon was not used to seeing Michael Irons in such a fancy wardrobe. Then Jon remembered that what was seen before was the real disguise. This was who Michael Irons was and who he always would be. He was a manipulator, a killer, *an enemy*.

"You," said Jon. He glared at Michael, who was the leader of this new organization known as The Over-Takers and who was designed to supplant the Doormen from the beginning. As Michael emerged, Jon felt as though he should have seen him all along.

He never really was hiding.

On the contrary, Michael Irons always was in plain sight.

"Hello, Jon."

Jon responded to Michael's call with venom. He couldn't imagine a greater adversary. The Fallen Sons were former employees, but Michael Irons and the OverTakers were bigger and badder than any other caste Jon could think of. They had resources, they had funding, and they were just as skilled as the Doormen were, if not more so. Worst of all, Michael Irons was elected to *take over* The Conquistador. The Keeper said their code of ethics and standards of practice were violated, and this required the intervention of a new party—another brigade of supposedly better bouncers.

Michael was not only a member of this new company; he was its leader.

Whether this was all coincidence or intentional, Michael had spoken highly of The Conquistador since the day he and Jon first met. He also indicated to Jon he knew of its secrets too.

The Conquistador was compromised, and its future was now uncertain.

"You did this," said Jon. "It was you...*all along?*"

"No," said Michael Irons. From now on, Jon would know him only as Irons. He had transformed in Jon's mind, and to Jon, Irons no longer deserved a first name. "Look at the footage. It was you. You did this, Jon. You broke the rules, and you led everyone astray. You failed."

"But you said...you—"

"I said nothing," Michael said. He cut off Jon completely. "I was just...*there.*"

"I trusted you," Jon declared. "My mom...we...we both trusted you."

After Jon admitted this, his fellow Doormen stood behind him to show they still had his back. Whatever their feelings were about what went down, they were still with Jon, just as they always had been.

"Didn't you learn the first rule of the club business? Never underestimate and never think you know someone, because more than likely...you really don't know them at all." Michael smirked and gave an obnoxious wink. Then, he stepped around Jon and proceeded into The Conquistador. With the Showdown now over and the next obstacle referenced, what lay ahead was something the Keeper had referred to only as *the schism.*

Whatever it was, it would be unchartered territory for the club.

Jon couldn't stand to think about it, and he didn't want to.

"I'll be seeing you around, Jon," said Irons as he

passed by. "I'll be seeing you...*real soon.*" He delivered another ominous warning that chilled Jon to the bone. Now fighting all his emotions, including peril, guilt, anger, and shame, yet it was failure Jon was fighting most of all.

Jon had failed. He didn't see clearly and was unable to settle his mind. No, the stress disorder had returned to Jon, and there was absolutely nothing he could do to stop it.

He was done.

"Jon," Addison called to the Marine. Addison was not angry. He reached for Jon like he wanted to touch him, but Jon was too far gone. While this was true in multiple ways, Jon was beyond grasping any of them now.

He walked and kept walking.

He brought his hand to his chest and grasped the crest—the symbol of all the Doormen. It was sewn into the fabric, which was less permanent than what was taken from the Fallen Sons. Still, to Jon, it had the same meaning. Fastening his grip around this crest, Jon ripped it clean off his shirt and let it go.

He let it *fall.*

"Jon, where are you going?!" Addison shouted for Jon but his voice was barely heard.

The farther Jon walked, the less he could hear. And, for the first time, Jon didn't look back. His decision was made and his fate was sealed. There was no going back. Jon didn't think about tomorrow, because he had no place left to go. All he could do was say goodbye, and that's what he did.

Goodbye, Conquistador. Goodbye, Doormen. Goodbye, *Kya.*

All his farewells had twisted in a cataclysm of endless doubt and perilous regret. Jon walked until the sun rose and then he continued. Worse than leaving, Jon quit. He abandoned, and now, he was outcast—AWOL in many ways. Still, Addison continued to call Jon's name, even though he refused to acknowledge him.

Jon couldn't stand to know what would happen, and he didn't want to think about it either.

He was out. He was gone. He was...*disappeared.*

ACKNOWLEDGMENTS

There are many people I would like to thank for helping to publish this novel, and I think the best way to do that is to start at the beginning. First, I would like to extend my warmest and most sincere gratitude to Jake Bray, Mike Bray, Patience Bramlett, Rachel Del Grosso, Ellie Folden, and everyone else at Wolfpack and Rough Edges who has worked hard to bring this book to life. It has been a long road, but you took a chance on me as well as on this story, and I am immensely grateful for everyone's patience and understanding. Long have I wanted to share stories about the enigmatic club, The Conquistador, as well as former Marine turned bouncer Jon Haze. And, because of your courage, these stories can now finally be told. I am also thankful to my fellow Goddardites, my Heebie Jeebie pals from Goddard College, for providing community and sanctity to a writer who was rejected by other MFA programs, and yet, it was you who gave me a path and a voice when I thought I had none.

I would also like to thank my writing teachers: John McManus, Douglas Martin, Jan Clausen, Melodie Campbell, and David Bergen, who—though they did not assist in the creation of this novel—still, nonetheless, sculpted me into the creative artist I am today. Next, I would like to thank writers Brian Drake, Mark Allen, and Michael Black—gentlemen who have generously donated their time and their knowledge and who provided feedback to someone who was a complete stranger. If not for your wondrous input and generosity, this book would not be where it is today and I would not be welcomed into such a glorious family of talented men and women. I also thank local writer friends, including Brent Van Staalduinen, who gave time and encouragement, and my great friend and confidant, Mark Jordan Manner. Mark, you guided me through this vast literary landscape, and without your help, I could not have navigated, conquered, or, for that matter, endured the many changes and challenges that come with this industry. I would also like to thank a man who is more than a friend but a mentor, Mr. John Corr. Candid and kind, receptive and lethal, you throw me on the mats, and still, you also help me both in and outside the dojo. I am thankful I met you when I did. I hope I might continue to train and learn alongside you in the years to come. I thank Naben Ruthnum, Lucy S. Snyder, Andrew F. Sullivan, and Amy Jones—writers who have taken time out of their busy schedules to look at my work and who have given me strength during tough and difficult times. I offer my gratitude to all my family and friends, including my teacher friends—good and decent colleagues. I thank my alma mater buds, Greg Zavitz, Brent Duguid, and Andrew Francella, someone who spends more time respecting my opinion than he does his own. I thank Dave Franciosa, Steve Legge, Christopher Barrett, and other like-minded geeks, and finally, all the Mazza-Anthonys as well. However, I owe an extreme debt of gratitude to Sharmaine Gobind, not just a reader but a guardian angel. Sharmaine, you came to my aid when I was at such a low point and you quite literally brought me and my stories back from the dead. I could not have done this without you and because you were there for me, I will always be there for you.

I thank the people on both sides of my splendid family:

My brother, Cody, my bud and forever pal.

My best friend and sister, Jenna, a relentless voice of concern.

My father, a decent man. My Bentley, my whole world. And above all else, my mother, Sheila. You are an amalgamation of encouragement, power, strength, and truth, which is often inconvenient, but most importantly you are love. Thank you for being my greatest fan, a great friend, and everything else in between. I thank you for following me on my many journeys. I always know where I'm going, and because of you, I am never lost.

A LOOK AT BOOK THREE:
OVERTAKER TERRITORY

After uncovering the shocking truth about his workplace, The Conquistador, former Marine Jon Haze has abandoned his fellow Doormen and removed his Crest—the badge of honor bestowed upon the club's elite brigade of bouncers. In doing so, Jon has done the unthinkable: he surrendered.

Lost, uncertain, and alone, Jon seeks solace from an old war friend, Lieutenant Dan. Through Dan's wisdom on loyalty and truth, Jon finds the strength to return to The Conquistador and finish what he started.

Upon his return, Jon discovers a transformed Conquistador, now ruled by brutal new bouncers who strip guests of their freedom. The once familiar faces of the Doormen are gone, replaced by a ferocious guild under the control of Michael Irons—the man who betrayed Jon during the Showdown.

With the Commission of Nightclub Codes and Conducts placing the club on temporary suspension, Jon must unite the Doormen for their greatest battle yet: to defeat the OverTakers and reclaim The Conquistador before all is lost forever.

Will Jon Haze overcome his past and emerge victorious, or will the OverTakers crush his spirit forever?

AVAILABLE SEPTEMBER 2024

ABOUT THE AUTHOR

Jarrett Mazza is a graduate of Goddard College's MFA in Creative Writing Program in Plainfield, Vermont as well as The Humber School For Writers.

Before completing his terminal degree, he studied writing at the University of Toronto School of Continuing Studies and comic book writing under Ty Templeton and Andy Schmidt. He has had stories published online in the GNU Journal, Bewildering Stories, Trembling With Fear, Aphelion, The Scarlet Leaf Review, and Toronto Prose Mill, The Fictional Cafe. His work is featured in anthologies by Silver Empire Publishing, a best seller, Zimbell House Publishing,NBH Publishing, MuseWrite Press, twice by Dragon Soul Press, Gypsum Sound Tales, Hellbound Books and The Ginosko Literary Journal. All are available on Amazon for purchase. He was also an Honorable Mention for the Freda Waldon Award for Fiction, nominated for an Indie Book award, and was featured as a visiting author for the nationwide We Read Canadian event in 2020. His mystery short story was published in an anthology under the editorial supervision of Michael Bracken and was published by Down and Out Books. He is currently a pulp fiction writer for the companies Airship 27 and Stormgate Press and Rough Edges Press.

He lives in Hamilton, Ontario.
You can follow him on Twitter @JarrettMazza